One
Amazing
Thing

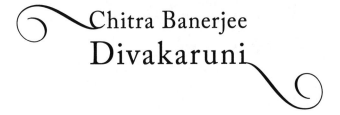

One
Amazing
Thing

Chitra Banerjee
Divakaruni

voice

Hyperion   New York

Library of Congress Cataloging-in-Publication Data

Divakaruni, Chitra Banerjee.
  One amazing thing / Chitra Banerjee Divakaruni.
    p. cm.
  ISBN 978-1-4013-4099-5
1. Earthquakes—California—Fiction. 2. East Indians—California—Fiction. 3. Disaster victims—Fiction.
4. Storytelling—Fiction. 5. Psychological fiction. I. Title.
  PS3554.I86O64 2010
    813'.54—dc22   2009024239

Hyperion books are available for special promotions and premiums. For details contact the HarperCollins Special Markets Department in the New York office at 212-207-7528, fax 212-207-7222, or email spsales@harpercollins.com.

Book design by Shubhani Sarkar

FIRST EDITION

10   9   8   7   6   5   4   3   2   1

THIS LABEL APPLIES TO TEXT STOCK

TO MY THREE MEN

MURTHY

ANAND

ABHAY

ACKNOWLEDGMENTS

My deepest thanks to:

My agent, Sandra Dijkstra, for support

My editor, Barbara Jones, for guidance

My mother, Tatini Banerjee,
and my mother-in-law, Sita Divakaruni, for good wishes

Murthy, Anand, Abhay, and Juno for love

Swami Nithyananda, Baba Muktananda, Swami Chinmayananda,
Swami Tejomayananda, and Swami Vidyadhishananda for blessing

We create stories and stories create us. It is a rondo.

CHINUA ACHEBE

If no one knows you, then you are no one.

DAN CHAON

One
Amazing
Thing

When the first rumble came, no one in the visa office, down in the basement of the Indian consulate, thought anything of it. Immersed in regret or hope or trepidation (as is usual for persons planning a major journey), they took it to be a passing cable car. Or perhaps the repair crew that had draped the pavement outside with neon-orange netting, making entry into the building a feat that required significant gymnastic skill, had resumed drilling. Uma Sinha watched a flake of plaster float from the ceiling in a lazy dance until it disappeared into the implausibly green foliage of the plant that stood at attention in the corner. She watched, but she didn't really see it, for she was mulling over a question that had troubled her for the last several weeks: Did her boyfriend, Ramon (who didn't know where she was right now), love her more than she loved him, and (should her suspicion that he did so prove correct) was that a good thing?

Uma snapped shut her copy of Chaucer, which she had brought with her to compensate for the Medieval Lit class she was missing at the university. In the last few hours she had managed to progress only a page and a half into "The Wife of Bath's Tale"—despite the fact that the bawdy, cheerful Wife was one of her favorite characters.

Now she surrendered to reality: the lobby of the visa office, with all its comings and goings, its calling out of the names of individuals more fortunate than herself, was not a place suited to erudite endeavors. She surrendered with ill grace—it was a belief of hers that people ought to rise above the challenges of circumstance—and glared at the woman stationed behind the glassed-in customer-service window. The woman was dressed in a blue sari of an electrifying hue. Her hair was gathered into a tight bun at the nape of her neck, and she wore a daunting red dot in the center of her forehead. She ignored Uma superbly, as people do when faced with those whose abject destinies they control.

Uma did not trust this woman. When she had arrived this morning, assured of a nine a.m. appointment, she found several people swirling around the lobby, and more crowding behind, who had been similarly assured. When questioned, the woman had shrugged, pointing to the pile upon which Uma was to place her paperwork. Clients, she told Uma, would be called according to the order of arrival for their interview with the visa officer. Here she nodded reverently toward the office to the side of the lobby. Its closed door bore the name *Mr. V.K.S. Mangalam* stenciled in flowery letters on the nubby, opaque glass. Craning her neck, Uma saw that there was a second door to the office, a blank wooden slab that opened into the sequestered employees area: the customer-service window and, behind it, desks at which two women sorted piles of official-looking documents into other piles and occasionally stamped them. The woman at the counter pursed her lips at Uma's curiosity and frostily advised her to take a seat while there was one still available.

Uma sat. What else could she do? But she resolved to keep an eye on the woman, who looked entirely capable of shuffling the visa applications around out of bored caprice when no one was watching.

NOW IT WAS THREE P.M. A FEW MINUTES EARLIER, THE WOMEN
at the desks had left on their midafternoon break. They had asked
the woman in the blue sari if she wanted to accompany them, and
when she had declined, stating that she would take her break later,
they had dissolved into giggles and whispers, which she chose to
disregard. There remained four sets of people in the room, apart
from Uma. In the distant corner was an old Chinese woman dressed
in a traditional tunic, accompanied by a fidgety, sullen girl of thir-
teen or fourteen who should surely have been in school. The teenager wore her hair in spikes and sported an eyebrow ring. Her lipstick
was black and so were her clothes. Did they allow students to attend
school dressed like that nowadays? Uma wondered. Then she felt
old-fashioned. From time to time, grandmother and granddaughter
fought in fiery whispers, words that Uma longed to decipher. She
had always been this way: interested—quite unnecessarily, some
would say—in the secrets of strangers. When flying, she always chose
a window seat so that when the plane took off or landed, she could
look down on the tiny houses and imagine the lives of the people who
inhabited them. Now she made up the dialogue she could not understand.

*I missed a big test today because of your stupid appointment. If I fail
Algebra, just remember it was your fault—because you were too scared to
ride the bus here by yourself.*

*Whose fault was it that you overslept six times this month and didn't
get to school for your morning classes, Missy? And your poor parents,
slaving at their jobs, thinking you were hard at work! Maybe I should tell
them what really goes on at home while they're killing themselves to provide for you. . . .*

Near them sat a Caucasian couple at least a decade older than Uma's parents, their clothes hinting at affluence: he in a dark wool jacket and shoes that looked Italian, she in a cashmere sweater and a navy blue pleated skirt that reached her calves. He riffled through *The Wall Street Journal;* she, the frailer of the pair, was knitting something brown and unidentifiable. Twice he stepped outside—to smoke a cigarette, Uma guessed. Sometimes, glancing sideways, she saw him watching his wife. Uma couldn't decipher the look on his face. Was it anxiety? Annoyance? Once she thought it was fear. Or maybe it was hope, the flip side of fear. The only time she heard them speak to each other was when he asked what he could pick up for her from the deli across the street

"I'm not hungry," she replied in a leave-me-alone tone.

"You have to eat something. Build up your strength. We have a big trip coming."

She knitted another row before responding. "Pick up whatever looks good to you, then." After he left, she put down the knitting needles and stared at her hands.

To Uma's left sat a young man of about twenty-five, an Indian by his features, but fair-skinned as though he came from one of the mountain tribes. He wore dark glasses, a scowl, and a beard of the kind that in recent years made airport security pull you out of line and frisk you. To her other side sat a lanky African American, perhaps in his fifties, Uma couldn't tell. His shaved head and the sharp, ascetic bones of his face gave him an ageless, monkish appearance, though the effect was somewhat undercut by the sparkly studs in his ears. When Uma's stomach gave an embarrassingly loud growl a couple of hours back (trusting in the nine a.m. appointment, she hadn't brought with her anything more substantial than a bagel and an apple), he dug into a rucksack and solemnly offered her a Quaker Oats Granola Bar.

It was not uncommon, in this city, to find persons of different races randomly thrown together. Still, Uma thought, it was like a mini UN summit in here. Whatever were all these people planning to do in India?

UMA HERSELF WAS GOING TO INDIA BECAUSE OF HER PARENTS' folly. They had come to the United States some twenty years back as young professionals, when Uma was a child. They had loved their jobs, plunging enthusiastically into their workdays. They had celebrated weekends with similar gusto, getting together (in between soccer games and Girl Scout meetings and Bharatanatyam classes for Uma) with other suburbanite Indian families. They had orchestrated elaborate, schizophrenic meals (mustard fish and fried bitter gourd for the parents; spaghetti with meatballs and peach pie for the children) and bemoaned the corruption of Indian politicians. In recent years, they had spoken of moving to San Diego to spend their golden years by the ocean (such nice weather, perfect for our old bones). Then, in a dizzying volte-face that Uma considered most imprudent, her mother had chosen early retirement and her father had quit his position as a senior administrator for a computer company to accept a consultant's job in India. Together, heartlessly, they had rented out their house (the house where Uma was born!) and returned to their hometown of Kolkata.

"But all these years you complained about how terrible Kolkata was," Uma had cried, aghast, when they called to inform her of their decision. Apart from her concern for their well-being, she was vexed at not having been consulted. "The heat, the dirt, the noise, the crowded buses, the beggars, the bribes, the diarrhea, the bootlicking, the streets littered with garbage that never got picked up. How are you going to handle it?"

To which her mother had replied, with maddening good humor,

"But sweetie, all that has changed. It's a different India now, India Shining!"

And perhaps it was, for hadn't her parents glided effortlessly into their new life, renting an air-conditioned terrace-top flat and hiring a retinue of servants to take care of every possible chore? ("I haven't washed a single dish since I moved here!" her mother rhapsodized on the phone.) A chauffeured car whisked her father to his office each morning. ("I work only from ten to four," he added proudly from the other phone.) It returned to take her mother shopping, or to see childhood friends, or to get a pedicure, or (before Uma could chide her for being totally frivolous) to volunteer with an agency that educated slum children. In the evenings her parents attended Rabindra Sangeet concerts together, or watched movies on gigantic screens in theaters that resembled palaces, or walked hand in hand (such things were accepted in India Shining) by the same lake where they had met secretly as college students, or went to the club for drinks and a game of bridge. They were invited out every weekend and sometimes on weeknights as well. They vacationed in Kulu Manali in the summer and Goa in the winter.

Uma was happy for her parents, though secretly she disapproved of their newly hedonistic lifestyle. (Yet how could she object when it was so much better than what she often saw around her: couples losing interest in each other, living in wooden togetherness or even breaking up?) Was it partly that she felt excluded? Or was it that by contrast her university life, which she had been so proud of, with its angst-filled film festivals, its cafés where heated intellectual discussions raged late into the night, its cavernous libraries where one might, at any moment, bump into a Nobel laureate, suddenly appeared lackluster? She said nothing, waiting in a stew of anxiety and anticipation for this honeymoon with India to be over, for disillusion and dyspepsia to set in. A year passed. Her mother continued as blithe as ever, though surely she must have faced problems. Who doesn't? (Why then did she conceal them from Uma?) Now and then she urged Uma to visit. "We'll go to Agra and see the Taj Mahal together—we're saving it for you," she would say. Or "I know the best ayurvedic spa. They give sesame oil massages like you wouldn't believe." In a recent conversation, she'd said, twice, "We miss you. Why don't you come visit? We'll send you a ticket."

There had been something plaintive about her voice that struck Uma in the space just below her breastbone. She had missed her parents, too. Though she had always decried touristic amusements, she felt a sudden desire to see the Taj Mahal. "I'll come for winter break," she promised rashly.

"How long is that?"

"Six weeks."

"Six weeks! Lovely!" her mother said, restored to buoyancy. "That should give us enough time. Don't forget, you'll need a new visa—you haven't been to India in ages. Don't mail them your passport—that takes forever. Go to the office yourself. You'll have to wait a bit, but you'll get it the same day."

Only after she had hung up did Uma realize that she had failed to ask her mother, *Enough time for what?* She also realized that her boyfriend, Ramon, whom her parents had treated affably once they got over the shock of learning that he and Uma were living together (her father had even given him an Indian nickname, Ramu), had not been included in the invitation.

She might have let it pass—tickets to India, were, after all, expensive—but there was that other conversation, when Uma had said, "It's a good thing you haven't sold the house. This way, if things don't work out, you'll have a place to come back to."

"Oh no, sweetie," her mother had replied. "We love it in India—we knew we would. The house is there for you, in case—"

Then her mother had caught herself deftly in midsentence and changed the subject, leaving Uma with the sense that she had been about to divulge something she knew Uma was not ready to hear.

MINUTES BEFORE THE SECOND RUMBLE, UMA FELT A CRAVING TO see the sun. Had the gossamer fog that draped the tops of the downtown buildings when she arrived that morning lifted by now? If so, the sky would be bright as a Niles lily; if not, it would glimmer like fish scales. Suddenly she needed to know which it was. Later she would wonder at the urgency that had pulled her out of her chair and to her feet. Was it an instinct like the one that made zoo animals moan and whine for hours before natural disasters struck? She shouldered her bag and stepped toward the door. A few more seconds and she would have pushed it open, run down the corridor, and taken the stairs up to the first floor two at a time, rushing to satisfy the desire that ballooned inside her. She would have been outside, lifting her face to the gray drizzle that was beginning to fall, and this would have been a different story.

But as she turned to go, the door to Mr. Mangalam's office opened. A man hurried out, clutching his passport with an air of victory, and brushed past Uma. The woman in the blue sari picked up the stack of applications and disappeared into Mr. Mangalam's office through the side door. She had been doing that every hour or so. For what? Uma thought, scowling. All the woman needed to do was call out the next name in the pile. Uma had little hope that that name would be hers, but she paused, just in case.

It was a good time to phone Ramon. If she was lucky, she would catch him as he walked across the Student Union plaza from the class he taught to his laboratory, wending his way between drummers and dim sum vendors and doomsday orators. Once in the laboratory, he would turn the phone off, not wanting to be distracted. He was passionate about his work, Ramon. Sometimes at night when he went to the lab to check on an experiment, she would accompany him just so she could watch the stillness that took over his body as he tested and measured and took notes. Sometimes he forgot she was there. That was when she loved him most. If she got him on the phone now, she would tell him this.

But the phone would not cooperate. NO SERVICE, the small, lighted square declared.

The man with the ear studs looked over and offered her a sympathetic grimace. "My phone has the same problem," he said. "That's the trouble with these downtown buildings. Maybe if you walk around the room, you'll find a spot where it works."

Phone to her ear, Uma took a few steps forward. It felt good to stretch her legs. She watched the woman emerge from Mr. Mangalam's office, shaking out the creases of her sari, looking like she had bitten into something sour. Uncharitably, Uma hoped that Mr. Mangalam had rebuked her for making so many people wait for so many unnecessary hours. The phone gave a small burp against her ear, but before she could check if it was working, the rumble rose through the floor. This time there was no mistaking its intention. It was as though a giant had placed his mouth against the building's foundation and roared. The floor buckled, throwing Uma to the ground. The giant took the building in both his hands and shook it. A chair flew across the room toward Uma. She raised her left arm to shield herself. The chair crashed into her wrist and a pain worse than anything she had known surged through her arm. People were screaming. Feet ran by her, then ran back again. She tried to wedge herself beneath one of the chairs, as she had been taught long ago in grade school, but only her head and shoulders would fit. The cell phone was still in her other hand, pressed against her ear. Was that

Ramon's voice asking her to leave a message, or was it just her need to hear him?

Above her, the ceiling collapsed in an explosion of plaster. Beams broke apart with the sound of gigantic bones snapping. A light fixture shattered. For a moment, before the electricity failed, she saw the glowing filaments of the naked bulb. Rubble fell through the blackness, burying her legs. Her arm was on fire. She cradled it against her chest. (A useless gesture, when she would probably die in the next minutes.) Was that the sound of running water? Was the basement they were in flooding? She thought she heard a beep, the machine ready to record her voice. *Ramon,* she cried, her mouth full of dust. She thought of his long, meticulous fingers, how they could fix anything she broke. She thought of the small red moles on his chest, just above the left nipple. She wanted to say something important and consoling, something for him to remember her by. But she could think of nothing, and then her phone went dead.

2

The dark was full of women's voices, keening in a language he did not know, so that at first he thought he was back in the war. The thought sucked the air from his lungs and left him choking. There was dirt on his tongue, shards under his fingertips. He smelled burning. He moved his hands over his face, over the uneven bones of his head, the stubble coming in already, the scar over his eyebrow that told him nothing. But when he touched the small, prickly stones in his ears, he remembered who he was.

I am Cameron, he said to himself. With the words, the world as it was formed around him: piles of rubble, shapes that might be broken furniture. Some of the shapes moaned. The voices—no, it was only one voice—fell into an inexorable rhythm, repeating a name over and over. After a while he was able to think past the droning. He checked his pants pockets. The right one held his inhaler. He pulled it out and shook it carefully. There were maybe five doses left. He saw in his mind the tidy cabinet in his bathroom, the new bottle waiting on the second shelf. He pushed away regret and anger, which for him had always been mixed together, and focused on positiveness the way the holy man would have, if he'd been stuck here. If Cameron was careful, five doses could last him for days. They would be out of here long before that.

His keys were in his left pocket. A mini-flashlight was strung through the chain. He stood and passed the pencil-thin ray over the room. A different part of his brain clicked into being, the part that weighed situations and decided what needed to be done. He welcomed it.

One part of the ceiling had collapsed. People would have to be kept as far as possible from that area in case more followed. Some folks were huddled under furniture along a wall. They could remain there for the moment. He searched for flames. Nothing. His mind must have conjured the burning smell from memory. He sniffed for the acrid odor that would signal a broken gas pipe and was satisfied that there were none nearby. Somewhere he could hear water falling in an uneven rhythm, starting and stopping and starting again, but the floor was dry. There were two figures at the door that led to the passage, trying to pull it open.

He sprang forward with a yell, shocking the weeper into silence. "Hey!" he shouted, though he knew noise was unsafe. "Stop! Don't open it! That's dangerous!" He sprinted as fast as he could through the rubble and grabbed their shoulders. The older man allowed himself to be pulled away, but the younger one flung him off with a curse and wrenched at the handle again.

A splinter of rage jabbed Cameron's chest, but he tried to keep his voice calm. "The door may be what's holding up this part of the room. If you open it suddenly, something else might collapse. Also, there may be a pile of rubble pressing against the door from the outside. If it's dislodged, who knows what could happen. We will try to open it—but we have to figure out how to do it right."

Something glistened on the young man's cheekbone. In the inadequate light, Cameron couldn't tell if it was blood or tears. But there was no mistaking the fury in his shoulders and arms, the lowered angle of his head. He came at Cameron, propelled by compressed fear. Cameron had seen men like him before. They could hurt you something serious. He stepped to the side and brought the edge of his hand down on the base of the man's skull—but carefully. Such a blow could snap the neck vertebrae. The men he had faced elsewhere would have known to twist away, to block with an upraised elbow. But this boy—that's how Cameron suddenly thought of him, a boy younger than his son would have been, had he lived— took the full force of the blow and fell facedown on the floor and stayed there. In the shadows someone whimpered, then stopped abruptly, as though a palm had been clapped over a mouth. Cameron massaged his hand. He was out of shape. He had let himself go intentionally, hoping never again to have to do things like what he had just done.

"I'm sorry I had to hit him," he called into the semidarkness. "He wouldn't listen." He repressed the urge to add, *I am not a violent man.* A declaration like that would only spook them further. He held up his hands to show that they held nothing except the minuscule flashlight. "Please don't be afraid of me," he said. He wanted to tell them what he'd seen in Mexico, where he'd gone to help after an earthquake in one of his attempts at expiation. People who had been too impatient and had tried to dig themselves out of the rubble often died as more debris collapsed on them, while people who had stayed put—sometimes without food and water for a week or more—were finally, miraculously rescued. But it was too much to try to explain, and the memory of all the mangled bodies he hadn't been able to save were too painful. He merely said, "If he'd yanked that door open like he was aiming to, he could have killed us all."

Silence pressed upon him, unconvinced, unforgiving. Finally, from underneath a chair, a woman's voice asked, "So did you kill him instead?"

Cameron let out the breath he'd been holding unawares and said, "Not at all! He's stirring already. See for yourself. You can come out from under your chair. It seems safe enough."

"I can't move too well," the woman said. "I think I've broken my arm. Can you help me?"

He felt a loosening in his shoulder blades at the last words, the corners of his mouth quirking up. Who would have thought he would find anything to smile about in a time like this? He stepped forward.

"I'll sure give it a try," he said.

MALATHI GRIPPED THE EDGE OF THE CUSTOMER-SERVICE COUN-ter with her left hand, carefully avoiding the broken glass that littered it, and raised herself surreptitiously off the floor, just enough to check on what the black man was doing. She needed to fix her sari, which had fallen off her shoulder, but her right hand was pressed tightly against her mouth, mashing her lips against her teeth, and she dared not relax it. Because then she wouldn't be able to keep in the cry that was also a supplication—*Krishna Krishna Krishna*—but most of all a prayer for forgiveness, for she might have been the reason the earthquake had happened. And if the black man heard her, he might decide to turn around and walk toward her. Who knew what he would do then?

When her relatives in India—aunties, grandmothers, spinster cousins—heard that she was coming to America, they had shuddered—with horror or envy, Malathi wasn't sure which—and warned her to stay away from black men, who were dangerous. (And they had been right, hadn't they? Look how he ran up to the door and attacked that poor Indian boy, who was half his size. For the moment Malathi forgot that the auntie brigade, ecumenical in their distrust of the male species, had gone on to caution her to stay away from white men, who were lecherous, and Indian American men, who were sly.)

No one, however, had thought to caution her about earthquakes. Where she came from, when people said *America*, many images flashed in their heads. But an earthquake was not one of them.

Malathi had followed the aunties' advice—partly because there was not much opportunity to do otherwise, and partly because she had other plans. She shared a tiny apartment with three other women who had been hired by the consulate and brought over from India around the same time. They spent all their spare time together, riding the bus to work and parting only at the elevator (the others worked upstairs in Tourism), walking to Patel Brothers Spice House to buy sambar powder and avakaya pickle, watching Bollywood movies on a secondhand DVD player, oiling one another's hair at night as they discussed hopes and plans. The other women wanted to get married. From their salaries, which had sounded lavish when translated into rupees but were meager when you had to pay for everything in dollars, they put money aside each month for their dowries, for even though dowries had been officially banned in India, everyone knew that without one you had no chance of landing a halfway decent man.

But Malathi, who had noted how her two sisters were ordered around by their husbands, had no intention of following in their foolish footsteps. She had set her heart on something different. When she had saved enough money, she was going back—though not to her hometown of Coimbatore—to open a beauty shop. At night she clutched her lumpy pillow, closed her eyes, and was transported to it: the brass bells on the double doors (curtained for privacy) that tinkled as clients came in, the deliciously air-conditioned room walled with shining mirrors, the aproned employees who greeted her with polite, folded hands, the capacious swivel chairs where women could get their eyebrows threaded or their hair put up in elaborate lacquered buns for weddings or relax while their faces were massaged with a soothing yogurt and sandalwood paste.

Then Mr. Mangalam had arrived at the visa office and de-railed her.

Malathi's roommates agreed that Mr. Mangalam was the best-looking man at the consulate. With his swashbuckling mustache, de-signer sunglasses, and a surprisingly disarming smile, he looked much younger than his age (which, Malathi had surreptitiously dipped into his file to discover, was forty-five). He was the only middle-aged man she knew without a paunch and ear hairs. But alas, these gifts that Nature had heaped on Mr. Mangalam were of no use to her, because there already existed a Mrs. Mangalam, smiling elegantly from the framed photo on his desk. (The photo frames had been provided by the consulate to all its officers, with strict instructions to fill and dis-play them. It would make the Americans who came to the office feel more comfortable, they were told, since Americans believed that the presence of a smiling family on a man's table was proof of his moral stability.)

Malathi, a practical young woman, had decided to write Mr. Mangalam off. This, however, turned out to be harder than she had expected, for he seemed to have taken a liking to her. Malathi, who harbored no illusions about her looks (dark skin, round cheeks, snub nose) was mystified by this development. But there it was. He smiled at her as he passed by the customer-service window in the morning. The days it was her turn to brew tea for the office, he praised the taste and asked for an extra cup. When, to celebrate Tamil New Year, he brought in a box of Maisoorpak, it was to her he offered the first diamond-shaped sweet. On occasions when she stepped into his office to consult him about an applicant's papers, he requested her to sit, as polite as though she were a client. Sometimes he asked how she was planning to spend the weekend. When she said she had no plans, he looked wistful, as though he would have liked to invite her to go someplace with him—the Naz 8 Cinema, maybe, where the latest Shahrukh Khan mega-hit was playing, or Madras Mahal, which made the crispiest dosas but was too expensive for her to afford.

Could anyone blame her, then, for visiting his office a little more often than was necessary? For accepting, once in a while, a spoonful of the silvered betel nuts he kept in his top drawer? For listening when he told her how lonely he was, so far from home, just like herself? For allowing his fingers to close over hers when she handed him a form? In idle moments it was her habit to doodle on scraps of paper. One day she found herself writing, amid vines and floral flourishes, *Malathi Mangalam*. It was schoolgirlish. Dangerous. Symptomatic of an inner tectonic shift that disconcerted her. She tore the paper into tiny pieces and threw them away. Still, she couldn't help but think the syllables had a fine ring, and sometimes at night, instead of visualizing her beloved beauty shop, she whispered them into her pillow.

Today, Mr. Mangalam had pulled her into his arms and kissed her.

Malathi had to admit that the action, though it surprised her, was not totally unexpected. Hadn't he, just yesterday, placed in her palm a small golden cardboard box? She had opened it to find four white chocolates, each shaped like a shell and tucked into its own nest. Try one, he urged. When she shook her head bashfully, he took one out, ran it over her lips, and pushed it into her mouth. The crust had been crunchy, but the inside—it was the softest, sweetest thing she'd ever tasted. Guilt and elation had filled her throat as she swallowed it.

That same guilty elation had made her scalp tingle as he pressed his lips against her mouth. If he had groped or grabbed, she would have pushed him away. But he was gentle; he murmured respectfully as he nuzzled her ear. (Oh, how deliciously his mustache tickled her cheek!) Though Malathi had never been kissed before, thanks to the romantic movies she'd grown up on, she knew what to do. She lowered shy eyes and leaned into his chest, letting her lips brush his jaw even as a worrisome thought pricked her: by dallying with a married man, she was piling up bad karma. When he drew in his breath with a little shudder, a strange power surged through her. But then her glance fell on Mrs. Mangalam's photo, which sat next to a small sandalwood statue of Lord Ganapathi. For the first time she noticed that Mrs. Mangalam's shoulder-length hair was exquisitely styled—obviously from a tiptop-quality beauty salon. She displayed on her right hand (which was artfully positioned under her chin) three beautiful diamond rings. Had the man whose face was currently buried in Malathi's throat given them to her? Mrs. Mangalam smiled sanguinely at Malathi—sanguinely, and with some pity. The smile indicated two things: first, that she was the kind of woman Malathi could never hope to become; and second, that no matter what follies her husband was indulging in right now, ultimately he would return to her.

That smile had made Malathi untangle herself from Mr. Mangalam. When he bowed over her hand to plant a kiss on the inside of her wrist, she had snatched her hand back. Ignoring his queries as to what was wrong, she had fixed her sari and her expression and hurried out of the office.

Before she had taken ten steps, the wheel of karma began rolling, and retribution struck in the form of the earthquake.

IN THE SPARSE GLOW OF THE MINI-FLASHLIGHT, MALATHI SAW the black man holding someone by the elbow, pulling her to the center of the room. It was the Indian girl—though could one really call her Indian, brought up as she had clearly been in decadent Western ways? From the first, Malathi had disliked her because of her hip-hugging jeans, the thick college book she carried, as if to advertise her intelligence, and her American impatience. But now when the man grasped her arm and the girl gave a yelp of pain, Malathi couldn't stop herself from sending out an answering cry. She regretted it immediately, because the man let go of the girl and started walking toward her. She ducked under the counter, though without much hope. The glass that normally sequestered her from the people who came into the visa office had shattered in the quake. It would be easy for him to lean over and grab her.

The man did lean over the counter, though he did not reach for her. He was saying something, but panic had siphoned away her English. He repeated the words more slowly. The syllables ricocheted around in her head, unintelligible. She shut her eyes and tried to imagine the beauty shop, with herself safe in its calm center. But the floor rose up, the mirrors cracked and fell from the walls, and the ground was full of shards like those under her hands.

Behind her she heard Mr. Mangalam's door open. Glass crunched under his unsteady shoes as he walked toward her and the black man. Though she had not premeditated it, she found herself flinging herself at him and pummeling his chest, crying out in Tamil, "It's our fault! It's our fault! We made this happen!"

When the earthquake had hit, Mr. Mangalam had ducked underneath his desk. Subsequently, the desk had slid to the other end of the room, trapping him against a wall. He had pushed and kicked for several minutes before managing to extricate himself. When he rose to his feet, disconcerted by how badly his hands were shaking, his eyes had fallen on his prize possession—no, not the photo, which lay on the carpet smiling with sly triumph, but the sandalwood Ganapathi that his mother had given him—*to remove all obstacles from your path*—when he had left home for college. The desk in its journey across the room had dislodged the deity and crushed it against the wall. He had felt a dreadful hollowness, as though someone had scooped out his insides. He, too, had been brought up with a belief in karma. Accusations similar to what Malathi was currently sobbing against his shirtfront had swirled like a miasma through his brain. No matter how resolutely he pushed them away as superstition, wisps kept coming back, weakening him.

Mr. Mangalam did not have any prior experience of earthquakes. He had, however, dealt with hysterical women before. He took hold of Malathi's shoulders and shook her until she fell silent. "Don't be stupid," he told her in Tamil, using the icy tone that had worked well in past situations. "It was an earthquake. Earthquakes have nothing to do with people." In English he added, "Pull yourself together and listen to what this gentleman is asking you."

Cameron didn't like how the officer had shaken the woman and wanted to say something about it, but there were more pressing issues. "Do you have a first-aid kit?" he asked again, enunciating the words as clearly as he could. "A flashlight? How about a radio with batteries? Tylenol? Is the phone working?"

"I checked the phone in my office," Mr. Mangalam said. "The line's dead." He repeated the other items for Malathi, substituting terms she would be familiar with—*torch, Anacin, medicine box*—until she nodded uncertainly and wandered off into the shadowy recesses of the office.

Dazed as she seemed, Cameron didn't expect much from her.

But in a few minutes he saw a bobbing circle of light moving toward him. She placed the flashlight on the countertop, along with a plastic Walmart bag that held two batteries and a white metal box painted with a large, red cross. Inside he found alcohol swabs, a few Band-Aids, a bottle of aspirin, some cold medication, a tube of antiseptic ointment, and a container of dental floss. It was better than nothing, though not by much.

He tried to order, in his head, the things that needed to be done. He had to check all areas of the room to determine if there were other possible exits. He had to check if anyone else was injured. He had to find out who might have food or water with them, and then persuade them to give it up. Were there bathroom facilities? If not, alternate arrangements would have to be made. He would have to walk around the room to see if there was a spot from which his cell phone worked. He would have to ask others to do the same. He would have to try to open the door, even though it might cause them to be buried alive.

His chest was beginning to hurt. The dust wasn't helping any. Soon he would be forced to use the inhaler.

It's too much, Seva, he thought. I can't manage it all.

Behind him he heard a swishing. He swung around, aiming his flashlight like a gun. Malathi had found a broom and was sweeping up some of the debris. He was not able to catch her eye, but at least she no longer seemed terrified. That was good, because soon he would have to ask her to do something she would hate him for.

He allowed his mind to move away from the demands of the present, to follow, gratefully, the rhythm of the broom, which sounded a little like something his grandmother, who had grown up as a house servant in a Southern home, had described for him: a woman walking down a staircase in a long silk dress.

3

Uma looked down at her hand, which was so swollen that she could no longer make out the wrist bones. Cameron had given her three aspirin tablets, which she had forced herself to dry-swallow, almost gagging in the process. They did nothing for the pain, which throbbed all the way up her arm into her shoulder, and which she could not separate from her fear. Under her skin, something jagged was grinding into her muscles. She imagined a bone—or maybe several, ends cracked and sharp and uneven, stabbing her flesh from the inside. She wanted to escape to something outside this dreadful prison of a room—the ocean, her parents, the pad Thai noodles that she had been planning to make for dinner, Ramon bringing her jasmine tea in bed—but she was unable to squeeze past the panic. Could one die of internal bleeding in the arm? By the time they were rescued, would her arm have to be amputated? She had believed herself to be the kind of person who could handle a crisis with cool intelligence. Now she was abashed at how quickly pain had eroded her resources.

Everyone was huddled in the center of the room, where Cameron had summoned them. Everyone except the bearded young man, who was still lying where he had fallen, although he was conscious now. He had turned onto his side so he could watch Cameron. His unblinking eyes were like black glass in the glow of the flashlight. His head lolled at an uncomfortable angle. When a wave of pain receded, Uma would think vaguely of placing something under his head, her backpack maybe. Then the next wave of pain would break over her and she would lose track of the thought.

Cameron was checking people for injuries. They sat in a chair, their faces docile and tilted up like children's, while he ran his pencil light over them. Almost everyone had cuts or bruises. The old woman had a nasty gash on her upper arm that was bleeding copiously. He handed swabs, Band-Aids, and the antibiotic cream to the older couple, Mr. and Mrs. Pritchett, and told them to do what they could to help those who were not too badly hurt. People had stammered out their names by now, all except the bearded man. But they knew his name anyway, because while he had been passed out on the floor Cameron had asked Mr. Mangalam, and he had asked Malathi. It was Tariq. A Muslim name. Uma wondered if that had anything to do with his violent outburst; then she was ashamed of such a stereotypical thought.

Cameron called the granddaughter, Lily, to hold the large flashlight for him as he cleaned the old woman's wound and pressed gauze on it. Uma could see Lily biting her lips as red soaked the gauze, but the girl did not look away. Cameron frowned as he worked on the wound. He had to use all the gauze before he could stop the bleeding. (*Who would have thought the old woman to have so much blood in her?* Uma longed to say to someone who would recognize the allusion.) Finally, he tore a strip off the bottom of his T-shirt and bandaged up the old lady's arm. He instructed her to lie down and keep the arm as still as possible. Then he lowered himself heavily onto the ground. Uma felt a stab of anxiety as she saw him lean his head against the customer-service wall and close his eyes. He fumbled for something in his pocket, held it to his mouth, and squeezed. Was he ill? *Be strong, be strong*, she thought between the bouts of pain that pulsed in the bones of her face.

In a while, Cameron pulled himself up and examined the back area for a door or window that might form a possible exit route. Perhaps a ladder that they could use to climb up to the large air vent near the ceiling? Failing to find anything, he deployed people with cell phones to move around (but carefully) in case they could catch a signal. Mangalam was put in charge of checking the office phones at regular intervals. Nothing there either. Cameron waited for the realization to sink in: they were stuck here until a rescue team arrived or until they decided to take the risk of pulling open the front door. Then he instructed people to pool whatever food or drinks they had, for rationing.

A reluctant pile of snacks formed on the counter, along with a few bottles of water. Uma, who did not have anything to contribute, felt improvident, like Aesop's summer-singing cricket. (But she was suspicious, too. Had people squirreled things away at the bottoms of their purses, deep inside a coat pocket, in their shoes? In their place, she would have done it.) For a moment she heard her mother reading her that old story, her voice indignant as the ant sent the cricket off into the winter to die. Right now, half a world away, her mother lay asleep on her Superior Quality Dunlopillo mattress, ignorant of her daughter's plight. But hadn't her mother always been that way, oblivious to trouble even if it lay down in her bed and placed its head on her pillow?

"Does anyone have pain medication with them?" Cameron called. "Something prescription strength? This young woman, Miss Uma, her arm is broken. I'd like to give her something before I try to set it. Legal or otherwise, I don't care."

But no one admitted to possessing anything.

Cameron turned to Mangalam. "I need some long strips of cloth for bandages and a sling. We're going to have to use her sari." He gestured with his chin toward Malathi. "You've got to explain it to her."

But when Mangalam spoke to Malathi, a rapid-fire set of staccato sounds that Uma did not understand, she retreated behind the counter and folded mutinous arms across her chest. "Illay, Illay!" she cried in a tone that was impossible to mistake. She continued with a wail of unfathomable words.

"She says it will destroy her womanly modesty," Mangalam reported. He looked flustered. Uma suspected that Malathi had said something more, something he was withholding from them. Then another wave of pain struck and she was no longer interested.

"Ma'am, you have to cooperate," Cameron said. "We're in a situation where the regular rules don't apply. I can't help Miss Uma here unless I have enough cloth." But Malathi had backed into a narrow space between two file cabinets at the far end of the room.

With her uninjured hand Uma groped in her backpack and pulled out a sweatshirt. The pain had taken over her head by now, making her dizzy. She walked unsteadily to the file cabinets and raised her swollen arm as best as she could for Malathi to see. The skin was turning a sick purple, visible even in the gloom. For a long moment Malathi did not move. Then she shot Uma a look of hate, snatched the sweatshirt from her hand, and retreated into Mangalam's office. A few seconds later, the blue sari came flying through a gap in the door. Uma heard the click of a lock.

The pain of setting the arm almost made Uma faint, but once her arm was stabilized—the enterprising Cameron had used two rulers to make a splint—and placed in a sling, she felt slightly better. She took two more aspirin tablets from Cameron, picked up her backpack, and made her way to Tariq. He accepted the tablets she held out and gave a nod of thanks. Then he grimaced and clasped the back of his neck.

"Does it hurt a lot?" she asked.

He gave a bitter bark of a laugh. "What do you think?"

"I'm sorry about what happened."

He shrugged. "I'm going to kill him."

His tone startled her. It was so casual, so chillingly certain.

"Don't talk like that," she said sharply.

She would have said more, but Mrs. Pritchett joined them. The older woman turned her body as though she did not want the others in the room to see what she was doing. From a bottle in her hand she tapped out two pills that glowed like tiny oval moons. "Xanax," she whispered. "Maybe they'll help." Tariq looked at her palm disdainfully. Uma, however, picked them up. She was hazy about what exactly Xanax did, but from where she stood, it could only improve things. She thanked Mrs. Pritchett, who gave a smile of complicity and took a pill herself. The pills glided across Uma's tongue with ease. She was getting better at this. She wished she could have had a sip of water to wash away the aftertaste, but Cameron had said that they should wait a few hours before eating or drinking, and she did not want to make trouble for him.

"I'm going to lie down," she announced to no one in particular. Cameron had used chairs to cordon off the area to the right of the customer-service cubicle, where the ceiling sagged open like a surprised mouth. Uma wandered to the other side, where the old Chinese lady was stretched out on the ground. Elsewhere the flooring had cracked into chunks and torn its way up through the carpet, but here it was fine and free of glass. She maneuvered herself into a prone position, placing her backpack under her head, where it made a lumpy pillow. After what the Muslim had said, she wasn't going to share anything with him. She should have told Cameron about the threat, though the man probably had not meant it. When people were angry and hurting, they blurted out all sorts of things that later made them feel sheepish.

In any case, it was impossible to summon the enormous energy she would need to get back to her feet. The pills were dissolving inside her, sending out little tentacles of well-being, jellying her muscles. Bless you, Mrs. Pritchett, unlikely angel! Cameron was crisscrossing the room very slowly, his cell phone held out like a divining rod. Uma angled her head so she could keep him in her line of vision. There was a restfulness to him. But a vast, misty lake had opened up around her. How enticing it was. Drifting onto it, she promised herself that she would warn Cameron as soon as she awoke. By then, most possibly, their rescuers would be here, and it wouldn't matter.

TARIQ HUSEIN SQUINTED AT THE LIGHTED DIAL ON HIS WATCH. It was seven p.m., past time for the sunset prayer. He had already missed the noon and afternoon prayers. The second time it was because the African American had attacked him from behind, the coward, and knocked him out. The memory made rage undulate in his stomach. Rage and futility, because if the bastard hadn't stopped him, they might all be outside by now. However, missing the Dhuhr prayer earlier was no one's fault but his own—Tariq was honest enough to accept that. His own weakness had kept him from pulling out the prayer rug and the black namaz cap from his briefcase and kneeling in the corner of the room, because he had not wanted people to stare. He would make up for it now.

His beard was itching again. He forced himself not to scratch it. He had abominably sensitive skin, easily inflamed, and he did not want to have to deal with that additional problem now. Ammi, who blamed the beard, was always asking him to shave it off. He smiled at the irony of that. For years Ammi had begged him to get more serious about his religion, weeping and praying over his bad behavior in high school—his drinking and fighting and getting suspended. But when he did change, his mother was too anxious to enjoy it, because America had changed, too: it was a time when certain people were eyed with suspicion in shopping malls and movie theaters; when officials showed up at workplaces or even homes to ask questions; when Ammi gave a rueful sigh of relief and told her friends when they came over for chai that perhaps it wasn't such a bad thing her son was so westernized.

The first sign of Tariq's change was arguments with friends (at that time, most of them had been white) about what had led to the attacks on the Towers, about the retaliatory bombings in Afghanistan, about what Muslims really believed. To argue better, he started reading up on these things. He visited websites with strange names and seemingly baffling views and stayed up into the small hours of the night trying to decipher them. He started e-mail conversations with people who held strong opinions and presented him with facts to back them up. Mostly as an experiment, he quit drinking. One day he rescued from its wrappings a salwaar kameez outfit his mother had bought him from India—and which he had promptly tossed into the back of his closet—and wore it to the masjid. He liked the glances he got from the young women, especially a certain young woman, and did it again. Yes, he might as well admit it: women had as much to do with his transformation as his political beliefs.

When Ammi was advised by friends to stop wearing the hijab, he sat her down on the sofa and took her hands in his. He told her she must do what she believed in, not what made the people around her feel better. And most of all, she must not act out of fear. It did not work. She folded the head scarves and put them away in a drawer. Still, sometimes he would catch her watching him adjust his black cap in the mirror before he set off for Friday prayers. Pride would battle with astonishment in her face. At unexpected moments, he would be struck by a similar astonishment. What made him change? Was it 9/11, or was it Farah?

Farah. The thought of her pulled Tariq off the floor. He tried to stand tall, but pain shot through his neck, making him curse the African American. He put the anger away in a small, dark closet in his mind. This was not the time. He needed to purify his heart now, to praise Allah, to ask for help, to request blessings, particularly for Abba and Ammi, may the angels enfold them in their protective wings. He groped through the darkness until he found his briefcase, still standing upright where he had set it down beside his chair, though the chair was gone. A small miracle whose meaning he would have to ponder. He unrolled the rug, pulled on the tight cap. He tried to ascertain in which direction Mecca lay, but he was confused by darkness and fear. (Yes, stripped of pride in front of God, he admitted to the fear that ballooned in his chest every few minutes, making it hard to breathe.) Finally he chose to face the door he had been prevented from opening.

"Allahu Akbar," he whispered. "Subhaaana ala humma wa bi-hamdika." He tried to feel on his tongue the sweetness of the words that had traveled to him over centuries and continents. Against the reddish brown walls of his eyelids, he tried to picture the holy Kaaba, which one day, Inshallah, he hoped to visit. (Sometimes the image would come to him clearly, edged with silver like a storm cloud: a thousand people kneeling in brotherhood to touch their foreheads to the ground in front of the black stone, fellowship like he longed to know.) Today, all he could see was Farah's face, alight with the ironic smile that, at one time, used to infuriate him.

Farah. She had entered Tariq's life innocuously, the way a letter opener slides under the flap of an envelope, cutting through things that had been glued shut, spilling secret contents. Her name was like a yearning poet's sigh, but even Tariq was forced to admit that it didn't match the rest of her. Boyishly thin and too tall to be considered pretty by Indian standards, she was smart and secretive, with the disconcerting habit of fixing her keen, kohl-lined eyes on you in a manner that made you suspect that she didn't quite believe what you said.

The daughter of Ammi's best friend from childhood, Farah had come to America two years back on a prestigious study-abroad scholarship from her university in Delhi. (Tariq, whose own college career was filled with stutters, was a senior then, trying to finish up classes he had dropped in previous semesters.) In spite of her brilliance, though, Farah almost had not made it to America. Her widowed mother, blissfully ignorant of what occurred with some regularity on the campuses of her hometown, had been terrified that American dorm life, ruled as it was by the unholy trinity of alcohol, drugs, and sex, would ruin her daughter. Only after a protracted and tearful conversation with Ammi had Farah's mother given Farah permission to come. These were the conditions: Farah would live with Ammi for her entire stay; she would visit the mosque twice a week; she would mingle only with other Indian Muslims; and she would be escorted everywhere she went by a member of the Husein family. Since Abba was busy with his janitorial business, which was growing so fast that he recently had to hire several new employees, and Ammi's day was filled with mysterious female activities, this member most often turned out to be the reluctant Tariq.

From the beginning Farah got under his skin. Though she was polite, a disapproval seemed to emanate from her, making him wonder if his disheveled lifestyle wasn't quite as cool as he'd thought. He couldn't figure her out. Unlike other girls who had visited them from India, she wasn't interested in the latest music, movies, or magazines. Brand-name clothing and makeup didn't excite her. One day, feeling magnanimous, he had offered to take her to the mall—and even clubbing, later, if she could keep her mouth shut. She needed to see what made America *America*. But she had asked if they could go to the Museum of Modern Art. What a waste of an afternoon that had been. He had trailed behind her as she examined, with excruciating interest, canvases filled with incomprehensive slashes of color or people who were naked, and ugly besides.

On the way back, she had been more exuberant than he had ever seen her, going on and on about how innovative modern Indian art was, too, with Muslim artists like Raza and Husain in the forefront. She had made him feel stupid because he had never heard of these so-called artists, not even the one with the same last name as his. In retaliation, he had listed for her all the things he had hated about India from his duty visits there. She was angry; he could tell that from the way her nostrils flared quickly, once. She said, "It's easy to see the problems India has. But do you even know what America's problems are?"

He was stung into that hackneyed retort: if America had so many problems, she was welcome to go back home. Right now. She had turned her face to the car window. After a few minutes, her hand had sneaked up to her face to wipe away tears. Her fingertips came away kohl-streaked. He hadn't felt like such a jerk in a long time, though he said far worse things to the girls he went out with. Perhaps it was that Farah didn't carry tissues, which he translated as meaning that she had not expected him to hurt her. He stopped the car and apologized. She didn't reply, but she gave a stiff little nod. The thin, curved rod of her collarbone reminded him, illogically, of a fledgling bird. That was when he started to fall in love.

Once when he was recovering from the flu, she had come into his room with a glass of barley water Ammi had boiled for him. She felt his forehead to check his temperature, and then touched the two-day growth of beard. "Looks good," she said. His defenses eroded by fever, he was caught in the inflection of her voice. Something ancient in it reached out and reclaimed him. He stopped shaving after that. When at the dinner table his parents pelted him with questions, asking him why he wanted to do something so controversial now, when it was absolutely the wrong time, Farah lowered her eyes demurely. The beard had become a code between them. Even now, a year and a half after she had returned to India (India, where she was waiting for him to come to her), he had only to close his eyes to feel her cool, approving fingers on his jawbone.

"FOLKS, PLEASE, I NEED YOUR ATTENTION!"

Cameron's voice crashed against Tariq's eardrums, shattering the memory and jolting him back to the present. He found that he was kneeling with his forehead to the floor. He had gone through the entire evening prayer without paying attention to the sacred words. This realization, along with losing Farah all over again, made him angrier with the African American.

"We need to eat and drink a little," Cameron was saying. "It'll keep hunger and thirst from overwhelming us later on. If you come up to the counter and make a line, I'll hand each of you your portion. It'll be small, I'm afraid—"

Tariq jumped up from the prayer mat, banging his knee on a piece of furniture because the African American had turned off the big flashlight and was, instead, holding up the pencil light—another part of his strategy for controlling them.

"Why should you decide what we're going to do?" he said. "Why should you order us around?" Even to his own ears, his voice bounced off the walls, too loud. He could see faces turning toward him in consternation. He bit his tongue to silence himself. They needed to realize that he was right. That way, he could have them on his side at the right time. "This is an Indian office. If anyone is to give orders, it should be the visa officer."

But Mangalam, hair hanging limply over his eyebrows, shook his head. Even in the thin light, his face was haggard. He had been trying the phones every five minutes and had come to the conclusion that service was unlikely to be restored any time soon. He did not want the responsibility for all these lives. In his youth, before marriage and the diplomatic service had snared him with false promises of glamour and ease, he had been a student of chemistry. It seemed to him that each person in this room—and the young man in front of him was a prime example—was like a simmering test tube that might explode if the minutest amount of the wrong element were added to it. He did not want to be in the forefront when the blasts came. He was no hero. Wasn't that why he had escaped to a post abroad rather than battling it out with Mrs. Mangalam?

"Mr. Cameron Grant here has been in the United States Army," he said. "He is used to handling emergency situations. He knows better than I do what precautions must be taken. I vote that we follow his strategy and offer him every cooperation." Other voices joined him, leaving Tariq stranded.

Tariq's mouth filled with a rusty taste. Fool, he thought, glaring at Mangalam. The man was typical of the worst kind of Indian. Let a foreigner appear, even a dark-skinned one, and immediately they bowed and scraped in front of him. He weighed the cost of disobeying the African American. But first he needed allies.

Patience, he told himself. After he ate and got the girl with the broken arm to fetch him more aspirin, he would undertake his own reconnaissance. Inshallah, maybe he would discover an opening the other man had missed, a possibility for escape. With God's guidance, he might be the one to lead his companions to safety.

4

Cameron portioned out the perishables: a turkey sandwich; three hard-boiled eggs, accompanied by salt in a little twist of paper; and most of a salad that Mrs. Pritchett had left uneaten. He set out nine napkins (BON VOYAGE! they proclaimed cruelly) and placed a few spinach leaves on each. He cut the eggs into nine pieces with a butter knife, trying hard to make the pieces the same size. He arranged them over the spinach, and sprinkled them with salt. He cut up the sandwich, too, but set it to the side because he wasn't sure if everyone ate meat. His movements were meticulous and gentle, as though that might make a difference.

Malathi had emerged from Mr. Mangalam's office after Lily, whose help Cameron had enlisted in this matter, had knocked on the door (but carefully, so she wouldn't jar any fragile structures). "Get over it and come eat!" she had said sternly. Perhaps being rebuked by a teenager had made Malathi rethink her conduct. Or perhaps she did not trust Cameron to save her share of the food. She maintained a sulky countenance and kept her arms crossed over the GO BEARS! sweatshirt she was wearing. Cameron, who had been reading up on India in preparation for his trip, understood that she felt embarrassed. It was ironic; the sweatshirt covered far more of her body than the midriff-baring blouse and thin sari had. But the ways in which cultural habits operated were mysterious.

Malathi's petticoat, pale blue and edged with ruffles, looked rather elegant. She had lost her red bindi—it must have been a stick-on—and that, along with the stray hairs that had escaped from her bun to curl around her face, made her seem younger. Though she was still not speaking to Cameron, she had provided him—without being asked—with the napkins and the knife.

Cameron asked Lily to hand out the food—partly to keep her occupied. She had been unusually calm through events that must have been terrifying for a young person. Her hand, holding the flashlight as he bandaged her bleeding grandmother and set Uma's broken bone, had been steady. She had asked only once if the old woman would be okay. But he felt a restlessness stirring under her skin, feelings she had tamped down. Some of the younger soldiers had been the same way. It was imperative to keep them occupied, to make them feel that they were central to the operation. Otherwise they could come unglued.

He'd put Lily in charge mostly because of Tariq's accusations. He had felt a bitter laugh spiraling inside as he listened to him. So the boy thought he was the Establishment, trying to take over! He wanted to hold his arm up against Tariq's, his far darker skin. He wanted to tell Tariq how it had been growing up with no money and skin that color in inner-city Los Angeles. Still, the accusations had cut into him.

Why did he feel guilty? Was it for having knocked Tariq out? For using violence when he should have found what the holy man called a better way? The word *ahimsa* rose in his mind because he had been studying Gandhi. He moved the thought aside apologetically. This was not the time for philosophy. Tariq could have killed them all if he had managed to wrench open the door. But the mind, the treacherous mind. It reminded him that he had killed far more people in his lifetime than Tariq ever would.

To keep the memories away, Cameron checked the water supply: four pint-size bottles, none of them full. If he gave everyone a half cup—and how could he give less?—it would be gone.

Mr. Mangalam was taking tiny bites of his egg with his eyes closed, savoring every morsel. Cameron asked him if there was anything else to drink. Maybe something they had overlooked? A gallon jug in the back? Some leftover tea? Mr. Mangalam opened his eyes reluctantly and shook his head.

Then Malathi said, "There is a bathroom." In the pencil light, her eyes gleamed, chips of unforgiving, as she pointed at Mangalam. "His."

THOUGH PEOPLE IMMEDIATELY SUSPECTED MANGALAM OF HAVing suppressed this crucial bit of information on purpose, it was not so. The earthquake and its aftermath had driven the presence of the bathroom from his mind. Very possibly, in a few hours, feeling natural urges, he would have recalled it and told Cameron. But perhaps there was something Freudian behind his forgetting, because the bathroom had always been his jealously guarded domain.

This bathroom, an anomaly of construction to which the only access was through Mr. Mangalam's office, was something Malathi's coworkers discussed often, usually as they made their way during their break down the long corridor to the women's restroom, which was drafty and smelled of mildew. Because none of them had seen Mangalam's bathroom, in their minds it assumed mythic proportions, filled with items culled from the pages of the glossies they bought, secondhand, from the newspaper stall near the subway. Floor-length mirrors, silken towels, perfumed liquid soap in elegant crystal dispensers, a braided ficus tree that reached all the way to the ceiling, a Jacuzzi tub—even a bidet. They spoke of these things with envy but not bitterness; in the universe they inhabited, it was expected that the boss would have a bathroom to himself while the underlings trekked to the other side of the building.

Malathi, too, had subscribed to this worldview until Mr. Mangalam began to single her out. As his attentions grew, an illicit hope blossomed in her breast. She found herself thinking, *If he really cares for me*... She changed her break times to match his, though she knew that people would gossip. Several times a day she went into his office to ask what to do with applications she knew perfectly well how to handle. Waiting for his response, she leaned against the closed bathroom door in a casual pose that showed off her curves. These strategies led to the gift of chocolate and to today's kiss, but not to the words she most wanted to hear: an invitation to use his bathroom, which would have countered the smug smile on the wife's face and proved to Malathi that Mangalam did not consider her just another time-pass girl.

Barricaded in his office today, Malathi had realized that this was her chance to explore it; once her eyes had grown accustomed to the dark, she went through it systematically. She discovered that the bathroom was nothing like the girls' fantasies. It was a tiny rectangle into which a sink and a toilet had been crowded. Like the rest of the building, it was old and dispirited. The mirror's edges felt uneven and worn under her fingers, and the toilet-paper holder wobbled. The only personal items in the bathroom were an air-freshening spray that smelled of chemicals and a bottle of mouthwash. Malathi had used it, swirling generous amounts around in her mouth. It was the least Mangalam and the universe owed her. The mouthwash tasted minty and bitter. Like love, she thought. Then she clicked her tongue, annoyed at having come up with a cliché like that. Finally, she had dipped into his file cabinets, not really expecting to find anything. But her fingers had closed around an item that made her grin fiercely in the dark. For now, she would keep that discovery to herself.

When Malathi led him into this sagging, cramped space, Cameron couldn't have been more delighted if he'd been ushered into a spa suite at a resort hotel. He checked the faucet to make sure that the water was running clean and asked if there were any containers that could be filled. There were. The party supplies for the consulate were housed, in spite of several memos of protest from Mangalam to the people upstairs, in a cabinet in the back of the visa office. Foraging, they discovered two fake-crystal punch bowls complete with ladles, a large saucepan for boiling tea and another for coffee (God forbid the flavors should be mixed), and one hundred BON VOYAGE! bowls purchased for the farewell party thrown for Mangalam's predecessor. There were also several matchboxes from Madras Mahal and sixteen packets of blue cake candles, which got everyone excited until Cameron pointed out that lighting any kind of fire was out of the question in case a gas line had ruptured somewhere.

Still, people felt better than they had in a long time, chatting as they lined up in front of the bathroom. Soon the countertop was lined with filled bowls. They shimmered like fairy pools when Cameron passed his flashlight over them, giving the room an unexpected festive aura. Cameron gave each person a BON VOYAGE! bowl that they could fill from the bathroom faucet any time they felt thirsty. This way, he said, the water in the containers could be saved for the future, though probably they would be rescued before they needed it.

Uma could tell Cameron was thankful that he could say something everyone wanted to hear. There were other words he was holding back. She heard them faintly in the back of her head. *The tap water might run out. There's food for only one more meal.* She was glad he did not say those things, allowing everyone happiness for the moment.

When it was her turn to use the bathroom, Uma looked at herself in the mirror in the pencil light, which Cameron had given her. (The bigger flashlight was to be used only for communal activities, such as handing out food, or in case of danger.) In its narrow, angled ray her face was gaunt and more interesting than it had ever been. She touched her cheekbones, which had taken on a sharp, tragic definition, and wondered what had gone through the minds of the others as they examined their reflections. She drank three cups of water and splashed water on her neck, amazed at how normal this simple action made her feel. The pain in her wrist was still there, but like a nagging old relative to whose complaints she had grown accustomed. With the ebbing of pain, her natural curiosity resurfaced; she found herself imagining the lives of her companions, their secret reasons for going to India.

Cameron suggested that people get some rest. If the phone lines were still down when they awoke, they would have to try to open the door. A murmur swirled through the room. Uma felt a prickle at the back of her neck, half anticipation, half dread. Then her mind moved on to the untold stories that lay around her, just out of reach. Would she get a chance to discover some of them before they made it out of here? The possibility invigorated her.

When Cameron said that they needed two people to keep watch, she volunteered.

MR. PRITCHETT, THE OTHER VOLUNTEER, SAT UP STRAIGHT IN his chair and looked out across the room. Though they had turned off the flashlights, he was surprised at how much he could see. Were

his eyes growing used to the darkness, like those of deep-sea crea-
tures? Or was he imagining the bodies, some passed out, exhausted
with worry, some tossing restively. Wherever possible, they huddled
under desks and chairs, forming small, compact mounds. Some slept
close to others, taking comfort from proximity. Some had staked
out the corners, their limbs splayed out. Ah, the alphabet of limbs.
How much it revealed of what people didn't want to give away.

Mr. Pritchett tried to ascertain which of the bodies was Mrs.
Pritchett's. He had been careful to note where she had been sitting
when Cameron turned off the light, but now he could not find her.
He scanned the room from one dark edge to the other. Had she
moved? He imagined her scuttling crablike through the debris into
the far recesses of the office, where she disappeared. Then he was
disconcerted at having conjured up such a bizarre image. But that's
how it had been since she had landed in the emergency room:
whenever he didn't know what she was doing, his brain, usually so
clear and orderly, ran amuck.

His fingers tightened around the lighter in his pocket. A
cigarette—even a few puffs—would have calmed him. An entire
pack of Dunhills sat in his other pocket, but smoking was impossible. The African American sergeant was right about the dangers of
a broken gas line.

"Mr. Pritchett," the young woman with the broken arm whispered. She sat on the floor two feet away from him, leaning against
the bottom of the customer-service counter. Her arm hung stiffly
in a makeshift sling the color of Lake Tahoe on a sunny day. He
had visited that lake as a child, the only vacation his mother and he
had ever taken.

"Are you all right?" the young woman whispered.

He felt a frisson of irritation. Of course he wasn't all right.

"Mr. Pritchett?"

He felt at a disadvantage because she remembered his name while he had let hers slip away. But he had to admit that it was kind of her to be concerned for him when she must be in significant pain herself. Hurting made most people selfish. Hadn't that been the case with Mrs. Pritchett?

"I'm fine," he said. To indicate appreciation, he added, "Call me Lance."

If Mrs. Pritchett had been nearby, she would have raised an eyebrow; he was not a man for rapid verbal intimacies. He liked formality. That is why he loved being an accountant. Early in their marriage, Mrs. Pritchett had protested that he wanted even the plants in their garden in neat rows, like entries in a ledger.

"Lance? Like a spear?"

"My full name is Lancelot," he found himself saying, to his surprise. Throughout his youth, he had insisted—in vain—that people call him Lance. When he moved away to college, he introduced himself only as Lance, and as soon as he was old enough to have his name changed legally, he had done so.

"Lancelot, like from King Arthur's court?" the young woman asked. She laughed in delight. In the dark, the sound was like a bell or a bird. He wondered that anyone could laugh under conditions like theirs. He surely was incapable of such—what would one call it? Strength? Levity?

"My mother was fond of the Camelot stories," he offered sheepishly, and this surprised him most of all because he never spoke of his mother.

"I am, too," the girl said. "I love the old tales—I have one with me right now." She patted her backpack. "Lancelot was my favorite among the knights, anyway."

"I'm not like him," Mr. Pritchett said. He considered romantic excesses undignified. He didn't like adventures.

"Sometimes we grow into a name," the girl said. "You might surprise yourself, Sir Knight."

Maybe she was right. Now that he thought of it, didn't he love the thrill of manipulating numbers, of balancing on the razor-edge of the law?

"It was embarrassing," he found himself saying. He wanted to say more. How boys had made fun of his name, how once they had put his head in a toilet. Where did that ancient memory spring from? He couldn't believe the things he wanted to pour out into this forgiving, pillowy dark!

His fingers twitched without a cigarette to hold. He marveled at the human mind, its tendency to crave what it could not have. Under normal circumstances, he smoked only two cigarettes a day, one after lunch and one while driving home from work. Mrs. Pritchett didn't like the smell, so on weekends he went out into the yard to smoke.

And she—what had she done in return? Betrayed him by trying to kill herself, that's what.

"I know about embarrassing," the young woman said. "My parents named me after a goddess. I'm going to India to see them. Why are you going?"

He could not bring himself to speak in the optimistic present tense. "Mrs. Pritchett wanted to visit India," he said, though this was not exactly true. "We were going to stay in a palace."

"Why, that's wonderful!" she said. "I'm planning to visit the Taj Mahal myself. I'm sure you'll love it."

Mr. Pritchett was not sure of any such thing. He wondered what the woman would say if he told her how the idea for this trip came to him.

AFTER MR. PRITCHETT HAD BROUGHT HER HOME FROM THE hospital, Mrs. Pritchett sat on the couch all day, looking at the window. She had always loved the view of the bridge and the sun setting beyond it, the entire vista framed by the camellias she had planted. But now she stared as though there was nothing outside but fog. The pills the psychiatrist had given her put a vacant smile on her face that was worse than out-and-out sadness. Mr. Pritchett was afraid to go to work and leave her, but when he was at home with her all day, that unasked question—*why?*—hung between them like a sword. He missed the efficient, antiseptic smell of his office, the obedient numbers adding up the way they were supposed to.

Mrs. Pritchett had been a meticulous housekeeper, priding herself on taking care of the big house by herself. But now there were dirty dishes stacked on the sideboards, unread newspapers spilling across the floor, dust bunnies in corners that smelled of despair. The maid who came in once a week didn't make more than a dent in the disorder.

Tidying up one evening, he had come across an old travel magazine Mrs. Pritchett must have picked up somewhere. There had been an article on old palaces in India being converted to hotels. A photograph of a spacious, marble-floored bedroom: a four-poster piled with red bolsters, a peacock perched on a windowsill, a curtain lifted in a foreign wind. On another day he would have found the room outlandish. This time, on an impulse, he had asked if she would like to go.

Something had stirred in her eyes for the first time since the hospital. "India?" she had asked. She had stretched out her hand and taken the magazine from him. Now they were trapped beneath several stories of rubble.

It was not Mrs. Pritchett's fault, but Mr. Pritchett couldn't stop himself from blaming her. But for her, he could have been in his office right now, its cool, white walls, its spare furnishings, its view of the Bay Bridge, those perfectly proportioned metal girders that he liked to contemplate while mulling over a tricky account.

He said none of this, but it seemed that the young woman sensed something. She fumbled in a pocket and handed him a stick of gum. How could she bear to perform this simple act? Didn't she realize they might not be rescued in time? He held the gum in his hand. In the dark, someone was sobbing quietly. It sounded like the Chinese teenager. Her grandmother spoke in a soft, cotton-wool voice until she grew quiet.

A lump formed in Mr. Pritchett's throat—no doubt an after-effect of shock. He wanted to tell the woman that he was afraid of dying in a slow, drawn-out way, from starvation or maybe lack of oxygen. He didn't feel too good about the possibility of a fast death, either. An image of himself being crushed under the rubble from an aftershock had flashed in his brain several times already. Instead of speaking, he got off his chair to sit cross-legged beside her, though he could not remember the last time he'd sat on the floor. He was embarrassed at how stiff his leg muscles were, his knees sticking up like little hills. And he so proud of being in good shape, of running on the treadmill for an hour at the gym, keeping up with younger men. Then he realized it did not matter. He opened the wrapper and bit down on the gum. The flavor of Juicy Fruit filled his mouth until his salivary glands ached.

"Feel," the young woman said. She took his hand in her good one. He mistook her intentions and his heart hammered with shock and contraband excitement. But she merely guided his hand all the way back to the edge of the carpet. His fingers came away wet. Water was seeping in from somewhere.

"Oh God!" he said. "We're going to drown." He scrambled to his feet to warn the others, but her hand closed around his ankle.

"Hush," she said. "The water isn't coming in that fast. I wasn't even going to tell you, but it was too frightening, knowing it all by myself."

In angry panic, he kicked at her hand. Stupid girl. She was going to get them all killed.

"Stop that!" she admonished him. "Let them rest. It's not like we can do anything about it."

The truth in her words pulled him down like gravity. When his heartbeat slowed, he could hear the sounds of sleep around him, breath moving in and out like waves in a cove. He felt a curious satisfaction, as though he were watching over fellow knights exhausted by a quest. As though he were responsible for their brief, trustful peace.

5

They awoke to dampness, the carpet smelling like a dog caught in rain. Everyone could see that the water was rising. And although it was happening very slowly, there was something about the slurping sound the carpet made as they stepped on it that caused panic to swirl in their stomachs. The phones were still dead. No one had tried to rescue them yet, which probably meant that the earthquake had done a huge amount of damage and the authorities were overwhelmed. The time had come to open the door. Cameron felt as though his lungs were filling with ice. He was not a praying man, but he closed his eyes and took a shallow breath (that's all he could manage) and tried to feel his center, as the holy man had taught him. Then he told them.

When he heard the African American's announcement, which was an admission that he had been right all this time, Tariq's heart leaped in vindication. But he conducted himself with admirable restraint, giving only a small, righteous sniff before he pushed past the others and laid a proprietary hand on the doorknob. He had scoured the entire area and found no other avenue of escape, but now they would get out, he was sure of it. He beckoned to Mr. Pritchett and Mangalam to hurry up and join him. They took turns pulling at the door, then tried it together. But the door was stuck fast. Tariq kicked at it—which, Mr. Pritchett pointed out, did not improve matters. The two men glowered at each other.

Cameron walked to the back with Mangalam to see if he could unearth any tools. He knew he should hurry, but a strange lethargy had taken him over. The squelch of his shoes on the wet carpet reminded him of a summer he'd spent with cousins out on a farm in East Texas, where his aunt had sent him to get him away from bad influences. That part hadn't worked. He'd found trouble there, too. He was a trouble magnet, as his aunt liked to say. Today, though, he didn't recall the problems. What he remembered was the rain coming down in silver sheets on the barn roof, the oaks draped in gray-green moss, the red mud in which you could sink up to your ankles if you weren't careful, the expanse of endless washed sky from the porch that made a strange hurt in your chest. He would stand on the porch for hours at a time. His cousins laughed at him, called him that daft city boy. He didn't care. It was the first time in his life that he was aware of nature as a seductive force.

But he couldn't afford the luxury of reminiscing. He wrenched his mind back to the task at hand, rummaging around on the shelves while Mangalam held the flashlight. Mangalam reeked of mouthwash. It was as though the man hadn't just swirled it around in his mouth but had splashed some on, like cologne. Oh well. People responded to stress in strange ways. More significant was the fact that they hadn't found a single strong tool, only another butter knife and a cake server.

What he wouldn't give for a crowbar, Cameron thought as he walked back. And as though the thought had split him in two, a voice inside his head said, *Would you give up Seva?*

He was familiar with the tricks of this voice, which had started speaking to him when he was in the war.

No, he said to it.

Not even if you were going to die? the voice persisted. *Not even if you knew everyone was going to die because of your decision?*

The second question gave him more pause than the first. *No*, he said finally. And then, *I'm not going to answer any more questions.*

How about your life? The voice continued, undeterred. *Would you give up your life for the lives of all these people?*

"Do you think it would help if we removed the doorknob?" Cameron asked Mangalam. He knew he was speaking too loudly. "We could take the screws out with the butter knife. Maybe we'd get a better grip if the hole is opened up—"

The voice grinned. *Later*, it said, before submerging itself.

Mangalam looked startled at having his opinion solicited, but after a moment he said, "I don't think that would help." Hesitantly, he added, "But maybe if everyone who wasn't hurt held on to one another, and we all pulled together, like when you play tug-of-war—"

That's what they did. Everyone except Jiang, Lily's grandmother, and Uma formed a line behind Tariq, who clasped the knob with both hands. Mrs. Pritchett tried to help, but Mr. Pritchett told her, curtly, to please sit down. Each person held the waist of the person in front. When Cameron gave the signal, they pulled as hard as they could. On the third pull, the doorknob broke off, so Cameron took off the screws with the butter knife and Tariq grasped with both hands the edges of the hole that was opened up. On the next pull, the door came unstuck all of a sudden; some people fell down and others fell on top of them. But a cautious cheer went up as soon as they had regained their breath, because the L-shaped bit of corridor that could be seen from the doorway was clear. Tariq gave a triumphant shout and ran out into the passage.

"Wait," Cameron cried, making a grab for the younger man, but

Tariq had already sprinted up the dark corridor. Others tried to follow, but Cameron blocked the doorway with outstretched arms.

"Folks! We've got to wait a few minutes to make sure the door wasn't holding up anything major, something that's shifting right now and might collapse on us," he said. They pushed against him. Mangalam was at the front of the crowd with the flashlight. The beam blinded Cameron. He could hear mutinous whispers, someone panting, impatience building like steam inside a cooker. There was a strong possibility that at any moment they would rebel against his cautiousness and trample him in order to follow Tariq. He braced himself for it.

Then they heard the rumble from down the corridor, and Tariq's cut-off cry.

IT WAS CLEAR TO EVERYONE, EVEN TO HER GRANDMOTHER, WHO was absolutely against it and clutched her tightly to make sure that everyone knew how she felt, that Lily was the only possible choice. She was the smallest and lightest; she might be able to crawl onto the pile of rubble that was now blocking the width of the corridor without starting a landslide and bringing down more of the ceiling. She could peer through the gap of about a foot and a half on top of the rubble and see what lay beyond. Cameron was hoping she would be able to glimpse Tariq, who he suspected was buried under the portion of the ceiling that had collapsed farther down the passage. He wasn't certain, though, because when he had cautiously called the young man's name, there had been no answer except for a warning drizzle of plaster from the hole above. Lily gently pried her grandmother's fingers from her shoulder and gave her a kiss, and nudged her back into the visa office, where Cameron wanted everyone to wait in case of further problems. She was surprised at the feel of her grandmother's cheek, so much more wrinkly than she remembered it, possibly because she hadn't kissed it in a while. She noticed with a thrum of worry that her grandmother's hurt arm felt hot. She would have to tell Cameron about it after she returned. She took the pencil flashlight from Cameron, who gripped her elbow.

"Climb only as far as you need to in order to look over the pile," he whispered. He had explained that out in the passage they must speak very quietly, if at all. Loud sounds could multiply through echoes and cause an avalanche. "If you don't see him, come back right away. Are you sure you want to try?"

She gave a small, stiff nod, though she was not sure at all. Her heart felt as though it was too big to fit in her chest. She could feel it beating up in her throat.

"Maybe you shouldn't," he said. "It's very—"

She didn't wait for him to finish, because then she would be too scared to do it. She pointed the thin, shaky beam of light at the jumble of Sheetrock, rods, and plaster ahead of her and took small, definite steps. She tried not to look at the gaping tear in the ceiling from which the debris had come—and from which more could drop at any moment—but it pulled at her eyes like a giant magnet. It was darker than anywhere else and huge, a black hole that could suck in entire solar systems. And was that something red shining deep inside it, like eyes? When she reached the pile, she started climbing, feeling carefully with her fingers because Cameron had warned her to watch for nails, some of which might be rusty. The pile shifted. She stiffened. Stopped. When it appeared to be holding, she went on. By the time she reached the top, she was sweating, but she had developed a rhythm of sorts, an understanding of the nature of debris.

She could feel the impatient anxiety of the group, as tangible on her back as heat from a blaze. There had never been a time when so many adults had depended on her for something crucial, something they could not do. It made her feel taller. Without turning her head, she whispered that she could see another pile. It wasn't very far, maybe three feet ahead. Something dark was sticking out of it. She thought it was a shoe. She would need to get closer to make sure.

"I'm going to climb down to the other side," she said.

"No." Cameron spoke with soft urgency. "Come back. Now that we know he's there, we'll clear this pile." When he realized that she wasn't going to listen, he said, "Be careful. Hold on to the light. If you start to fall, curl into a ball and remain still."

Lily lay flat on top of the debris for a moment, left hand fisted around the pencil light. She'd have to swing her legs over to the other side before she climbed down, and she wasn't sure what that would do to the pile. *I'm Gulliver,* she told herself. *This is a mountain in Lilliput.* Making it into a fantasy helped a little. She turned her body cautiously and inched her legs across until they hung down. Almost immediately, she began to slip. Her feet couldn't find a hold. She grasped a piece of wood with her free hand, but it came with her. The entire pile teetered. She felt herself sliding down in a noisy rush of plaster. *It's a small mountain,* she kept saying. *It's a small mountain.* Then she hit the floor, the blessed, solid floor, with a thump, a fog of dust rising around her. Amazingly, the rest of the pile held. She clamped a hand over her mouth to muffle her coughs and dragged herself into the small clearing between the piles.

"Tell Grandma I'm okay," she whispered as soon as she could speak. She could hear the chain of whispers on the other side, people relaying her message back into the visa office. She crawled forward until she reached the blob—it *was* a shoe—and grasped it. Carefully, she inched her fingers up over its edge, and sucked in her breath when she felt an ankle. Was it her first dead man she was touching? The thought jerked her hand back even though she hadn't intended to.

"He's here," she whispered.

"Ask him to move his foot," Cameron said.

She did. There was no response.

It hit her that she was stuck here in the passage with a corpse, that she had gone through all this for nothing. Now she couldn't stop the hiccuping sobs. Knowing how dangerous they were just made her cry harder.

"It's okay," Cameron said. "You did really well. Better than any of us could have. Try one more time, then come back."

She made herself touch the dead foot. She shook it, feeling the bile rise in her mouth. Just when she thought she would throw up, the heel turned a little.

"Tariq," she cried, forgetting to be quiet. "I'm here."

There it was again, the tiniest swivel of the heel, as though he had heard what she was saying.

"Brave girl!" Cameron said. "Come back now so we can start clearing the debris."

Lily imagined herself buried under that pile, wood and metal and pieces of glass pressing against her backbone, her mouth stuffed with dirt. She imagined feeling a hand around her foot, and then that hand going away. "I'll wait here," she said. It wasn't heroism. When she thought of her journey in reverse, slats of wood coming loose again in her fingers, that uncontrolled sliding, it made her body heavy with terror.

Cameron didn't waste time trying to persuade her. She could hear him whispering instructions. She removed a little debris from the side of the pile under which Tariq was buried but stopped when a chunk of Sheetrock slid menacingly toward her. Instead, she thought about Beethoven. When deafness began to descend on him, it must have been like being buried under auditory darkness. But somehow he found a spark, the music sounding inside his head. As she waited for Cameron to arrive, Lily tapped out the rhythm to the *Danse Villageoise* on Tariq's heel.

MANGALAM WAS NOT AFRAID AS HE HELPED CAMERON AND MR. Pritchett clear the passage. He did not look up at the hole from which grainy dust drizzled intermittently. He did not wonder what might happen if they pulled the wrong piece of wreckage from the pile that teetered in front of them like a crazy giant's Jenga tower. (Mangalam loved American games and had bought several since he arrived here. If they required more than one player, he played against himself.) Right now, his brain was a file cabinet where he had shut all the drawers except one. The open drawer held a single folder, titled *What the Soldier Says to Do,* and that was what he focused on.

In the past, this particular talent of Mangalam's had enabled him to enjoy moments of forbidden pleasure without worrying about consequences. Today it was bolstered by a bottle of Wild Turkey that had miraculously escaped the wrath of nature and was safely hidden inside his file cabinet. Over the last several hours, he had been making surreptitious pilgrimages to it, followed by guilt-ridden mouthwash sprees in the bathroom. The guilt was two-pronged. First, he had been brought up in a strict Hindu household on scriptural verses that declared that the consumption of alcohol was a primary symptom of the depraved age of Kali. And second, though it didn't exactly fall under the category of food, he felt that he should have turned the bottle in to the soldier.

Under normal circumstances, Mangalam was not a drinker. He had the bottle in his office only because he had received it last week, a gift from a grateful client whose visa he had expedited through a less-than-legal shortcut. He had planned to take it back to India, where the price of Wild Turkey was astronomical. He hadn't yet decided whether he would sell it or re-gift it to someone important who might extend his overseas assignment. But now India had receded from his life, and the best he could hope for was that an aftershock would not shatter the bottle before he had the chance to empty it.

Mangalam hauled off beams that had splintered like the neem sticks his parents had used as toothbrushes, yanked at metal rods twisted into skewers, and spat out with Zen dignity pieces of plaster that had found their way into his mouth. As he did so, he wished that Mrs. Mangalam, who used to denounce his ability to compartmentalize as callous and cowardly, could observe him now. Since that was not about to happen, it wasn't unreasonable of him (was it?) to hope that Malathi would notice his single-minded, stoic demeanor. Although when he thought of her, the drawers in his mind shrank. He could not fit her into any of them. He thought of how he had kissed her, her soft mouth opening under his, her tongue tasting of fennel seed, which she must have chewed after lunch. Later, he had gripped her by the forearms and shaken her. He remembered how her head had snapped forward and back, how astonished she'd looked before hatred had heavied her features. He wished he could tell her that he was sorry. But even if the perfect opportunity for it arose, he would never take it. Apologize to a woman and she would gain the upper hand. Mangalam knew better than to let that happen.

IT TOOK THEM THREE HOURS TO MAKE THEIR WAY TO TARIQ and dig him out. Throughout, Lily stayed with them in the passage. When Cameron told her she was taking an unnecessary risk, distressing her grandmother, she put on her sullen teen face. Once they uncovered Tariq's hand, she clutched it as though it rightfully belonged to her. She had to let go when the men made their way, carrying him single file, through the tunnel they'd dug in the Lilliputian mountain, but as soon as they were on the other side, she grasped it again.

Back in the room, Tariq said nothing. Though he was conscious, he kept his eyes shut and refused to answer the questions Cameron asked him in order to figure out if he had a concussion. By now, the floor of the visa office was too wet to lay him down, so they seated him in a chair. Lily held his hand, which she patted from time to time. Malathi propped him up while Mrs. Pritchett cleaned him off with a wet piece of what had once been a blue sari. But they were both distracted.

"Why isn't anyone trying to get us out?" Malathi whispered to Mrs. Pritchett. "Do you think they've forgotten us? Do you think we're going to die down here?"

Mrs. Pritchett wiped cursorily at Tariq's face, missing a large patch of grime on his cheek where his skin had been scraped raw. "God hasn't forgotten us," she said, staring into the distance with concentration, as though attempting to read a billboard that wasn't adequately lighted. "He knows our entire histories, past and future both, and gives us what we deserve."

If the words had been meant to comfort, they failed. Malathi gave a moan and backed away. Tariq began to slide sideways. He might have slipped off the chair if Lily hadn't grabbed a fistful of his shirt. She gave the two women her best evil-eye look, but they didn't seem to notice.

The sudden movement had jolted Tariq into a more alert state. When Cameron came back with some ointment, he strained away until the other man threw down the tube with an expletive. It was Lily who rubbed the salve into Tariq's face and forearms and bandaged him the best she could, admonishing him for his misbe-havior. Afterward, she delved in her backpack and found a pink comb and smoothed down his hair. Her own once-spiky hair had wilted, falling over her forehead, making her look waiflike. She asked if she could get him anything else, and bent close to his mouth to listen. When, eyes still shut, he whispered something, she found his briefcase and put his Quran in his hands. She made him drink some water and recommended that he open his eyes. "No need to feel embarrassed. We'd probably all have done the same thing and rushed out." When he didn't respond, she said, "Jeez! Quit behaving like a baby. No one's looking at you."

This was true. Cameron had just informed the group that be-yond the pile that had trapped Tariq, the stairwell was blocked, floor to ceiling, by chunks of debris too large to be moved without the help of machines. He had reminded them not to talk or move about too much. He wasn't sure how good the air was down here. How much oxygen they had left. People were trying to deal with the fact that their greatest hope—that the door, if only they could open it, would lead them to safety and sunlight—had evaporated. Until now death had been a cloud on a distant horizon, colored like trouble but manageably sized. Suddenly it loomed overhead, blotting out possibility. Panic darkened each mind, and Malathi's questions—*Have they forgotten us? Will we die trapped down here?*— beat inside each chest.

Tariq heard Lily, but he kept his eyes shut. He was mortified by having caused more trouble, by having required rescuing—by the African American, no less—when he'd hoped to lead their band to safety. That's why, although he wanted to, he wasn't able to tell Lily how grateful he was for what she had done for him out in the pas-sage, when terror had spread through him like squid ink. She had been brave, far more than he. He had sniveled and sobbed under the weight of darkness and debris. Even if no one else found this out, he knew it.

Holding the Quran in his lap, he tried to pray. God was the only one he could bear to connect with, because surely over the ages He'd seen more contemptible behavior than Tariq's and forgiven it. But Tariq couldn't recall any of the traditional words. He would have to make up his own prayer. He couldn't remember the last time he had undertaken that. Removed from the elegant choreography of the chants he depended on, he was stumped. What did people say to their Maker, anyway? In which tone did they register their complaints or pleas? How did they (not that it appeared that Tariq would have a reason to do this anytime soon) offer their thanks? *Allah,* he tried tentatively. But even inside his head his voice sounded querulous, and he fell silent.

WHEN MRS. PRITCHETT HEARD ABOUT THE BLOCKED PASSAGE, she backed away from the group until her shoulders came up against a wall. How could this be? She was *meant* to go to India. She had felt intimations stirring within her since the time the night nurse had appeared in her hospital room. They had coalesced into certainty when Mr. Pritchett, who disliked travel because it was messy and uncertain, had held out that magazine, offering her a palace. But now unsureness stirred within her, muddying things, and she collapsed into a chair. With no way out but the imagination, she closed her eyes and let a memory take her over. In it she sat at her mother's yellow Formica kitchen counter with her best friend, Debbie. They were both eighteen; they had just graduated from high school; they each had in front of them a piece of peach pie that Mrs. Pritchett (except she wasn't Mrs. Pritchett yet) had baked from a recipe she had created herself.

The peach pie was excellent, with a light, flaky crust and the golden taste you get only when you combine fresh peaches of just the right ripeness with a cook who has that special touch. But the girls had barely taken a bite. They were too excited. Each of them had a secret, and the telling of that secret would change their futures.

How tangible and powerful hope had been in that kitchen, like freshly grated lemon zest on her tongue. Every dream that came to her in those days was possible—no, *more* than possible. Even dreams she had been unable to imagine yet waited like low-hanging fruit for her grasp. What happened then? How did she get from there to here, waiting against a wall like a deer dazed by headlights? If she took birth again (she had been thinking about reincarnation a great deal since her time in the hospital), would she regain her early ebullience? Would she know not to let it slip through her hands this time?

Yes, I would, Mrs. Pritchett told herself. She visualized, once again, the palace bedroom, its plush pillows fit for the gods. It gave her new strength, though she did not particularly wish to visit a palace once she reached India. She had other plans. Still, the image reminded her that all she had to do was remain happy and calm, and rescue would arrive.

She made her way to the counter, where water twinkled on and off in a hundred BON VOYAGE! bowls, depending on the direction in which Cameron's flashlight was pointing. She chose a bowl and walked to a chair located as far from the others as possible. Even so, she could feel the desolation they emitted as they milled around Cameron, demanding to know what would happen next. So much agitation. And for what? All that negative energy only attracted bad luck into your life. But she knew better than to try to explain. They would learn when they'd been through the fire themselves.

She placed the bowl on the ground, arranged the pleats of her skirt daintily from old habit, and shook out a couple of Xanax tablets from the bottle in her pocket. Three fell out on her palm. Four. She didn't put them back. The universe wanted her to have them. The pills would allow her to be hopeful. And the power of that hope would draw the rescuers to them.

She tucked the bottle into her pocket and took a sip of water. And then, just as she was about to release the pills into her mouth, a hand clamped itself around her wrist and jerked them away.

"What are you doing?" said Mr. Pritchett's low, furious voice.

"Let go of me," she said, equally furious. He was spoiling everything.

"Why? Don't we have enough trouble here already, without trying to take care of you on top of that?"

She peered at him through the gloom. People you had once loved knew the best ways to hurt you. "You don't have to take care of me. I've been managing on my own."

He stared, astonished at her ingratitude. He considered all those precious hours of work he had given up, waiting in her hospital room while she lay in a daze. And later, moping around the house with her, asking which TV show she wanted to watch, fixing lunches that she abandoned half-eaten, offering to pick up books from the library. The time and money he had spent planning this trip to India, the tickets he had booked. Just because her eyes had shone for a moment when she saw that cursed picture. The words were in his mouth: *If it weren't for trying to take care of you, I wouldn't be stuck down here, about to die. Everything I worked so hard for brought to zero.* With an effort that could only be described as heroic (though no one else would know), he held the retort back. If she did something to herself, he didn't want it on his conscience.

Instead he said, "Haven't I worked hard all my life to give you everything you wanted, everything—"

"You don't know the first thing about caring," she said. "Relationships aren't businesses that can be made healthy by pouring money into them. As for things—okay, I enjoyed them. But I never wanted them that much. What I wanted—" She shook her head as though he were some kind of moron, incapable of understanding what she was trying to explain. "It doesn't matter what I wanted," she said. "All I want now is for you to leave me alone."

A trembling had started deep in his body. If only he could have a cigarette, he could handle this better. He tried to twist the pills out of her hand, but she made a stubborn fist. "Stop it!" she shouted. Like they were in a scene in a bad movie. "Stop trying to control my life!"

He could see people looking up, distracted from their own troubles by this little marital drama. He hated her for making them stare. He had always disliked attention, and she knew it. Then he saw something that gave him a brilliant idea. He let go of her hand and lunged for the bulge in her sweater pocket. Sure enough, it was her bottle of pills. He held it up like a trophy.

"Give it back!" she cried. This time the panic in her voice was real. She lunged for the bottle, but he raised his arm so that it was beyond her reach. "You can't take my medication!"

"I'll give it to you, in the right dosage, when you need it. You just have to ask me."

He started walking away. He could hear her sobbing behind him, a sound like soft cloth tearing. It almost made him turn around and give the bottle back. But her behavior had just proved she couldn't be trusted with the pills. For her own good, he had to hold on to them. Didn't he?

What was that she was saying, between sobs? *Now you've ruined everything.* Next she'd be blaming him for the earthquake.

Preoccupied, he didn't notice Malathi standing in the half-dark until he was almost upon her. "Sorry," he said, moving to the side. But she moved with him. "Give her back her medicine," she said.

He stared at her, taken aback. Except for a few terse instructions when he had approached the counter yesterday, these were the first words she had said to him. As far as he knew, she hadn't spoken to Mrs. Pritchett at all. Now she blocked his path, her hands on her hips, her hair loose and wild around her face, wearing a ruffled underskirt and a blue-and-gold sweatshirt.

"Give it back," she said again. "You have no right to treat her like that just because you're her husband."

Under different circumstances, he would have told her it was none of her business, but he was weakened by Mrs. Pritchett's continued weeping. He started to explain that Mrs. Pritchett was a danger to herself, but he was interrupted by Mangalam.

Mangalam had overheard Malathi's words as he returned from another trek to the bathroom; he pulled at her arm. "Have you gone crazy?" he whispered angrily in Tamil. "This isn't India. You can't interfere in people's lives like this. Leave them alone."

She shook him off. "You leave *me* alone," she said in English.

He reached for her arm again.

"Don't you touch me," she said, her voice rising. "Don't you tell me what to do. What do you men think you are?"

Out of the corner of his eye Mangalam saw people watching. The teenager was moving toward them. Her grandmother said something sharp and forbidding in Chinese, but the girl kept coming. Embarrassed, he resorted to officiality. "Malathi Ramaswamy," he said in the icy voice that had worked so well earlier. "As your superior I am most displeased with your behavior." He used English: he wanted Mr. Pritchett to understand what he was saying. "Kindly wash your face and compose yourself before you speak with any of our clients again. Mr. Pritchett, please accept my apologies for this woman's unprofessional conduct."

Malathi bowed her head—suitably chastened, he thought. Then, as he turned away, she said, "Only just wash my face, sir?" In Tamil she added, "Or shall I take a little whiskey drink also, like you? And what would our clients think if they knew about your *professional* conduct behind closed doors?"

He was shocked that she had discovered the bourbon. She must have snooped around when she had locked herself in the office. He felt light-headed. His mind hovered over a suspicion: the air was getting harder to breathe. But he was distracted by rage. She was planning to expose him in front of these people whose opinion mattered to him because they were probably the last people he would see before dying. She was going to tell them about his drinking, about the advances he had made. She was going to take their kiss, which in spite of its doubtful ethical nature had been something beautiful, a first kiss freely given between a man and a woman, and make it sordid. That was what made him most angry. His hand, moving faster than his brain, swung out and caught her on the side of the face. He felt the flesh give under the impact. She cried out sharply and raised her arm, belatedly, to shield herself. He moved toward her to inspect the damage, queasiness and guilt churning inside him, and as he did so, like echoes, he heard two other cries.

One of them rose from Mrs. Pritchett, somewhere on the floor behind him. The other came from Lily, who was somehow in front of him. She launched herself at him, spitting expletives. Disgraceful, the language a young person used these days. Before he could turn away, her nails raked his cheek, leaving a line of burning. He clapped his hand over it. Would it leave a scar? He had always been so careful with his face. It was the one thing that he had going for him, that had brought him this far. His life was unraveling. His god, his career, his reputation, his looks—they were all deserting him. He pushed Lily from him. She landed on the floor with a thump and a gasp, and then someone else was on him, pummeling furiously. Had everyone gone crazy? Through the rain of fists he saw Tariq's face, so distorted with rage that Mangalam almost didn't recognize him.

"Hitting her after she risked her life!" Tariq panted between blows. "Aren't you ashamed?"

Mangalam wanted to point out that he had just been standing there. Lily was the one who ran up and attacked him. Did a man have no right to self-defense just because he was a man? He wanted to remind Tariq that he, too, had been part of the rescue team that had dug Tariq out. He, too, had—in his own small way—risked his life. But the moment was not suited to logical parley. He punched Tariq back, partly to protect himself and partly because it felt so good to finally *do* something. Hands were on them both, trying unsuccessfully to pull them apart. The alcohol gave him an exhilarating agility. He skipped from foot to foot and jabbed at Tariq's face. But then his body betrayed him. He stumbled. Tariq wrestled him to the floor and grabbed his throat.

"Don't—ever—hit—her—again!" Tariq gasped.

Bright swatches of color pulsed in and out of Mangalam's vision. He thought he saw Malathi beating her fists on Tariq's back, yanking Tariq's hair, trying to get him off Mangalam. Would the world never cease to surprise him? He heard someone—it was the girl with the broken arm—crying, "Stop! What's wrong with you? God! You've all turned into savages!" Somewhere in the back, the grandmother was keening. He didn't understand the Chinese words, but he knew it was a chant for the dead. Where was the soldier? What was the soldier's name? The pressure on his throat made him forget. If Mangalam could only have called his name, the soldier would come. The ancient words fell, covering him, soft (he thought) as snow. When he'd been given this chance to start over in America, he had hoped to see snow, to lift his face to the swirl of flakes as he'd observed people doing in foreign movies. He had been disappointed to learn that snow almost never fell in this part of the country. That was his last thought before the colors pulsing in his eyes were suddenly switched off.

6

Uma lay on a row of three chairs, using her backpack as a pillow. A sharp edge from inside the pack poked her neck; she suspected it to be her Chaucer. The pain was on its way back—she could feel its early forays in her bones. She shivered. The heating system had been broken for—was it thirty-six hours now? The room had grown very cold, and it didn't help that water had seeped into her shoes.

She longed to remember something beautiful and warm, and what came to her was a summer walk she had taken in the hills with Ramon. But before she could recollect anything more than a sloping trail of slippery orange gravel and a wicker basket filled with picnic supplies, a commotion rose in the room.

She heard voices raised in protest and the unmistakable sound of a slap. Had they gone mad? Didn't they remember their precarious situation? Lily ran past her. In the shaky ray of the flashlight, which Cameron had turned toward the quarrel, she saw Mangalam fling the teenager to the ground with a thwack and Tariq launch himself at Mangalam. Plaster drizzled from the broken ceiling in protest, and her throat constricted with terror. But consumed by their passions, the two men were oblivious of the danger in which they placed the entire company.

When Cameron hurried toward the melee, Uma followed. She was worried about him: after digging Tariq out, he had coughed until he was forced to use his inhaler again. She also realized that she had forgotten to warn Cameron of Tariq's threat.

I'm going to kill him.

It was as she feared. When Cameron tried to pry Tariq's hands from Mangalam's throat, Tariq punched him hard. Blood gushed from Cameron's nose. Malathi was sobbing, pulling at Tariq's hair. Tariq swatted her away. For some reason, Cameron wouldn't hit Tariq back (Uma was sure he could have knocked him out again) but tried to grab his arms. Tariq's eyes were crazed. He butted Cameron hard with his head and Cameron reeled back, gasping. It was like their very own *Lord of the Flies*! Uma couldn't let it go on. She jumped into the fray, though she was terribly afraid for her broken arm, and caught Tariq's shoulder. He turned, swinging, before he saw who it was. His fist hit her upper arm—her good arm, thank God. Still, she fell with a cry of pain. Perhaps that fall did some good because Tariq was startled into lowering his fists long enough for Cameron and Mr. Pritchett to catch him by the arms. He lunged at them, his mouth a snarl. But Lily added her efforts to the men's, whispering fiercely into Tariq's ear words that no one else could decipher, until he went limp and allowed her to lead him away.

THEY WERE SITTING CLOSE TOGETHER (CAMERON HAD INSISTED on it), trading distrustful glances in the half-dark. The larger flashlight had fallen to the ground. Cameron let it lie there. He was wheezing. He wiped his nose on his shirt, but the blood kept coming.

This propelled Uma to stand up. She wasn't sure what she was going to say, only that she needed to say something. For a moment her heart pounded. She had never liked speaking in front of a crowd. Even the lectures she had to give as a teaching assistant, with carefully prepared notes and jokes she had practiced in the bathroom mirror, had made her nervous. Then an ironic calm descended on her. Only a few things mattered when you were about to die, and what people thought of your speaking abilities was not one of them.

"Folks," she began, "we're in a bad situation. It looks like the earthquake was a serious one. We don't know how long we'll be stuck here. I'm scared, and I guess you are, too."

She could see that no one wanted to listen. Mrs. Pritchett turned her face away. Mangalam was busy massaging his neck. Tariq had shut his eyes again. Malathi worried the sleeve of her sweatshirt. Lily, who was stuffing Cameron's nostrils with clumps of Kleenex, scowled at her.

But she had to go on. "Unless we're careful, things will get a lot worse. We can take out our stress on one another—like what just happened—and maybe get buried alive. Or we can focus our minds on something compelling—"

"Like what?" Mr. Pritchett said. "It's not like we have cable TV down here."

Uma refused to let him annoy her. An idea was taking shape in her mind. With a little burst of excitement, because she sensed the power behind it, she said, "We can each tell an important story from our lives."

Mr. Pritchett looked offended. "This is no time for games."

Mangalam grunted in agreement. Malathi crossed stubborn arms over her chest.

"It's not a game," Uma said. She hugged her backpack, wanting to tell them how powerful stories could be. But they were staring at her as though she were half-witted.

"What if we don't have a story to tell?" Mrs. Pritchett asked, sounding anxious.

"Everyone has a story," said Uma, relieved that one of them was considering the idea. "I don't believe anyone can go through life without encountering at least one amazing thing." A shiver came over her as she said the last words, a blurry déjà vu. Where had she heard the phrase before?

"You don't know my life," Mrs. Pritchett said.

"I've never told a story," Mangalam announced flatly. His tone indicated that he wasn't going to start now.

"It's not difficult," Uma said. "I'm sure you remember the stories your parents told you when you were little." But at the mention of his parents, a shuttered look came over Mangalam's face.

"I'm not good at explaining," Malathi said. She looked unconvinced when Uma promised to help her find the right words.

"What if no one likes my story?" That was Lily.

Though Uma assured her they would love it, she shook her head and busied herself with rummaging in her backpack.

Tariq opened his eyes and glared at Uma. "Did you consider that we might not want everyone to know our business?" Before she could think of a rejoinder, he shut his eyes again.

One volunteer, Uma thought in desperation. That was all she needed. But even Cameron, whom she had counted on, was examining the lines on his palm.

Then she heard a voice, quavery, speaking English with a rusty Indian accent.

"I will be first."

It was Jiang. They stared at her with varying degrees of incredulity.

"Gramma," Lily began, "You can't even speak English."

Jiang blinked in the ray from the flashlight that Cameron had trained on her. Uma thought an impish expression flickered over her face. Had the old woman pretended, all these years, not to know the language of America?

Jiang said, "I am ready. I will tell my tale."

THE RULES UMA SET DOWN WERE SIMPLE: NO INTERRUPTIONS, no questions, and no recriminations, especially by family members. Between stories, they would take breaks as needed.

They arranged the chairs into a circle. Malathi came out with a tin of Kool-Aid fruit punch. (Where had she hidden it? What else was she hiding?) She mixed it into the bowls of water sitting on the counter, placed the bowls on a tray, and served them as though she were the hostess at a party. The sugar made people more cheerful, though Uma guessed it would ultimately make them feel worse. Oh, well! Carpe diem. Cameron switched off both flashlights. But in spite of the claustrophobic dark that fell on them, Uma sensed a new alertness in her companions, a shrugging off of things they couldn't control. They were ready to listen to one another. No, they were ready to listen to the story, which is sometimes greater than the person who speaks it.

"WHEN I WAS A CHILD," JIANG BEGAN, "I LIVED INSIDE A SECRET." From outside her house, in the narrow alley lined with the smelly gutters typical of Calcutta's Chinatown, an observer would have seen the ugly, square front of a building, windowless and muddy red like its neighbors. In the center of this façade was a low, narrow door of cheap wood, painted green. The door opened only a few times

each day—for the children, who walked a few blocks to the Chinese Christian school, or for the father, who was picked up for work by the monthly taxi he shared with two other Chinese businessmen. Sometimes in the afternoon the grandmother might undertake a visit by rickshaw to her friends, all of whom lived within a mile of the house. Or a guest would arrive unexpectedly, causing a flurry of excitement and a dispatching of the cook to the market for bean cakes or fresh lychees. Should the observer have peered into the interior of the house, he would have seen only another brick wall— the spirit wall, built for the express purpose of deflecting the outsider's gaze.

"But no one ever looked," Jiang said. "No one gave the Chinese any thought—not until much later. Indians considered us below them because many of us were in the tannery business or owned leather-goods stores. That was okay with us. We had our own people, and we got from them everything we needed."

Had the observer walked through the door and around the spirit wall though, he would have been astonished. Inside was a large and beautiful courtyard, the heart around which the rest of the house was structured, its windows and balconies looking down benignly on mango trees and roses. At the courtyard's center, a fountain rose and fell. Parties were held here on full moon nights, with much drinking of wine and reciting of poetry, while children played catch around the sculpted lions.

Jiang and her brother never spoke about the courtyard—or about the other parts of the house. The banquet hall with the carved rosewood table that could seat twenty-four people. Their father's bedroom, which had a large photograph of their dead mother and was still hung with the silks she had chosen as a bride, embroidered with herons and good-luck koi. His study with the antique calligraphy scrolls he loved to collect. The hidden safe in which, because he didn't quite trust the banks, he kept gold coins, their mother's jade and pearl jewelry, stacks of rupees, and important documents (all except one, which he would later realize was the most important). There was no reason to tell the other Chinese of these things. They already knew, and many of the children's friends' houses mirrored theirs. And as for the non-Chinese—the ghosts, as they were called— the children were taught from the beginning to stay away from them. To keep family secrets safe.

"I would be the first in our family to break this taboo," Jiang said.

IT IS AN EARLY SPRING DAY IN 1962 IN CALCUTTA AND JIANG, twenty-five years old, stands in the doorway of her father's shoe store inside New Market, under the sign that reads FENG'S FINE FOOTWEAR. She is proud of the sign, of which she is the author. That sign had led to some heated arguments, her grandmother claiming that such an arrogant declaration would attract bad luck. Look at the other Chinese businesses with their noncommittal nomenclatures: LUCKY ORCHID, JADE MOUNTAIN, FLYING DRAGON. None of them draw attention to their family name by blazoning it over their storefront. But her father had taken Jiang's side, the way he had ever since her mother had died when Jiang was five, leading her grandmother to lament that he was nothing but a soggy noodle in his daughter's hands.

Secretly, Jiang admits that her grandmother is right. And thank God for it, because otherwise Jiang would not be standing inside Feng's, breathing in the smell of shoe leather, which is her favorite smell in all the world. She would be married off like her classmates, toting babies on her hip. Instead, she manages the family business, in which her older brother Vincent, a dentist with a spacious office off Dharmatala Street, has shown no interest. Though he is too loyal to the family to say such a thing, Jiang suspects that he looks down on shopkeeping.

And that is just fine with Jiang, who loves every aspect of her work. She opens the store each morning so her father, whose gouty leg has been bothering him, can sleep in. She decides which designs to order. She checks the quality of the work sent in by the shoe-makers and ruthlessly sends back pieces that do not meet her strin-gent standards. She visits every convent school in Calcutta and speaks to the appropriate personages so that their students will be directed here to purchase uniform shoes. (The priests and nuns are happy to recommend Feng's. The quality is excellent, and it doesn't hurt that Feng's provides the holy ones with free footwear.) She haggles ruth-lessly with the men from the Chinese tanneries in Tangra, squatting over the leather samples they have brought in. She quells, with a sin-gle glance (as she is doing now) the two salesgirls who have a ten-dency to dissolve into giggles at the slightest cause.

The cause, this time, is a young man who is approaching the store. Jiang notes that he is taller than the average Indian and clean-shaven, unlike the usual scruffy Bengali male who operates under the delusion that beards are the emblems of intellectualism. His blue shirt is crisply ironed, but his sleeves are rolled up. This gives him a holidaying look that Jiang finds surprisingly attractive, per-haps because her father and brother, both formal men, would never do something like that. She decides to attend to him herself and dismisses the disappointed salesgirls with a flick of her wrist.

The man is accompanied by a wide-eyed girl of about fourteen, who clearly adores him. Jiang guesses her to be his younger sister. Just as they enter the store, he bends and whispers something funny in her ear—or is it that the girl finds everything he says funny? She bursts into laughter, then claps a self-conscious palm over her mouth. The man pulls it away. "Stop that, Meena!" he says. "It's okay to laugh!"

Jiang is struck by his words. Has anyone in her family ever encouraged her to abandon herself to laughter? Even her father, who loves her dearly, is a cautious man. Letting her work in the store is probably the riskiest act he has undertaken in his life. And this is a temporary recklessness, because sooner or later Jiang's grandmother will wear him down into setting up a match for Jiang. As for her brother—Jiang pictures him in his starched white shirt and face mask (to keep out germs and the ubiquitous fishy odor that he insists pervades Bengali mouths) as he bends gingerly toward a patient. A sigh escapes her and she feels a twinge of jealousy toward the girl. Then the businesswoman in her takes over. A caring brother such as this man, she thinks, would buy high-quality shoes for his sister rather than look for a bargain.

As she expects, they are here to buy uniform shoes. For Loreto House, which is the poshest of the convent schools in Calcutta. The girl moves to the foot measurement stool, but already Jiang has called out to the salesgirl to bring A-22 and 23, and C-601 and 602, in youth size 3, narrow. Four pairs of shoes arrive, two black and primly laced for schooldays, two white with tiny silver buckles for holy days. They fit perfectly. The sister offers Jiang an awed glance, and even the young man is impressed. He chooses A-23 and C-602, which are the more expensive designs, and then as Jiang is about to lead them to the sales register, he tells her that he would like to buy another pair for Meena. Her first set of high heels. Would Jiang be so kind as to pick out something suitable, since she has such fine taste? Here he glances at her feet, at the elegant square heels she is wearing, their dark blue leather a perfect match for her pencil skirt. But his glance does not stop there. It flickers (but not disrespectfully, she decides) over the skirt, which shows off Jiang's trim figure to advantage, over the lace blouse with the tiny puff sleeves, over her neck, her chin, her mouth, and comes to rest on her eyes. Jiang is not totally inexperienced with men. She has attended numerous socials sponsored by the China Club, where she has had occasion to fend off dozens of ardent would-be suitors. But today, as she calls out for L-66 and P-24, in beige and dark brown, she finds that her throat is dry. Meena tries on the shoes; Jiang recommends the P-24 in brown; the brother declares that it is the perfect choice.

While a delighted Meena takes a wobbly walk around the store in her grown-up footwear, her brother hands Jiang his card. Jiang has never known a man who carries a card. She looks down at the white rectangle in her hand—how heavy, how smooth—to find that his name is Mohit Das, and that he is a manager—at such a young age!—at National and Grindlays Bank. He is thanking her for being so helpful; he is asking if she would like to go to Firpo's with him after work tomorrow for coffee and dessert; he is asking for her phone number; he is asking her name. Jiang? he says. In his mouth it sounds elegant, more exotic than she could ever have imagined herself to be. At the end of the corridor, he turns to wave. Everything has happened so fast that she is almost too stunned to wave back. But she manages. She raises her hand—still holding his card—and smiles.

Thinking back on those days, Jiang will most remember the food. The delicate flavor of marzipan and petits fours on her tongue. And later, crisp moghlai parathas eaten in tiny hole-in-the-wall restaurants where you could sit safely in a "family cabin" curtained off from the other diners. When they grew bolder, there were clandestine coffees and steamy vegetable cutlets among students at the Coffee House on College Street, and crisped-rice-and-potato chaat bought from street vendors because he wanted her to learn what real Bengalis loved to eat. The streetside snacks were so pungent that they made her eyes water, but even as she dabbed at her face with Mohit's handkerchief, she had to admit the taste was worth every tear.

"I FELL IN LOVE, OF COURSE," JIANG SAID. "WHAT IS FORBIDDEN is attractive. Also what is different. Also, when it is the first time. Put all of them together, they make strong wine."

Whatever Mohit's original intentions, he, too, succumbed to that intoxication soon enough. Additionally, as he observed her at work (sometimes, daringly, he would come to the store), he was taken by her fierce business acumen, her canny bargaining, her ability to match customers with the product best suited to them. Then there were the stories she told, about growing up in what he thought of as the Forbidden Palace. Were there really such fantastical places in Calcutta? He had to see for himself. And so, after a few months of clandestine meetings and stolen kisses in restaurants and movie theaters and the dusty carrels in the backs of university libraries, he armed himself with a box of Flurys cream pastries and persuaded Jiang to take him to her father so he could ask for her hand in marriage. The expected fireworks ensued. The grandmother threw a fit and threatened to return to China. (No one was too concerned by this, however; the family had migrated to India generations ago and did not even remember the name of their ancestral village.) But what surprised Jiang was that her father, usually so malleable, dug in his heels.

"He told me my marriage would fail," Jiang said. "When I told him I loved Mohit, he said, *Can fish love birds?*"

Finally he couldn't withstand her tears. He gave Jiang and Mohit reluctant permission to keep seeing each other. After a year, if they still felt the same way, he would reconsider the matter.

Mohit's family proved tougher. Devout Hindus and staunch Bengalis, they were devastated by the prospect of their only son, carrier of the generations-proud Das name, marrying a Chee-nay heathen. The thought of slant-eyed, octopus-eating grandchildren sent Mohit's mother's blood pressure rocketing, confining her to bed. Mohit's father sat him down for a man-to-man talk, in the course of which he informed him clearly that he would never give permission for such a perversion to occur in his family. *The girl must have bewitched you*, he said, *to make you forget your responsibilities as a son and a brother. I've heard the Chinese have sorcerers that specialize in such things. How will we ever get Meenakshi married into a decent family if you persist with this ridiculous idea?* Later he added, *Have an affair, if you're so besotted. Get her out of your system. Then we'll look for a proper match for you—a woman I won't be ashamed to introduce to Calcutta society as my daughter-in-law.*

An incensed Mohit moved out of his parents' house to stay with a college friend in his hostel. Soon after that, three men showed up at the shoe store and informed Mr. Feng that bad things would happen to his daughter if she didn't leave Mohit alone. A shaken Mr. Feng forbade Jiang to leave the house. Chafing in her confinement, Jiang began to hate the home she had cherished until now. She was able to call Mohit at his office for only a few minutes each day, speaking in hurried whispers when her grandmother was taking her bath.

Mohit assured her of his love. He wasn't going to buckle under his father's pressure. They would elope. They would go to Darjeeling or Goa. He told her to pack her valuables and be ready. But he sounded harried. She could tell he missed his family; she understood how torn he felt. As she hid an old suitcase under her bed and filled it with clothes and the few jewels she owned, the thought of her father's face when he discovered her defection pierced her with guilt.

As she lay awake at night, imagining her life with Mohit in a hill town, or in a seaside cottage awash with bougainvilleas, she worried that one day each might blame the other for what that life cost them.

Who knows how things would have turned out? But both Jiang's grandmother and Mohit's mother, convinced of the imminent ruin of their families, sought divine intervention. The grandmother lit joss sticks at Kuan Yin's shrine; the mother offered hibiscus garlands to the goddess at Kalighat. They both asked for the same boon: *May Mohit and Jiang's relationship break up, and may they subsequently marry someone suitable from their own communities.*

Over millennia, people have bewailed with some justification the tardiness of the mills of the gods, but in this case they began grinding at once, though perhaps not quite in the way the requesters had envisioned. Three days after the petitions, a unit of the People's Liberation Army of China attacked an Indian patrol in the Aksai Chin region of the western Himalayas, setting into motion the Sino-Indian War of 1962. The PLA advanced south past the McMahon Line into Indian territory, attacks spread to the eastern Himalayas and thus closer to Calcutta, and Chinese forces took over both banks of the Namka Chu River. Intelligence reports cited massive Chinese war preparations along the border. News of dead or captured jawans appeared in the papers. The Chinese consulate shut down, rumors of Mao's plan to bomb Calcutta ran rampant, and panic flared in the city.

People stopped patronizing Chinese businesses. Stores were vandalized. A popular Chinese restaurant was set on fire because a group of customers got food poisoning and believed it was part of a deliberate plot to kill Indians. Chinese banks failed. Crimson slashes of graffiti denouncing Chinese spies appeared on the walls of houses where Chinese families were known to live. The government ordered individuals of Chinese origin to register themselves and present papers for identification. Jiang and her brother were lucky. They had been born in a hospital and had Indian birth certificates. But many others, whose families had been in the country for generations—like their Indian counterparts—had never thought of acquiring official papers. Jiang's father was one of these.

"He was placed under house arrest," Jiang said. "We had to lock up Feng's and let the employees go. We didn't know what would happen to our property, or to us. Our friends had similar problems. Vincent quit his practice. No one trusted a Chinese dentist anymore. We spent our time at home glued to the radio, trying to guess our fate. There were terrible rumors. Many friends abandoned their property and left the country. Every day the Calcutta port was jammed with Chinese trying to get berths on ships.

"I called Mohit again and again. He wasn't there. Once a coworker picked up his phone and told me Mohit had taken leave because his mother's health was worse. He asked my name. I didn't give it, but I could tell he was suspicious. After that I was afraid to call, but I couldn't bear not to. If someone else answered, I hung up. Then one day Mohit called me from a public phone. He told me to get out of Calcutta as soon as possible. He had heard that the Chinese were being sent to internment camps. Then he said that he couldn't phone or see me again. Already he had received threats because people knew about me. He was afraid his family would be targeted as sympathizers. The worry was making his mother sicker. *Forgive me,* he said. *I love you, but I can't fight a whole country.* Then he hung up.

"I felt like my world had ended. I couldn't believe Mohit could let me down like this. I couldn't even tell my family (who had their own problems) how much it hurt."

Mohit's sources had been accurate. Within a couple of days, Jiang's family was notified that they must leave the country or relocate to an internment camp in Rajasthan, all the way across India. Those who did not obey would be forcibly deported to China. Jiang's father knew that going back to China under the yoke of Mao's Communist regime was out of the question. From refugees in the 1950s, he had heard stories of the labor camps rife with starvation and disease, the massacre of those labeled traitors to the Party. And he no longer trusted the government of India, this country that he had mistakenly loved as his own. He tried desperately to get his children out of the country—Vancouver or Brazil, San Francisco or Sydney or Fiji— it did not matter where. (Paperless as he and his mother were, he knew they had no hope.) But the Chinese exodus was at its peak. There were no airplane tickets, no ocean berths. Mr. Feng was willing to pay a hefty bribe, but he discovered that others had already paid equally hefty bribes.

Two days before the family was to board the train that would transport them to the hot, dry quarry town of Deoli, Vincent managed to locate a friend—an acquaintance, really—whom he had met a couple of times at the Chinese Dentists Club. Curtis Chan was the lucky possessor of a berth on a ship that was to leave for America in the morning—and he was a bachelor. That evening, unknown to Jiang, her father and brother bribed the guard posted outside their house and went to Curtis Chan's home. They took with them Jiang's photograph, a stack of dollars that Mr. Feng had managed to procure by calling in favors, several of his rare calligraphy scrolls, and all her mother's jewelry.

Curtis Chan was a practical man. He had been approached by two families with unmarried daughters earlier that day, and at the very moment the Fengs rang his doorbell, he had been getting ready to phone one of them. But perhaps he had a romantic streak in him, too, or a love of art. Otherwise why would he, after examining

Jiang's photograph and one of the scrolls, agree to Mr. Feng's proposition, even though one of the other families had offered him as many dollars, more valuable jewelry, and, additionally, a bag of gold Krugerrands? Vincent was dispatched home to fetch his sister. Mr. Feng and Mr. Chan—it is appropriate that we should address him in this manner, because as Jiang was about to discover, he was decidedly older than her brother and going bald, besides—hurried to the Buddhist temple in Tangra.

"And, just like that," Jiang said, "I was married."

Under normal circumstances, Jiang would have balked at the summary manner in which her father had decided her fate, yoking her to this middle-aged, stocky stranger, without even asking her opinion. But since Mohit's phone call, she had been walking around in a numb haze that gave way periodically to fits of furious tears. One moment she wanted a bomb to obliterate all of Calcutta, or at least the Das household. The next moment she wanted time to rewind itself to that day at Feng's so that she could leave the shop before Mohit arrived, and thus avoid the entire heartache of loving him. At other times she longed for Mohit to break down the door of the Feng mansion and carry her away to a place where her Chineseness would not matter. Buffeted by contradictions, she stood in the Buddhist temple, under the ominous shadows thrown by a single, shaky candle (Calcutta was under blackout orders), and did as the priest instructed, her motions jerky as a puppet's. It was only the next morning, as she was about to board the *Sea Luck*, that she seemed to realize the enormity of what had happened. She threw her arms around her father, insisting that she would not leave him, that she would rather that they died together. It took her brother and her new husband all their strength to get her up the gangplank while her father, himself in tears, tried to console her. *I'll be fine. I'll be back in the house once the government sorts things out. Then I'll come to America to pay you a visit. And your brother will join you soon. We'll get him on another ship in a few days.*

None of the things he promised came to pass. Within a year, he died of a heart attack at the camp, his devastated mother following him soon after. As for Vincent, he did get on a ship, but one bound for Australia, and it was years before he and his sister found each other.

"That was the last time anyone would see me cry," Jiang said.

The monthlong voyage seemed endless, with the Chans cooped up in a minuscule cabin with another newly married couple. (Upon boarding they had discovered that the captain, taking advantage of the helplessness of his customers, had double-sold tickets.) Mr. Chan and Mr. Lu, understanding that they had no recourse, made the best of it. They divided the little space they had with a blanket that served as a curtain, made up a bed on the floor where each couple slept on alternate nights, and created a strict timetable for the use of the cabin so that they would each get some privacy with their wives. This had a twofold result. Mr. Chan and Mr. Lu formed a lifelong friendship, and by the end of the voyage, Jiang was pregnant.

How did she feel about this last development? Did joy course through her as the baby grew? Or did she feel sick with worry at the prospect of having a child in a place where she knew no one who could support her through childbirth and into motherhood? Did she feel fondness for the child's father—or perhaps even the beginnings of love? Did she resent him for imprisoning her in a bloated body that would no longer fit into the pretty clothes she brought from Calcutta? Did she compare him with someone else who had kissed her more tenderly? Or did she tolerate him with resignation, because what choice did she have?

In America, they moved from city to city until Mr. Chan was forced to accept the fact that his dentist's degree was worthless here. Finally, they sold Jiang's jewelry and bought a small grocery in a Chinatown. Jiang helped in the store, dividing her attention between the customers and the babies—one, then two, in the playpen in the tiny back room. She was so good at managing the business that by the time the babies grew into children, the store had expanded into a supermarket and the Chans lived in a comfortable apartment above it. The family bought another supermarket and then a third; the children were sent to private schools; they moved to a large and lavish apartment in a gated building.

Everything Jiang required for daily life lay within the boundaries of Chinatown—markets, movie theaters, the houses of friends, the children's schools. Was there another need? If so, she buried that hankering deep within herself. In this new, compacted existence, there was no necessity for her to speak English, so she let it go. And, along with the language she had once prided herself on speaking so well, she let go of that portion of her past where English had played an important part. By the time her grandchildren were born, she communicated only in Mandarin.

Sometimes in the evenings Mr. Lu, now a widower, visited Mr. Chan. Jiang served them tea and dim sum but never joined in their wistful reminiscences. Her brother, Vincent, having finally managed to locate her, paid them a visit from Australia, where after decades of hard work he had risen to be the manager of—ah, ironic world!—a shoe factory. She was happy to see him, if in a bemused kind of way. (This stooped, tobacco-chewing man with a shock of salt-and-pepper hair did not seem to her to be connected in any way to the young man she had left behind on the docks of Calcutta, dressed in a crisp white button-down shirt.) When he brought up their childhood, waxing poetic about the hidden mansion in which they were raised, she refused to indulge in nostalgia with him. Only fools chewed the cud of the past.

But something was dislodged inside her as she listened to her husband and her brother conversing. After Vincent left, she found herself sitting by her bedroom window, staring out. Instead of the busy streets of Chinatown she saw an enclosed courtyard, roses spilling over a stone bench, children running around a fountain, screaming with laughter. The moon rose, shaking her heart with its beauty. Her father recited poetry, and she mouthed the words along with him. Each day she could smell the mango trees more distinctly. Inside her, emptiness grew until she felt like a hollowed-out bamboo. So when Mr. Chan passed away and Vincent wrote that he was planning a trip to Calcutta to decide whether he wanted to retire there, she wrote back impulsively—surprising herself, because she had thought herself long done with impulsiveness—that she would meet him in the city of her youth.

"Why am I going?" Jiang said. She shrugged and spread her hands. "Not sure. End of story."

7

I n the silence that shimmered in the wake of Jiang's story, each member of the company—for listening had made them into that—was busy with his or her thoughts. They went about their tasks, which had been assigned by Cameron or dictated by their bodies, but inside them the story still traveled, glowing and tumbling end over end, like a meteor in a slow-motion movie clip.

Malathi stirred a pan of Kool-Aid in the weakening light that Cameron had switched on—for only a few minutes, he warned— and thought of Jiang's parting from her father. It pulled up uncomfortable memories of the last time she had seen her own family, outside the security gate at the airport in Chennai. They had forgiven her and traveled by train all the way from Coimbatore to say good-bye, although she had indicated that it was quite unnecessary. How embarrassed she had been by their garish clothing, their loud, provincial accents. Her mother's teary hugs, her father's admonitions to be a decent girl and keep out of trouble, her sisters' lists of items they wanted from America—all of it had made her glad she was leaving. Now she would probably never see them again. With that realization, every item on the lists her sisters had compiled in their innocent greed (items she had pushed out of her mind even before she boarded the airplane) came back to haunt her: Hershey's Kisses, bars of Dove soap, Revlon lipsticks, copies of *Good House-keeping* and *Glamour,* and diaries with a little lock and key.

Then she thought of Mohit's fickleness, typical of men. This made her so angry that she almost upset the pan of Kool-Aid.

Tariq had not moved from his seat, not even to raise his feet onto the rungs of the chair as Cameron had advised, although he could feel water seeping into his shoes. He, too, was thinking, his forehead scrunched from contemplation. He should have been checking his cell phone, but instead he considered the nature of governments. How they couldn't be trusted. How they turned on you when you least expected it, when you had been a law-abiding, good-hearted citizen, and locked you up as though you were a criminal. Why would anyone want to live in a country that did that to their father?

Mangalam tried the office lines, but only half his mind registered that they were still dead. With the other half of his mind he was thinking about the passion with which the young Jiang had loved Mohit, a passion frozen into foreverness by the destiny that separated them. A passion that he suspected, by the tremor in the old woman's voice, still existed. Jiang had cursed fate for separating them, but wasn't she lucky, in a way? Had they married, at best their love would have been like the comfort of slipping one's feet into a pair of old shoes. At worst, it would have been like his life. (Mangalam, too, had loved his wife in the beginning. He remembered the fact of that love, though not *how* it had felt. That memory was gone completely, like a computer file wiped out by a virus.) Love, when alive, is a garland, he thought. When dead, it's a garotte. He felt rather pleased with himself for having come up with the metaphor.

Lily and Uma were helping Cameron check the condition of the ceiling.

"Gramma *really* fooled us all these years, pretending she didn't know what we were saying, forcing us to speak Mandarin!" Lily said as they slopped through the water to the storage area in the back. "And all those things that happened to her." She whistled softly, eyes sparkling in the dim light. "Now I want to go with her to India and see that house."

"I want to see that house, too," Cameron said.

If people could be compared to houses, Uma thought, then Cameron was as secretive as Jiang's former home. Who lived within his shuttered inner rooms? In the bleakness that Uma's life had shrunk to, the mystery of Cameron gave her something to anticipate. Ramon, now—he would be a traditional Japanese home, walls built of rice paper so that light could shine through and reveal every silhouette. Perhaps that was what she had loved about him, his transparency. He never tried to hide anything, not even how much he cared for her.

But why was she thinking of him in the past tense?

Mrs. Pritchett had locked herself in the bathroom, though she didn't need to use it. Jiang's matter-of-fact voice, speaking of love crumpled up and thrown away like a letter with too many mistakes in it, of families blown like spores across the desert of the world, had calmed her and made her remember something that she needed to check on. She searched through the inner compartment of her purse and came up with a small Ziploc bag that she had secreted there weeks back, just in case. It held a few pills. Mrs. Pritchett congratulated herself on the superior intelligence with which she had foiled Mr. Pritchett. She considered taking a pill but decided she would save it for later. Right now, she had to think about the story.

For Mrs. Pritchett, one item in Jiang's story had shone out like a lighthouse in a storm. It was the bakery-restaurant, the site of a slim, pencil-skirted girl's first forbidden date with a boy whose shirtsleeves were rolled up with holiday abandon. *Flurys*, she whispered to herself in the mirror, a delicious name that melted in one's mouth like the lightest of pastries. Was it large and cool and old-fashioned, set inside a high-ceilinged colonial building with pillars and chandeliers, protected from the harsh sun by a striped awning? Or had it been modernized into gleaming metallic sleekness? She hoped not. If she got to India, she would somehow make it to Flurys and offer them her services. If they demurred, she would give a demonstration on the spot, baking for them—she'd carry the ingredients in her suitcase—her irresistible white chocolate–macadamia nut cookies.

CAMERON GAVE THEM A TERSE UPDATE ON THE SITUATION. HE didn't sugarcoat the facts—he wasn't that kind of man: the phones were still nonoperational; the water was rising, though very slowly; the air quality seemed safe; there was food for one more meal. People looked glum at his assessment, but Uma noted they didn't press around him as they had earlier, bumping into one another like befuddled moths, demanding to know what would happen. When she asked if they wanted to continue with the storytelling, they returned to their chairs at once.

"Who would like to be next?" Uma asked.

"First I must tell you one more thing," Jiang said, surprising them again. I left this out because I was embarrassed. But without it the story is not true.

"The first night on the ship, Mr. Chan and I lay on the floor. I could not stand to think of him as *husband*. Every time I closed my eyes, I saw Mohit's face. That made me angry with myself. Mohit was not thinking of me, I was sure.

"The Lu family was on the bed, on the other side of curtain. We could hear them. Mr. Chan put his hand on me. I pushed him away. I felt like I would vomit. If he forces me, I thought, I will jump from the deck tomorrow.

"But he did not force. He put his hand on my head and stroked my hair. I realized he knew I had a boyfriend! Most Chinese men would not have married a girl who had a boyfriend. I started to cry. He did not say anything, not even tell me to stop. He just stroked my hair. For seven-eight nights it was like that.

"One night I kissed him. I thought, He is so kind to me, I must give him something. What else did I have to give? So even though I did not love him, we made love. I thought, It could be worse. It is possible to live without love with a gentle man.

"Finally we came to Chinatown. He could not be a dentist, even though he longed for it. Instead, we were working day and night in the grocery. Also, I was sick with the pregnancy. Some days we were so tired, we had no strength to say even one word to each other. There was no time to think of silly things, moon and roses and romance.

"Four years went like that. One night he was very sick. The flu had killed many people that winter, so I was worried. I gave him medicine. Put a wet cloth on his forehead. He was burning up, babbling nonsense. Suddenly he went stiff. His eyes rolled back. I thought, He's dying. My insides turned cold. *Don't die, don't die,* I shouted. *I love you.*

"Maybe he heard me. His eyes cleared for a moment. He lifted a hand. I clutched it. But he was trying to pull it away. Then I understood. He wanted to stroke my hair. I bent over so he could do it. Who knows why, next day his fever was less. In a week he was better.

"Later I thought I had said those words out of fear. Or because that is what they say in movies to dying men. But I had not been afraid. I knew I could take care of the store and the children, with or without a husband. And movies are foolish fancies. Then I knew I really loved him.

"When had it happened? Looking back, I could not point to one special time and say, *There!* That's what is amazing. We can change completely and not recognize it. We think terrible events have made us into stone. But love slips in like a chisel—and suddenly it is an ax, breaking us into pieces from the inside."

NO ONE SPOKE FOR A WHILE. MAYBE THEY WERE TRYING TO decide if they had ever been similarly ambushed by love. Maybe they were wondering if they had it in themselves to be as honest as Jiang. Then Lily said, "I'll go next."

"Would you wait a bit, sweetheart?" Cameron said. The endearment sounded natural in his mouth, though it was the first time Uma had heard him use it. *Sweet my heart,* they would have said in Chaucer's time, an expression that bound the speaker and the listener together, in one body. "We'll need your story more after a while."

Lily, who under normal circumstances would not have suffered anyone to call her sweetheart, flashed him a gamine smile. "What makes you think it's that kind of story?" But she nodded yes. Her eyebrow ring must have fallen off during the tussle. Without it, she looked more vulnerable. But at the same time, as she leaned over to stroke her grandmother's shoulder, she was more grown up. Then she said, her voice fearful, "Gramma's arm is hot."

When Cameron checked Jiang's arm, his lips thinned into a line.

He gave her two aspirin, though they all knew she really needed antibiotics. "Let's get started with the story," he said brusquely.

Mrs. Pritchett straightened her shoulders and drew in her breath. But before she could volunteer, Mr. Pritchett said, very quickly, "I would like to go now."

8

In the boy's earliest memories, his mother is always asleep, like Sleeping Beauty in the picture book she bought for him at a garage sale. And even though the boy loves his mother—loves her so much that sometimes he feels breathless, as when he's trying to blow up a stiff, new balloon—already he realizes she isn't that kind of pretty. She sleeps stretched out on the nubbly salt-and-pepper couch with a phone book wedged under the corner where one of its legs used to be. Her own legs are propped up on the frayed armrest because they tend to swell by the end of her shift, and when the boy is sure she's fast asleep he sometimes presses down on her shinbone with a finger and watches the dip that forms. Her mouth is slightly open, its corners pulled down as though she's just been handed a surprise of the less-than-pleasant variety. She snores softly. The sound comforts the boy, partly because it's soothing and familiar, and partly because it's so much better than those moments when she stops breathing and he's afraid she's died and left him alone.

Sometimes there's a bottle of Hires Root Beer on the floor beside her outflung arm. Sometimes (but rarely, because this is before the days of serious drinking that are waiting around the corner) there's a bottle of real beer, which smells and tastes so awful that he wonders why anyone would want it. But mostly there's nothing, because by the time his mother gets home from Mickey's Diner and Take Out she's too tired even to make it to the fridge. She shucks off the uniform right there, by the couch—she has only two uniforms, and the washateria is too far away and too expensive for more than one trip per week. Besides, she doesn't like doing laundry and waits until the last possible moment, a fact that will earn him certain unpleasant nicknames when he begins kindergarten next year. It's his job to pick up the brown pants and tunic and hang them over the back of the couch. If the night is warm, she sleeps in her underwear. If not, he fetches her nightie for her. She wrestles with the worn cotton shift, which is getting tight under the arms. (His mother is involved in a long-drawn-out, losing battle with her weight.) Once it's on, she thanks him with a hug for being her sweet boy. At those moments, her voice never fails to send a thrill through him. It's the one part of his mother that's more beautiful than Sleeping Beauty. Sometimes on the weekends, when she's in a good mood, she sings to him about a lady with green sleeves, a song that she says is hundreds of years old. And, best of all, she reads to him.

The boy knows how to dress and undress himself, how to brush his teeth (which he does in the bathtub because he can't reach the sink yet). He gets his own dinner, mostly cereal, which he has learned to eat dry on the days when they're out of milk. If he feels ambitious, he'll fix himself a peanut butter and jelly sandwich, but he's not too good at spreading the peanut butter and usually ends up tearing the bread. His mother eats at Mickey's—one of the perks of working there—and sometimes she's able to sneak home a hamburger or French fries or a bit of leftover pasta for him in the oversize tote she carries for that purpose.

The boy eats and watches his sleeping mother—the way her chest rises and falls with each breath, the line of hair that runs from her bra line, down her stomach, to the wavy elastic of her faded pink panties. Her body twitches from time to time like that of the animals he watches on the wildlife shows on TV. Those are his favorite shows, even more than *Howdy Doody,* and sometimes he and his friend Jimmy get into a fight about this. Should anyone ask him what he wants most in life, the boy wouldn't hesitate. A dog, he would say—though this is not completely true. He would prefer a tiger. But already he has learned that some desires must be held unspoken in the dark core of one's being.

When he is sure his mother has sunk into sleep, the boy will turn off the TV. Mostly she watches *I Love Lucy,* with its baffling jokes. (As he grows older, he will recognize this about himself: most things that people find funny fail to amuse him.) He'll go to the old tape player with reels as big as his head and carefully rewind the tape that's on it. He'll curl up on the floor with his blanket and listen to *Lassie Come Home,* which his mother recorded for him one week when she hurt her foot and couldn't go to work. There's a bed in the other room, but he'd rather lie here so that he can keep an eye on that undependable breath of hers while he follows Lassie over a thousand dangerous miles, determined to find her little boy. In the middle, he'll fall asleep, secure in the knowledge that before he wakes she would have concluded her quest.

Is the boy unhappy? No. When you've known only one thing all your life, you accept it as natural. It isn't until Mary Lou brings them the stolen math workbook that he will figure out that happiness is a whole different feeling.

THE BOY'S MORNING MEMORIES ARE OF MARY LOU BANGING ON the door of the apartment, shouting his mother's name—*Hey Betsy, are you dead or what*—and his mother stumbling bleary-eyed to the door, still in her underwear and cursing, but under her breath because she doesn't want her son to pick up any bad words. Jimmy runs in through the crack of the open door, shouting, "LL, look what I got."

In the background he can hear Mary Lou saying, "Shoot, girl, you look like death warmed over. You better go see the doctor."

The boy's chest hurts until his mother says: "Now don't start, Mary Lou. Nothing wrong with me except too many hours at a crappy job."

Jimmy pulls at his arm. "Look! look! You ain't looking."

Jimmy is here because the boy's mother and Mary Lou, who lives a few apartments over and works in the cafeteria of their neighborhood elementary school, babysit for each other. The boy likes Jimmy. He's fun to play with, even though he's always wanting the boy to look at things the boy doesn't find particularly interesting. Besides, Mary Lou, at whose apartment he eats dinner when his mother works overtime, is a great cook, and her lasagna (though the boy would never admit this, not even if someone tortured him using a cattle prod, like he once saw on *Gunsmoke*) is way better than anything the boy's mother cooks. The boy's mother, who is responsible for lunch, usually serves them canned soup and hot dogs wrapped in slices of white bread. Right after payday, they get real hot-dog buns, along with apples.

When the weather is good, the boy's mother sends them out to play, warning them to stay where she can see them, to not venture off the sidewalk. Playing cops and robbers, the boy watches her watching them as she talks on the phone, smoking, although she's told Mary Lou she really wants to quit. "Bang! Bang!" shouts Jimmy. "You're dead."

"Am not!"

"Are, too! I shot you in the head. Your brains are splattered all over the ground."

On days when it's too cold, they look at the books Mary Lou brings them from the school, claiming they've been discarded. "Yeah, right!" her mother says, though not in Mary Lou's hearing. But she, too, likes the books. Sometimes between phone calls, she sits beside the boys on the couch and exclaims over things she doesn't know. She doesn't know a lot of things. One day they go through a workbook titled *Fun with Math,* in which a chipmunk uses nuts to teach baby squirrels about addition and subtraction. The boy's mother loses interest after two pages, Jimmy after five, but the boy is riveted. Inside his head, the numbers fall into place with little clicks. His body buzzes as though it is filled with electricity. The chipmunk fades away. He does not need it to understand what's going on. He asks to keep the workbook, and that night, instead of listening to *Lassie,* he goes over multiplication and division. Though the terms are unfamiliar, within a few minutes he finds that he can work out the problems in his head long before he turns to the page where the chipmunk has written the answers on a blackboard hanging from a tree.

ON WEEKENDS THEY SLEEP LATE AND WHEN THEY WAKE, THE boy lying next to his mother in the bed in the back room, the two of them snuggled in a quilt with blue spouting whales on it, she reads to him. If they've had time to go to the library, she reads him new books. If not, as is more often the case, she reads to him from their dog-eared *King Arthur and His Knights of the Round Table,* a book that with its small print and no illustrations isn't really for children. But he loves its complicated cat's cradle of stories, loves how the familiar names roll off her tongue, Guinevere, Parsifal, Gawain, the sword Excalibur, the Questing Beast, the Chapel Dangerous, and, most of all, his own name. When she speaks it, she gives him a kiss.

Later they go to the grocery in Mary Lou's car, which rattles excitedly when it hits a pothole and sometimes dies at a stoplight. On the way back they stop at the bakery outlet and the boy's mother buys them powdered doughnuts. Jimmy eats his right away, but the boy takes tiny bites so the doughnut will last until they reach home. In the front seat, his mother and Mary Lou discuss the no-good men they've been dating, bursting into such loud laughter that the boy smiles in the back even though he doesn't understand most of the things they say. He knows about dates, though. That's when his mother wears a flared skirt and a sleeveless top (his favorite one is black, with lace over the chest). She sprays herself with perfume and swipes bright lipstick across her mouth and squeezes her feet into shoes with tall, dangerous heels, though later she'll complain that they hurt. But recently she hasn't been wearing heels because her new boyfriend, Marvin, is shorter than her and sensitive about the issue.

After they laugh for a while, the women get quiet. They turn up the music and talk in whispers, but the boy knows they're lamenting the fact that they aren't getting any younger, and that it's hard to find a man out there who wants a serious relationship with a woman who's carrying baggage. The boy wants to ask what kind of baggage, but he doesn't. He's afraid he knows already.

The boy doesn't mind so much when he's dropped off before a date at Mary Lou's. But when Mary Lou has a date, too, he and Jimmy are deposited at Mrs. Grogan's apartment, and that's not so good because Mrs. Grogan doesn't have a TV, only a radio that she keeps covered with a lace doily. Mrs. Grogan doesn't have teeth, either. The boys can't understand much of what she says, and that makes her angry. Besides, her apartment smells like pee, but when he complains of this to his mother, she says, "We'll all get old like her—if we're unlucky enough to live that long!"

(The boy's own mother will not be unlucky, not in that way. When the boy is in fourth grade, she will collapse at work one day, dying of an aneurysm before the ambulance can get her to a hospital. Later the boy will look up the word in the dictionary, but it will still baffle him.)

When the boy is five and a half, Mary Lou and Jimmy abandon them for Memphis, which is clear across the country. They're going to live with Mary Lou's mother, although she constantly bitches at Mary Lou, because Mary Lou can't make it on her own anymore, and she's just too tired trying. She cries as she tells the boy's mother this, wiping at her eyes, smearing mascara over apologetic cheekbones. The boy's mother doesn't say anything, but he sees something flicker in her eyes. He thinks it's anger with Mary Lou for quitting on them. But later he wonders if it's fear, and that makes him afraid, too. Then Mary Lou and Jimmy are gone, and his memories get a lot worse.

IN THIS AFTERNOON MEMORY, THE BOY IS ABOUT EIGHT, WITH long, untidy hair and clothes that aren't quite clean. He's playing by himself in the empty field behind the apartment building that doubles as a junkyard. The junkyard is off-limits—his mother thinks it's dangerous—but she's at work and isn't going to know. Marvin, who lives with them now, is aware of the boy's disobedience, but Marvin isn't going to tell his mother. Because then she would insist that the boy stay inside after school, and Marvin wouldn't like that. In the afternoon, when the boy's mother is at work, Marvin's friends come over to the apartment. The boy isn't sure what they do there, though from the sweetish smoke-smell that lingers after they have left, he can guess at some of it. In any case, he is playing alone in a field overgrown with brambles because there aren't any kids his age who live around here. If there were, they probably wouldn't be friends with him, like the children at school who sometimes make fun of his name or shove him around during recess when the teacher on duty isn't watching but mostly just ignore him.

The boy pretends he's Robinson Crusoe, alone on his island except for the cannibals who are after him. From behind an abandoned freezer, he trains his binoculars on them, watching them laugh with their pointy cannibal teeth. But they won't get him; he knows his way around the entire island, the caves and mountain passes where people must travel single file. He has his M1 semiautomatic and one hundred clips of ammo, and he knows how to move quiet as death. He raises his rifle and takes a step forward, then jumps back with a yelp because something furry has just brushed against his shins. It is a kitten.

The kitten is small and scrawny and meows loudly, opening its mouth wide and displaying tiny cannibal-sharp teeth and a very pink tongue. It skitters away when the boy reaches for it, but then lets itself be picked up. Its claws are sharp, too, but the boy doesn't mind. He thinks it looks like a miniature tiger, and he holds it and strokes its back while the kitten squirms in an attempt to get away. The boy remembers something he read in a book. He sets it down, breaks off a bramble branch, and bobs it up and down. The kitten swipes at it, entranced. They play like this for a while, but then the kitten starts mewing again—with hunger, the boy is sure. So he tucks it inside his shirt—he is afraid he'll lose it if he leaves it out here—and goes to the apartment. Inside, Marvin's friends, who scare him, observe him through a haze of smoke. One of them beckons him, asking if he wants a beer. The boy's face goes hot. Marvin's friends laugh. He almost backs out. Then he feels the kitten trying to climb up the inside of his shirt. Its tail tickles his chest. He tightens his shoulders and strides past their stares to the fridge—it is *his* fridge, he reminds himself. *His* apartment. He pours milk into a bowl. His hand shakes and milk spills on the sticky counter, but only a little. He carries the bowl out to the field.

The kitten laps up the milk and licks the boy's fingers. Its tongue is sandpaper-rough against his knuckles, and the boy shivers with pleasure. They play some more with the branch, the boy pulling it backward and the kitten pouncing on it so fiercely that right then and there he names it Shere Khan, after the character in *The Jungle Book*. They play this game for hours, even after the sun sets and the boy shivers in his too-small jacket. Finally he hears the sound he's been waiting for, the roar of trucks. Marvin's friends are leaving, and when the boy peers around the edge of the apartment building, he sees to his delight that Marvin is going with them.

It's simple enough, after that, to carry into the apartment the discarded kitchen drawer that he has already picked out, to hide it behind the couch where he sleeps nowadays, beside the cardboard boxes that hold his clothes and books. He lines the drawer with an old shirt and places the kitten in it, admonishing it to stay put while he does his homework. The kitten promptly climbs out, scampers to his chair, and clambers up his jeans leg onto his lap. That's how he does his homework, with the kitten curled into a ball of warmth against his stomach and him not daring to move because he doesn't want to disturb its sleep.

He has never loved anyone in the world as much as he loves this kitten. He will never love anyone this way again, with nothing held back.

When he hears the key rattle in the door, he squeezes his eyes shut and prays it's his mother, and, miracle of miracles, it is. He stuffs the kitten into his shirt and fetches her a soda pop, and when she puts out a tired hand to rumple his hair, he tells her

about it in a rush, because he knows he has only a little time before Marvin returns.

"Can I keep it, please, please? I'll take care of it. It won't cost
you anything."

Holding the kitten carefully in both hands, he offers it to her.
She puts out a finger to scratch behind its ear. It closes its eyes and
purrs, and butts her finger with its head when she stops. She laughs
and his heart leaps. But then her face fades and she shakes her head.
"We don't have enough room," she says. "And Marvin doesn't like
pets."

All his pent up resentment comes out in a rush. "Why do we
have to do what *he* says? This isn't his place. Why does he even
have to live with us?"

She's angry, he can tell that by the way her nostrils flare and little
blotches of red appear on her cheeks. But then her shoulders sag.
"He pays part of the rent," she says. "He watches you in the afternoon in case there's a problem or something." He's about to protest
hotly, but she goes on. "This way I don't have to get a babysitter.
Plus—" She shakes her head. "Oh, you won't understand."

He wants to tell her she's the one who doesn't understand that
things were so much better when there were only the two of them,
snuggled in their whale quilt. Her raspy, lovely morning voice reading to him on Saturdays is only a memory now. Instead, at night,
wriggling around on the lumpy couch, he hears noises from the
other room that make it hard for him to look her in the eye the next
morning.

The door swings open, banging against a chair, and the possibility of telling her anything ends. Marvin throws a fit when he sees the
kitten, going on and on about how he's allergic to cats, and is the boy
trying to kill him. Scared by the noise, the kitten pees on the boy's

hand. He doesn't care, but some of the pee drips onto his mom's uniform and now she's shouting, too. He's forced to take the kitten out on the porch, where he puts it into the drawer, tells it to stay, and covers the drawer as best he can with a cardboard box. The box is too small and he's afraid the kitten (already scrabbling madly inside) will escape. He hunches beside the box, trying not to cry, shivering, hating Marvin, wishing he would die. Alongside Marvin, he hates his mother—this is a first—and wants her to die, too. Then he can go and live with a different family, one that will let him keep his kitten. He hates them even more when she yells at him to get inside before he catches a cold and when Marvin stomps out and yanks him into the apartment, telling him to mind his ma. His hatred swells through the broken dreams of a night he will never forget.

In the morning, he runs out to discover the kitten gone. In school he is unable to pay attention—even to math. He rushes from the school bus to the junkyard, searches frantically through piles of garbage, and finally discovers the kitten shivering under a bush. Even when he hugs it hard against his thumping chest, hatred simmers inside him.

HE WILL REMEMBER THIS HATRED THE DAY HIS MOTHER DIES. Guilt will press down like a ball of iron on his chest no matter how much he rationalizes it, telling himself that he wasn't responsible, because look at Marvin, wasn't he still walking around hale and hearty in spite of all the boy's wishing?

He will be sent to live with foster parents. They'll turn out to be an older, childless couple, a bit strict but clean and organized. They will not get him a pet—and that's good, because surely then the iron ball would crack his chest. They will make sure he gets to school on time and does his homework and has nutritious meals. They will take

him to art museums and classical music concerts and will not up-
braid his indifference to such things. They will recognize his talent
and enter him in math contests—regional, then state, then national—
and winning these contests will begin to change the way he feels
about himself.

He knows his mother would have done none of this. Why then,
lying in a bedroom all his own, the wallpaper of flying dragons that
he picked himself lit ghostly blue by the night-light—a room he
couldn't have imagined when he lived in the old apartment—should
he give in to tears?

FOR A WHILE AFTER THAT TRAUMATIC NIGHT, THINGS GO WELL.
The boy cleans out the abandoned freezer in the junkyard and lines
it with his old clothes. He keeps inside it a bowl of water and a dish
of cat food bought with money he has stolen from his mother's purse
and Marvin's wallet, a couple of cautious dollars at a time. After
school each day, he takes Shere to the other end of the junkyard and
plays with him, keeping a wary eye out for his mother and Marvin,
because he doesn't want them to know what he's doing. When it's
time for him to go in, he reluctantly puts Shere in the freezer, bids
him good night, and wedges a stick under the lid—enough to allow
the kitten to breathe without letting it escape. This way, the raccoons and wild dogs that roam the junkyard at night can't get to it.
The kitten learns to recognize the boy. It launches itself at his chest
as soon as he opens the freezer lid, purring so loudly that its whole
body vibrates. The boy steals more money—what else can he do
when his mother will not give him an allowance?—to buy Shere a
catnip ball and can't stop grinning as he watches the kitten go crazy
over it. Then one day he returns from school to find the stick with
which he had wedged the lid open lying on the ground. The freezer

lid is shut, and when he opens it, he discovers that the kitten has suffocated.

He does not tell his mother. From this time on, he speaks to her as little as possible. She tries at first to engage him in conversation; then she gets angry. She doesn't have time for this nonsense, this sulking without a reason when she's knocking herself out to provide for him. He finds a pie server in a bottom drawer, digs a hole in the junkyard, and buries the stiff kitten-body though he can hardly bear to touch it. He can't eat anything the rest of the day or the next, but no one notices because he fixes his own meals. At night he lies in bed, going over the moment when he had last wedged the stick in the freezer door. How could it have fallen out? Had he been in a hurry? Had he been careless? Had someone followed him and pulled the stick out on purpose? Who would do something like that? There are no answers, and perhaps that's why the questions keep replaying in his head. Sometimes when people are talking to him, the questions come back, very loud, and he is unable to hear anything else. He gets in trouble at school for this; a couple of his teachers wonder if he's mentally handicapped. But they're overworked; since he doesn't cause trouble like the others, they let him be. At home he gets clouted on the head when he blanks out while Marvin is talking to him. Once his mother sees this and it leads to a huge fight between her and Marvin. Earlier, such a development would have pleased the boy. Now he hardly notices.

The only time he can forget the feel of the kitten's fur under his palm, or the way it butted its head against his shins, is when he's doing math. So he does more and more of it, asking his teacher for extra worksheets that he brings home, fractions and decimals, and word problems about Aunt Anna who's driving from Boston to Philadelphia at a certain speed, or a bathtub where the stopper doesn't quite fit, and how long would it take to fill. The words transform themselves into numbers that line up like acrobats, numbers that can be trusted to perform the way they're supposed to. He begins to understand their nature. They are ancient and immortal, not frail and easily broken. As long as he offers them his full attention, they will never abandon him. They sing their answers to him, and the inside of his head fills with light as he writes them down.

THERE HAD BEEN A NAKEDNESS ABOUT MR. PRITCHETT'S STORY, the feeling of a wound not yet healed. Perhaps that was why no one said anything, Uma thought. Or were they hoarding energy and oxygen for their own tales?

The noise of water had grown louder, more uneven, a *chug-chug* followed by a silence, then a gurgling, swallowing noise. Uma tried to visualize what might be happening. Cameron told them to roll up their pants legs or hitch up their skirts and remove their shoes and socks before getting off their chairs.

"Once you've taken off your socks, you need to put your shoes back on so you don't cut your feet on broken glass. Keep your socks in your pocket, along with these." He handed out pieces of blue cloth, the last bits of Malathi's sari. "We have to move to the employees area and sit on the tables there. The ceiling at this end of the room is sagging more than before." They stared up at the hole that yawned above. In the near blackness, Uma couldn't tell how much worse it really was. "Use the cloth to wipe your feet before wearing your socks again," Cameron said. "Stay as dry as you can so you don't get chilled."

Everyone did as Cameron instructed. Maybe they were grateful for these small, concrete acts that they could successfully perform. When Uma pulled off her socks with an awkward hand, she almost dropped one. Lunging to grab it, she hit her broken wrist against the chair. Pain shot through her and she cursed out loud. Standing, she saw that the water reached above her ankles, and the inevitability of that rising, more than the pain and the cold, made her want to cry. The group shuffled to their new location and pushed the tables around until they formed a triangle with gaps. Lily helped Jiang, who was holding her arm out stiffly, onto a table, and beckoned to Tariq to join them. Uma climbed onto the second table. Cameron wiped her feet for her and pulled her socks back on. Uma had expected Mrs. Pritchett to join them, but the older woman went to the third table, where her husband was sitting. Uma wondered if his story made her do this. Mrs. Pritchett perched on the edge, leaving the center spot for Mangalam.

Uma moved closer to Cameron to make room for Malathi, who was climbing onto their table. Three to a tabletop was a snug fit. But it would keep them warmer. Cameron was asking if anyone suffered from diabetes. No one confessed to it because Mangalam was holding a big plastic bag filled with sugar packets. When Cameron nodded, Mangalam passed the bag around. Uma took three packets. Greedily, she tore open the corner of one with her teeth and poured some onto her tongue. She was looking forward to the taste, but it was overly sweet and made her want to throw up. The unfairness of this made her want to cry.

Everything was making her want to cry. No matter what her own problems were, Mr. Pritchett's mother should have taken better care of her son. And why did the boy love her so, in spite of everything? Uma thought of her own mother, who had watched out for her with a hawk-eyed vigilance that she had ungraciously tolerated through childhood and rejected as a teenager. Did one always take for granted what came easily and long for what was impossible?

Cameron disappeared into the storage area, returning with a small stack of disposable tablecloths. He divided them among the three groups, to use as communal blankets. They weren't very warm, not even with two or three of them layered atop each other. But there was something comforting, Uma thought, something childlike and innocent, about sharing them.

HALFWAY THROUGH MR. PRITCHETT'S STORY, MRS. PRITCHETT had been broadsided by a memory. Years back, when she first realized they weren't going to have children, she had asked her husband for a dog. He had dragged his feet, pointing out that it would mess up their beautiful new carpet. He didn't have time to help her take care of it. And what would they do with it when they traveled? But she had begged and begged because she was lonely. Finally he had given in to her entreaties and taken her to the animal shelter.

A few minutes into their visit, before Mrs. Pritchett had taken a single dog out of its cage, Mr. Pritchett had complained of shortness of breath. He had rushed out of the building, and when she followed, concerned, she found him inside their Mercedes, bent over the steering wheel. His hands, when she had grabbed them, had been clammy.

She had guessed the problem to be an allergy, a severe one. To get to the dogs, they'd walked through a room filled with cat cages. Maybe that had set it off. *Very convenient!* a part of her had thought angrily. Then, ashamed of her selfishness, she had busied herself with rolling down the windows and getting him water. She had put away this disappointment like many others and had busied herself with the garden, the golf lessons he wanted her to take so they could join the local club, and the dinner parties he loved for her to throw. Now she was filled with sorrow and anger: sorrow for the boy he had been and anger because he had not ever trusted her with the truth.

ENTANGLED IN THEIR THOUGHTS, LOST IN THE HYPNOTIC GUR-
gle of water, they were startled when Lily said, "I'm glad you had
your math, Mr. Pritchett. It made you special when everyone
thought you weren't good enough." She glanced at Cameron. "Can I
tell my story?"

"Hold on a little longer," he said. He peered at the faces around
him, checking for responses.

Uma wanted to say something about the treacherous nature of
memory, how one painful event can overpower the many good ex-
periences that came before. But a dangerous lethargy arising from
cold and hunger prevented her from speaking. It was imperative that
someone start telling a story before the feeling overpowered them all.

With relief she heard Malathi's voice. "I will give you my story.
But my English is not so good, and I want you to understand everything properly. So Mr. Mangalam must translate it from Tamil."

Mangalam jerked up his head, frowning with wary surprise. He
looked like he was about to refuse, but Malathi spoke as though he
had assented already. "Better not change even one word. I know
enough to catch you if you do."

9

When I failed tenth grade for the second time, my parents figured it was no use wasting more money on my school fees and decided to marry me off. I had no objections; it was not as though I had anything else to do. Having navigated their way through the weddings of two daughters already, my parents knew that the local matchmaker would ask for a photograph. If they could provide her with one in which I looked better than normal, my chances of finding a husband—and theirs of negotiating a smaller dowry—would be highly improved. Though in general thrifty and suspicious, they knew the importance of a well-chosen investment. That is how I ended up at Miss Lola's Lovely Ladies Salon, the premier beauty shop in Coimbatore.

My mother had been to Lovely Ladies only twice, but Miss Lola knew her right away. "The bridal photo special, again?" she asked. When my mother nodded, Miss Lola looked me up and down and pronounced that I would require more work than my sisters. My mother gave a sigh but did not disagree, and the two of them fell to bargaining about the price of my beautification. When they had reached an agreement, Miss Lola gave a volley of staccato instructions to the pink-uniformed girls who worked for her, ending with "Bridal Special Silver Level with Hair Oil."

Two girls whisked me to an inner sanctum filled with elegant women undergoing the complex and painful process of improving upon nature. I was settled into a reclining chair and shrouded in cotton sheets. And it was here, in this moist, air-conditioned room decorated totally in shades of pink (Lola's favorite color) and fragrant with astonishing and exotic substances which my naïve nose was incapable of identifying, that I saw as though illuminated by lightning the path of my future.

Until this day, I had thought of marriage as an inevitable destination. The only other choice a girl from a middle-class Brahmin family, handicapped by respectability, had in our sleepy town was to teach at the Sree Padmavati Girls Higher Secondary School. But teachers were meagerly paid and resembled chewed-up sticks of sugarcane, and I had no desire to become one.

I confess: sometimes from our veranda I spied on other kinds of women, receptionists and typists who worked for Indian Oil and Godrej, and waited across from our house for the company vans to pick them up. Torn between disapproval and envy, I noted the dresses that exposed their knees, their shoes with platform heels, their permed hair. They wore lipstick even in daytime, erupted in laughter at frequent intervals, whispered prodigiously when men in expensive cars drove by, and ignored the lascivious remarks aimed their way by lesser males. But they were Kerala Christians—members of a forbidden, scandalous species that I could never join.

Lola's girls, though, with their perfectly arched eyebrows, glowing skin, and prettily coiffed faces hanging over me like radiant moons, were different. As they plucked and exfoliated and massaged oil and pinched blackheads and slathered my cheeks with Fair & Lovely cream, clucking soothingly when I yelped and assuring me that the end result would be worth it, I felt a strange kinship with them. They camouflaged me with sufficient foundation, face powder, kohl, lipstick, blush, and Vatika Pure Coconut Hair Oil to pass as one of Lola's lovely ladies. They attached a glistening bindi to my forehead and clipped fake diamond earrings to my ears. They pinned a sequined sari, kept in the salon for this very purpose, to my upper body (since that was all the photo would show) to manufacture curves where none had existed before. One of them ran to fetch Lola's nephew, who ran the photography business next door, while the others demonstrated facial expressions guaranteed to delight mothers-in-law, causing me to burst into laughter, something I never did in the presence of strangers. But they were no longer strangers. They had charmed me with their daring jokes, their code words for particular beauty procedures, their gallant laughter in the face of the drudgery that I guessed awaited them once they stepped out of the magical perimeter of Lola's salon.

The next morning, when my mother armed me with a parasol to protect my newly lightened skin and dispatched me to the bazaar to buy bitter gourd, I used the money to rent an auto rickshaw. Half an hour later I was at Lola's, begging her to let me work for her. Lola must have seen something—perhaps a glint of determination in my eyes reminded her of her own younger self. Although she had a room full of clients, she took the time to listen to my pleas. When I finished, she asked, "What's the matter? You don't want to be a bride?"

To which I answered, "I'd rather be a bride maker."

Lola, who had been divorced twice and thus knew what was what, said, "Smart thinking."

And just like that—although she hadn't really needed another employee—I became one of Lola's girls.

There was a dreadful hullabaloo at home, as you might imagine.

My parents stormed into Lola's, demanding that I be handed over. But she coolly informed them that the wife of the police high commissioner (her client for many years) was due in that very day for a gold-leaf facial. One word to her, and my father could end up in jail with charges of harassment. Once they crumbled, she took pity on them and pointed out that I would be excellently compensated. And if I should change my mind and wish to take on the yoke of domesticity, I would be provided with a Bridal Special Diamond Level photo, gratis. A Diamond Bridal photo was not to be sneezed at. My parents gave grudging permission, expecting me to tire soon of catering to spoiled society ladies.

Freed of parental interference, for the next six months I soaked up everything I could learn, from eyebrow threading to hot waxing to clay masking to hair perming. This last, most difficult skill Lola taught me herself. It was a job she entrusted only to her top girls. Pride filled me as I memorized the different kinds of rolls and tongs and end papers, the distinct amounts of time that provided Lola's clients with various degrees of curliness, and the secret proportions of potent chemicals that, if used wrongly, could exact a heavy penalty.

AMONG THE CREAM OF COIMBATOREAN LADIES WHO FREquented Lola's, the richest and most powerful was Mrs. Vani Balan. Wife of an industrialist who had made his money in cement, she visited Lola's every two weeks and underwent our most expensive regimes. In spite of the substantial tips she left, the girls avoided her. They didn't like the way she flicked the rupee notes at them. Besides, she was finicky and hot-tempered and had been known to throw things if a treatment did not turn out the way she had envisioned it. Only Lola was capable of handling her at such times, and even she would pour herself a full glass of rum and Coke after Mrs. Balan exited the premises.

For some reason that no one at the salon was able to fathom, Mrs. Balan took a liking to me and began to ask specifically for me when she came in. Although I was nervous around her, I was flattered, particularly when, one time after I assisted Lola in perming her hair, Mrs. Balan said I had a gentle touch.

I was not Mrs. Balan's sole favorite. She had a maid named Nirmala who often accompanied her to the salon and sat in the waiting room looking through the latest American magazines, which Lola's other nephew, who worked in a government office in Hyderabad, procured for her through unorthodox means. A slim, sweet-faced girl with surprisingly elegant hands, Nirmala would turn each page with attentive consideration, although she could not read. When Mrs. Balan emerged from the inner sanctum, she was ready with a flask of chilled juice. When they left, Nirmala carried with utmost care the packages of expensive foreign cosmetics Mrs. Balan had purchased. Once, in preparation for a wedding party, Mrs. Balan was undergoing a whole-body makeover that would take several hours; I asked the girl if she wanted a snack. She shook her head shyly, though I could see that she was hungry. When I brought her an orange, she was taken aback. "For me?" she said, as if she could not believe someone would consider her important enough. She thanked me several times, calling me Elder Sister. The appellation touched me. I could see why Mrs. Balan, who was surrounded by people who believed that the world owed them everything and then some, would find her refreshing.

MRS. BALAN TALKED INCESSANTLY ON HER CELL PHONE. SHE had perfected the art of speaking without moving her facial muscles and could thus continue to destroy reputations from under a substantive swath of seaweed or a coating of alpha-hydroxy peel thick enough to render most women immobile. Thanks to her, I became privy to all manner of skeletons lurking in the closets of our fanciest mansions. Were I so inclined, I could have blackmailed large numbers of addicted husbands, unfaithful wives, and grown offspring with questionable sexual preferences. But we at Lola's had our code of honor. And we knew that to meddle in the affairs of the powerful was akin to riding the proverbial tiger.

Mrs. Balan wasn't the only gossip at the salon. On days when she was absent, I learned from the conversations of the other women, who viewed her with a mix of hatred and adulation, that her husband (whom she ignored) was overly fond of the young secretaries at his corporation, and her son, Ravi (whom she adored), was studying abroad. She had gone into a deep depression when Ravi insisted on going to America—to get away from her, some of our less charitable clients suggested. She had revived only after a spate of shopping trips to Chennai and Bangalore. Now Ravi was returning to Coimbatore, with a degree in psychology and a head full of Western notions.

"You tell me now, what good is a degree in psychology of all things, that also from, what's that place, Idahore, that nobody has heard of?" Mrs. Veerappan said.

It was a rhetorical question, but her friend, Mrs. Nayar, was happy to respond. "No good. No good at all. But then, *he* doesn't need to make a living, not like our sons."

"I hear he wants to open a school for poor girls," Mrs. Subramanian ventured from the corner.

"Pouring money down the toilet hole, that's what he'll be doing," Mrs. Veerappan pronounced. "Oh well, that family certainly has no lack of it. Some of it might as well go to poor girls—the father has ruined enough of them."

MRS. BALAN GAVE US FURTHER DETAILS. "WHAT TO DO, MY RAVI
has always been a sensitive boy, gets it from my side of the family.
Wants to improve the lives of suffering people, just like Mahatma
Gandhi. I said to Mr. Balan, how can we stand in his way, let us
buy him the old Sai Center building like he is asking. Mr. Balan
didn't want to do it. Finally I told him, keep your money for those
secretary girls—what, you thought I didn't know about them? I'll
sell my diamond set and buy the school myself, and don't think
people won't hear about it. He signed the papers right away, but
grumbling all the while, as if Ravi wasn't his own flesh but some
beggar child we picked up from the street."

On a suitably auspicious morning, coconuts were broken; prayers
were chanted; camphor was burned; ribbons were cut by political
dignitaries; applause was offered by the newly hired teachers; copi-
ous amounts of idli-sambar, bondas, and coffee were consumed by
the invitees; and Vani Vidyalayam was open for business.

"Can you believe, Ravi named the school after me," Mrs. Balan
told us when she came in to get her hair styled for the celebratory
dinner party she was throwing. There were tears in her eyes, something we'd never seen before. She blew her nose, not caring that it
turned red. "He wants me to volunteer there. Maybe I'll do what he
says." It struck us that we might have been too quick to dismiss Mrs.
Balan as heartless and shallow. Perhaps mother-love would work a
transformation upon her.

AT FIRST, THINGS WENT WELL. LURED BY THE PROMISE OF FREE
education, along with a free lunch and two uniforms, a good number of parents sent their children to the Vidyalayam. Mrs. Balan

started visiting the school once a week at lunchtime, when she would walk up and down the canteen wearing a starched hand-loomed sari that Gandhiji himself might have woven, gingerly patting the heads of the cleaner children. Then she would go into the office and terrify the clerks into efficiency. Who knew where this might have led? But just when we conceded that Mrs. Balan had surprised us, Ravi decided to expand his philanthropy beyond the boundaries of the school compound. He insisted that the Balans' servants should attend, each evening, an English reading and writing class. He would teach it himself, on their terrace. Mrs. Balan was not happy about this disruption to her household, but she was unable to refuse her son.

The servants were, at first, intrigued by this novel development, especially as it afforded them an hour's break from their duties. But they soon tired of it. The older ones didn't see how their lives, into which they were comfortably settled, could be improved by reciting sentences out of children's books. The younger ones were bored, because in spite of his noble intentions, Ravi was a poor teacher. The servants came to class late and left early, pretending to be busy with housework, until finally they did not come at all. But by then Ravi did not mind because he had found his star pupil, Nirmala.

Who can guess what had been in Nirmala's mind when she started attending the class? It is possible that she longed for the education that birth had deprived her of. Can you blame her if, along the way, she fell in love with the way Ravi looked earnestly into her eyes as he urged her to remember the strange sounds of English, the shapes of its contorted letters? He was as close to a prince as anyone she knew. Aided by the romantic movies she had seen, she might naturally have cast herself in the role of the beggar maid whom he rescues. But all this is conjecture. The only thing we know for certain is what one of Mrs. Balan's servants witnessed.

One evening Mrs. Balan, home early from the club, climbed to the terrace to check on the progress of her servants' education. To her shock, she discovered Ravi and Nirmala sitting side by side, heads almost touching, his hand guiding hers as she traced letters into her notebook. She saw the girl's shining face as she completed her task and looked up to be complimented, and she saw Ravi put his arm around the girl and give her a hug.

If Mrs. Balan had curbed her temper, sent Nirmala downstairs, and spoken quietly with Ravi, the situation might have been resolved. But seeing her beloved son's lips just a few inches from those of her maid drove strategy from her mind. She strode forward and delivered a stinging slap to Nirmala's cheek, screaming at the cringing girl for being a conniving hussy. She would have hit Nirmala again if Ravi had not grabbed his mother's wrists and told her to pull herself together.

Mrs. Balan went a little crazy then, calling Nirmala worse names, threatening to make sure everyone in her home village knew how she had repaid Mrs. Balan's many kindnesses with treachery. Then she turned on Ravi. Had he lost all sense of proportion, living in America? Had he forgotten that servants needed to be kept in their place? Couldn't he see that a low-class girl like Nirmala had probably been planning all along to trap him?

Ravi made threats of his own, delivered in a quiet voice. If his mother fired Nirmala, he would return to America. She would never see him again.

Faced with this ultimatum, Mrs. Balan was forced to allow Nirmala to remain. The defeat confined her to bed for several days. She rose a different woman, older and frailer. At first she avoided her son. But when he apologized for the harshness of his words (though he did not take them back), she wept and embraced him. In a few days, things seemed to have returned to normal in the Balan household.

Nirmala carried out her regular duties, even accompanying Mrs. Balan when she went shopping.

"The lessons were stopped, of course," Mrs. Veerappan told Mrs. Nayar as they both underwent Hibiscus Oil Hair Therapy. "But in a big house like that, is it difficult for a young man and woman to meet in secret?"

"Not difficult at all," Mrs. Nayar said. "Do you think they are . . . ?"

"Oh no," said Mrs. Veerappan. "It's much worse." She went on to relate what her sweeper girl had heard from the Balan cook. One evening, when his wife was away at a bridge party, Mr. Balan, who noticed much more than his wife gave him credit for, asked Ravi to join him for a glass of whiskey-soda. He then inquired whether the young man would like to set Nirmala up in a little flat where he could visit her without disrupting the peace of the household. Scandalized, Ravi said he had no intention of taking advantage of Nirmala. He praised her intelligence, her belief in the goodness of the world, and her willingness to improve herself. He ended by stating that he thought rigid class boundaries were the bane of Indian society and should be broken down.

"You think he means to . . . ?" Mrs. Nayar asked, aghast.

Mrs. Veerappan spread her newly manicured hands to indicate the thoughtless perfidy of children. "Naïve, idealistic, stubborn, and rich—when a young man's like that, anything can happen."

THOUGH NEWS OF THE FATHER-SON TÊTE-À-TÊTE MUST HAVE reached her, Mrs. Balan did not seem overly concerned. A few weeks later, she swept into Lola's with Nirmala in tow, as high-nosed as ever. I scrutinized her from behind a beaded doorway as she informed everyone that she was going to Chennai to attend the fiftieth birthday celebration of her cousin-brother, Mr. Gopalan, who owned a five-star hotel franchise. The festivities would go on for an entire week. Gopalan, a bachelor and a playboy of sorts, loved parties and spared no expense. Mrs. Balan was leaving this evening, though Mr. Balan and Ravi couldn't join her until the weekend. She had to have a facial and a manicure at the very least, and perhaps a deep-steam cleanse as well. She insisted that Lola take care of her personally for this important occasion.

"Are you taking your maid with you?" Mrs. Veerappan asked sweetly.

Mrs. Balan replied, equally sweetly, that she was. She couldn't do without Nirmala for even one day. Who would iron her clothes, keep track of her jewelry, carry her packages from the best shops in Chennai, remove her makeup, and give her a bedtime foot massage? "No doubt you're accustomed to doing all these things for yourself, dear Mrs. Veerappan," she ended, "but I'm afraid Mr. Balan has quite spoiled me." Then she stated that she wanted Nirmala to get a facial, too.

A collective gasp went through the room at such blasphemy.

"Give her the Ayurvedic Herbal Pack," Mrs. Balan said, causing Mrs. Veerappan, whose face was currently slathered with that exact mixture, to come perilously close to a seizure.

I was the one to whom Lola assigned the task of removing Nirmala to a private room where she would not offend the sensibilities of our regulars. Some of Lola's girls would have balked at working on a servant, but I didn't mind. Since the day she called me Elder Sister, I'd felt strangely protective toward Nirmala. I worked to make her as beautiful as possible, silently wishing her luck. If things worked out, she would need it, with a mother-in-law like Mrs. Balan. If things didn't, she would need it even more.

Once she got over the wonder of being seated in a chair just like the rich madams, Nirmala chattered excitedly about going to Chennai. She had never been anywhere, apart from her village and Coimbatore. She was looking forward to the air-conditioned malls with moving staircases. And Gopalan-saar's house, which was supposed to be twice as big as the Balans'.

As I shaped her eyebrows and massaged her firm, unblemished skin, so different from the faces I usually worked with, she confided something else to me. Mrs. Balan had given her several old silk saris to wear during the trip. Surprise must have made me frown. She hastened to add that they were very fine, and wasn't she lucky to have such a generous mistress?

"She even gave me a fake ruby set she bought last year, for me to wear the first night when Gopalan-saar will throw a party at the house, for close friends. Madam wants me with her in case she needs something."

I was thankful that the relationship between Nirmala and her mistress seemed as good as before. Mrs. Balan wasn't the kind to let go of a grudge easily. Perhaps, having met her match in her stubborn son, she had decided it was best to be on friendly terms with her might-be daughter-in-law.

Nirmala examined her burnished skin in the mirror. She asked whether her face would still look as good by the weekend—which, I recalled, was when Ravi was to join them. I told her the truth, which was no. The first couple of days, with the skin still toned and shining from the massage, were the best. She bit her lower lip, deep in thought. I guessed she was trying to figure out how to meet Ravi before she left for Chennai. Then she smiled. That's how I would remember her: glowing in the mirror, the light from the ceiling casting an asymmetrical halo around her head.

NONE OF US SAW NIRMALA AGAIN, THOUGH BITS OF HER STORY blew back to us on the winds of rumor. Piecing them together, I felt stupid. Worse, I felt responsible. She had trusted me, called me Elder Sister. I should have seen what was coming and warned her. Though I had never been religious, I went to Goddess Parvati's temple and prayed for forgiveness. But I knew it wasn't enough.

This is what I guessed: That first night, by dressing Nirmala far above her station and keeping her constantly at her side, Mrs. Balan made sure that Gopalan noticed the maid. Nirmala herself must have piqued his interest with her amazement at the extravagance of his house. Admiration is a powerful aphrodisiac. After the guests left, it would have been easy enough for Mrs. Balan to complain of a headache and send Nirmala to Gopalan's room for some medicine. Who knows what transpired between the two of them there? Only these facts are certain: Long before Ravi and his father joined the festivities, Nirmala was moved from the servants' quarters to a suite of her own in another wing of the house. Her fake jewels were replaced with real ones, her hand-me-down clothes with designer saris studded with sequins and deep-cut blouses that showed off her charms. And from the manner in which he patted her behind when she fetched him his gin and tonic, it was clear to his guests that Gopalan had found himself a new girl.

MRS. BALAN CAME IN TO LOVELY LADIES A COUPLE OF WEEKS later. She informed Lola that she wanted the softest, most natural-looking curls. Ravi was getting engaged to the youngest daughter of Kumaraswami, a real-estate tycoon from Bangalore. They had met on the last day of Gopalan's birthday celebrations. The marriage would take place in the girl's hometown, but the engagement party would be held this weekend at the Balan residence—a small affair, really, no more than three hundred guests.

"Do you like the girl?" Mrs. Nayar asked.

"Of course! After all, she comes from an excellent family. A bit short, and a trifle plump, but smart as a whip. Already she's talked Ravi into handing over Vani Vidyalayam to a manager and going to work for her papa. I'm a little disappointed that he'll be moving to Bangalore—but I'm not one to hold a son back from his happiness. Now, Lola, can you make sure I'm the chicest, youngest-looking mother-in-law ever?"

Lola assured Mrs. Balan that she could. I watched amazed, because when Lola first heard the news about Nirmala, she had kicked a table and used several colorful expletives to refer to Mrs. Balan and her ancestors. Yet now, with the utmost politeness, Lola pointed Mrs. Balan to the best salon chair. I realized that the secret of Lola's success was a perfect separation between business and personal emotion.

"No, not here," Mrs. Balan said. "I don't want everyone seeing what you do and then asking for the same look. You must keep this a secret. I don't mind paying extra. And I want only Malathi to assist you."

Lola called my name.

"Where is that girl hiding, anyway?" Mrs. Balan said.

For a moment, I considered disobedience, but when Lola called again, I followed them to one of the private rooms in the back. My heart lurched as we entered. It was the room to which I had brought Nirmala. I felt as though the goddess was sending me a message. An idea pushed through the muck of confusion in my brain.

Mrs. Balan was in high spirits. "If you do a good job," she told me, "I'll give you the biggest tip you'll ever earn." Lola entrusted Mrs. Balan's tresses to my care while she went hunting for youth-inducing unguents. I combed out Mrs. Balan's hair with trembling fingers. But by the time I started mixing the chemicals for the perm, they were rock-steady.

"Smells funny," Mrs. Balan said. "Are you using something different?"

"Yes, madam," I said, applying carefully. "This is a special occasion, no?"

"It stings."

"As you know, madam, beauty has its price."

"Be careful," she warned. "I don't want to end up looking kinky-headed, like some Andaman aborigine."

"Such an outcome is most unlikely, madam," I said.

AS SOON AS LOLA WALKED INTO THE ROOM, SHE SENSED THAT something was wrong. I could see it in the way she scrunched up her nose. Would she order me to unwind Mrs. Balan's hair and wash it out at once?

"Give madam a pedicure while you wait for the perm to set," she said. She busied herself with scrubbing Mrs. Balan's face with an imported and extremely expensive exfoliant.

Mrs. Balan's hair started falling out as soon as I ran water over it. By the time I finished rinsing, clumps of it lined the sink like dead seagrass. The shriek she emitted when she opened her eyes brought the girls—and any clients who were not attached to machines—rushing to the back room. Several shrieked in sympathy. About half of her scalp was as bald as a baby's bottom and covered with a rash. The other half sported wilting sprouts. I swayed between terror and exhilaration. Mrs. Balan spewed invectives as she attempted to simultaneously strangle me and gouge out my eyes. Lola, who had been vainly trying to calm her, instructed two girls to remove me from the premises. As I left, I could hear her declaring that I would never set foot in Lovely Ladies or any other beauty shop in Coimbatore again.

I lay awake all night. I would sorely miss the salon and the company of the girls. What would I do now? I was barred from the only profession I was good at or cared about. Probably, I would have to find a husband—and that, too, without the benefit of a Diamond facial. Worse, I feared I had landed Lola, who had understood my dreams better than anyone in the world, in deepest trouble.

All morning, I stayed in my room, pretending to be sick, not confessing to my parents that I had been fired. But after a while I felt like I was suffocating. I had to go to the salon, no matter how angry Lola was with me. She would probably throw me out without hearing my apology. But I had to try. I wanted to tell her how I had felt responsible for Nirmala's fate, and how, therefore, I had to even the score no matter how much bad karma I accrued in the process.

I went around to the dingy back entrance of Lola's, which was used only by the sweepers. I had never been there before. It took me a while to find the unmarked door. The stinking garbage piled along the open drains was symbolic of the turn my life had taken. The girl who answered my knocks looked anxious when she saw me. I said I would wait outside. Would she ask Lola to see me for just a minute?

Standing in that alley for what seemed like a lifetime, I wondered if Lola would even come. Finally, she opened the door, hands on her hips, her face stern. I whispered my explanation and apologies, my eyes on the ground. Halfway through, I was distracted by strange gasping noises. Was she apoplectic with anger? Or could she—the Amazonian Lola I had hero-worshipped—have been reduced to tears? Perhaps Mrs. Balan had threatened to sue her. Perhaps Lola would lose her beautiful salon. When I dared to look up, I saw her hand over her mouth. She was trying to keep her laughter in check.

"Did you see her head?" Lola managed to choke out finally. "And her face? It was priceless!" Both of us burst into hysterical peals.

When I confided my fears for the salon, Lola waved a dismissive hand. "Mrs. Balan won't dare do anything to me. I have too many influential clients, and I know too many indiscreet things that she's said in here. If I decided to open my mouth, she wouldn't be invited to another party as long as she lived. Besides, she needs me. Without me, within a month, she'd look fifteen years older.

"I had to fire you, of course. I had no choice. Though I hate to lose you—you have the instincts of a true beautician. But you must leave Coimbatore right away. It isn't safe here for you anymore. Mrs. Balan can't harm me, but you're a different matter. She could easily hire a goonda and have him throw acid in your face—"

I panicked. "Where will I go?"

Lola dug into the pocket of her smock and took out an envelope and a pouch. It struck me that she had known, before I knew it myself, that I would come to see her. "Here's a letter of introduction to my nephew who works in Hyderabad. I spoke to him about you, and he said that he would help. He told me some of the Indian consulates abroad are looking for employees. One of the hiring officers is an old classmate of his. But the employees have to know English." She handed me the pouch. "Take this money. My nephew and his wife have agreed to rent out a room in their house to you. He'll find you an English teacher. And when your English is good enough, he'll take you for an interview."

I didn't have the words to thank her, so I hugged her instead. She patted me awkwardly on the back. She was uncomfortable with displays. "Just keep your temper, the next place you go," she said. "And when you've saved enough dollars, come back and open a salon in a better city." She looked as though she might say something more, but then she didn't.

At the end of the alleyway, I turned to wave, but she had gone inside. She was a practical woman, with a roomful of clients waiting.

10

After Malathi finished her story, Uma didn't want to return to the present. It was so pleasant in Lola's pink salon, moist and cool, with its herbal shampoos, sandalwood paste, and the calm, ministering hands of Lola's girls. Even the heat that ambushed you when you emerged from air-conditioning onto the noisy street was a gift. She wanted to know what it was that Lola had almost said to Malathi at the end.

The others were discussing Malathi's characters with vigor. Mrs. Pritchett puzzled over Mrs. Balan's Machiavellian tactics. How could one woman be so cruel to another? Jiang said Mrs. Balan really couldn't feel for Nirmala because she had been brought up to dismiss a servant as a lesser being. Lily thought Lola was cool, and she, too, would have liked to work at Lovely Ladies and listen in on high-society scandals. The beauty shop that Lily's mother frequented on Van Ness was run by a mousy Taiwanese woman with braces. The one time her mother had forced Lily to get her eyebrows done there before a school musical performance, Lily had almost died from boredom. All the aunties talked about was how well their children were doing in school, and who had won which award. Did Malathi remember any of the tricks she had learned at the salon? Malathi's teeth glimmered in the beam from Cameron's flashlight. (Had he changed the batteries? Uma wondered. She tried to recall how many batteries had been in the bag, but she couldn't remember that far back, and trying made her head hurt.) Malathi promised Lily that if they ever got out of here, she would give her a hibiscus oil head massage that would make her feel like a princess.

No one spoke of the two people who were most on their minds until Tariq, in his blunt way, said, "Why would Nirmala do something so stupid, give up Ravi for a creep like Gopalan?"

"Maybe he offered luxury that a girl like her, brought up in a shack, just couldn't turn down," Mrs. Pritchett said. "You can't blame her."

"That night at Gopalan's house, she must have realized that Mrs. Balan would not let her son marry a servant," Jiang said. "Perhaps she thought, if I do not take this offer, next thing, my body will be in a ditch somewhere."

"Maybe she couldn't imagine refusing a man as powerful as Gopalan," Uma said. She wondered if Gopalan had raped Nirmala. Coming from a background where virginity was the paramount virtue for women, Nirmala would have had no option after that.

"But what about Ravi?" Mrs. Pritchett said, with some force.

"I don't think Ravi was in love with Nirmala," Lily said. "It was probably infatuation because she was so different from the girls he knew. Maybe he was secretly relieved because she went with Gopalan—like when you have a boyfriend you don't really like anymore, but you can't tell them, and then they start going out with someone else."

Malathi said, "I suspect Ravi saw Nirmala with Gopalan and felt she was spoiled for him. He didn't want her anymore. But his ego was hurt that she was with someone else. So he picked the first girl his mother sent near him."

"Could be Ravi's heart was broken," Mangalam said. Uma heard a snort from Malathi, but Mangalam continued. "Could be he felt betrayed by Nirmala after he had taken such a risk for her, going against his parents. That must have been hard for him, being the only child and knowing they had all their hopes pinned on him. I think he chose that other woman because he was hurting."

Malathi drew herself up, ready to debate the issue. But just then Cameron said, "Hush. Listen." In the silence carved out by his imperative, they heard a creaking, yawing sound—like an abandoned ship rolling back and forth on a misty sea, Uma thought. The sound filled her with an eerie melancholy.

"What is it?" Mr. Pritchett asked, his voice sharp with distrust.

"The ceiling on the other side of the room; you can't see it because of the partition," Cameron said. "A part of it—hopefully not a very big one—is getting ready to come down. Don't panic—the portion above our heads"—here he swung the flashlight up—"seems stable enough. But we must have a plan ready in case that ceiling, too, starts breaking apart. Under normal circumstances, I would tell you to get under the tables—not that we'd all fit. But the water's risen too high. It'll soak your clothes. It's too cold in here to remain in wet clothes."

He pointed down with the flashlight and Uma saw that the water had reached halfway up the first drawer. It was very dark. Looking at it made her shiver. And Cameron was right—it had grown very cold in the room.

Cameron said, "Keep your pants rolled up and your skirts tucked high, so you can jump down at a moment's notice. Our best bet is to stand in the doorways. We can't use the door leading into the passage—it's too close to the damaged ceiling. That leaves us the two doorways into Mangalam's office and the bathroom entrance. We should be able to squeeze everyone into them. But there's no point sitting here waiting for that to happen. Let's listen to our next story."

Mr. Pritchett had not taken part in the discussion about Ravi and Nirmala. When he had finished telling his tale, a great lightness had taken over his being. But that high had faded. Now he felt more depressed than ever. He had been hoping for a comment from his wife, a validation for the suffering of the boy he had been. She had said nothing. Disappointment increased his craving for a cigarette. Within his body, things were beginning to shake. Soon they might start coming apart. He was almost certain there weren't any broken gas lines nearby. A few puffs, with the bathroom door tightly shut, couldn't harm anyone. He would spray the bathroom with the deodorizer afterward. No one would even know. As soon as this tiresome discussion ended, he was going to head for the bathroom.

"Tell us why you picked this story," Uma said.

"It was the only time in my life I did something brave," Malathi said, "even though it was a big cost for me. I don't think I can do that again. I am too selfish. So it is special to me."

At the mention of selfishness, Mangalam's head jerked up as though he had not expected her to confess to such a vice.

"Does anyone need a bathroom break?" Cameron asked. People looked down at the water, weighing their need against its darkness. Mr. Pritchett waited, trying not to fidget. He didn't want to go if there were other trekkers to the bathroom. There was only one flashlight allowed for such errands, and they would have to wait around to walk back together. They might smell the smoke.

"Well, then," Cameron said, "let's start a story."

"I want Tariq to be next," Lily said. Tariq looked startled and not particularly pleased. Uma was sure he would say no. But he nodded at Lily and cleared his throat.

"Excuse me," Mr. Pritchett said, jumping down before Tariq could begin. "Back in a moment." He took the pencil light—very dim by now—that Cameron handed him. He was glad he hadn't had to tell a lie about the purpose of his trip. He did not like lying. He sensed Mrs. Pritchett's eyes on his back as he made his way through the icy water. Did she guess? When he thought he was out of the range of Cameron's big flashlight, he put his hand into his pants pocket and caressed his lighter. He had almost reached the door to Mangalam's office when he heard a splash. He turned and saw that Mangalam, too, had climbed down. "Wait for me," he called as he hurried toward Mr. Pritchett.

Mr. Pritchett felt a futile fury surge through him. He rubbed his thumb against the serrated wheel of the lighter as though it were a magic lamp and tried to come up with another plan. Failing, he offered the pencil light to Mangalam. "You go first."

But Mangalam, who had plans of his own, gestured solicitously and said, "No, no. After you, please."

Mr. Pritchett walked into the bathroom and pushed the door through the water until it closed. He had to use all his self-control to keep from slamming a fist into the wall. He grabbed the edge of the sink in both his hands and held it tightly, trying to decide what to do. Could he take the chance that Mangalam wouldn't smell his cigarette when he walked in here? No. No amount of deodorizing spray could disguise the odor of burned tobacco that quickly. Would Mangalam report him to Cameron? Very possibly. The visa officer seemed to hold the sergeant in some awe. What could the sergeant do to him, though? What could any of them do?

Nothing, Mr. Pritchett said to his sallow reflection. At most, they would confiscate his cigarettes, but he had already hidden a few. If they took the lighter, he could sneak a book of matches. He took out a cigarette and placed it between his lips, his hands trembling from anticipation. He could already taste the smoke.

A knocking on the door made him jump. Voices. Mangalam—and someone else. Their words were unclear but insistent. One of them jiggled the handle.

Mr. Pritchett cursed under his breath and stuffed the cigarette back into its packet, hoping he hadn't injured it. He splashed his face with water, gasping at its coldness, and pulled the door through the water.

Cameron was standing there, his hand on the doorknob. "Are you okay? Mangalam said he called you a couple of times, but you didn't answer."

"I'm fine," Mr. Pritchett said. He knew he sounded snappish, but he couldn't help it. How much time had he spent in there? Cameron stared at Mr. Pritchett's dripping face. Mr. Pritchett pushed past the two men into the dark. Behind him, he could hear Cameron telling Mangalam, "We'll have to insist that people not lock the door when they go to the bathroom." Hah, thought Mr. Pritchett. Insist away, Sarge. I'll do what I need to. The smell of bourbon seemed to be all around him. Was nicotine withdrawal messing with his senses? In his hurry he banged his hip into something hard and metallic. Pain shot through him. He stumbled and felt one of the men grab his arm.

"Careful, buddy!" Cameron said. "The world has handed us enough problems already."

Hadn't he said almost the same thing to his wife a while ago? Mortified, Mr. Pritchett trudged to his table. But he wasn't too mortified to decide that while everyone was eating, he would try his luck again.

11

When Ammi called on my cell phone, I was sitting out on the quad with Ali and Jehangir, watching the girls walk by in skimpy outfits. It was the first warm day in weeks, with the sun out, and the girls were making the most of it. We were, too. Truth to tell, I didn't enjoy girl-watching as much since Farah and I had become close. But I didn't say this. Already my buddies teased me about her, though it was gentle compared to the things they would have said if I had been going with a girl who was non-Muslim and non-desi.

Farah? She's my mother's best friend's daughter from India. She spent a semester with us last year. More about her later.

Out on the quad, we were ranking the girls one to ten, with ten for the hottest. For us, "hottest" meant the ones that we thought would end up in the hottest circle of Islamic hell. The things we considered were: how much of their bodies they exposed, how much makeup they wore, how loudly they laughed, and how much public display of affection they allowed. I felt guilty about this, too. If Farah knew what we were doing, she would have been mad. Though she was serious about her religion, she believed in live and let live, and she didn't appreciate crude comments about women. I consoled myself with the thought that the white guys I used to party with earlier would have said cruder things.

I'm not sure when I stopped paying attention to the girls and began daydreaming about Farah. We had kept in touch through e-mail since she left last year. She was a good writer, not like me. Her notes brought the smallest aspects of her daily life alive: the posters of Indian art that she had put up on the walls of the bedroom she shared with her sister; the roadside stall in Nizamuddin East that sold the best kebabs in Delhi; the intercollegiate debate where she presented arguments against the Narmada Dam Project and won a trophy; a visit to her grandmother who lived in their ancestral village where you had to hand-pump water. I had to admit that the India of her letters sounded pretty interesting.

Farah's sister was getting married in a couple of months, and her mother had invited us to come and stay with them for the week of festivities—and for as long afterward as we could spare. Ammi was dying to go. She hadn't been part of a traditional wedding in years. I agreed to accompany her, though I didn't let on how excited I was at the thought of being with Farah again (and seeing her wear the zardosi lengha she had already bought for the wedding). Ammi had a tendency to jump to conclusions and then share those conclusions with the world.

Ammi had been trying to persuade Abbajan to go with us, too. His assistant manager, Hanif, she pointed out, was very trustworthy, and anyway, business was really slow. She was right. Jalal's Janitorial Services, which my father had built from scratch into a flourishing enterprise, had lost many of its biggest customers since 9/11. Though no one came out and said it, people weren't comfortable having Islamic cleaners going into their offices when they weren't around. It didn't matter that the same men had been cleaning those offices for over a decade. Abba was too proud—or maybe too hurt—to try to persuade his clients to change their minds.

Out on the quad, when the phone rang and I saw that it was Ammi, I didn't take the call. It was almost time for my Calculus class. The professor took off points for lateness, and I couldn't afford to lose any points. Ammi called me almost every day, usually to ask me to pick something up from the grocery, and if she got me on the line, she would talk for a long time. She had become used to Farah's company and was lonely now with no one at home. I figured she could leave me a message with her shopping list.

But Ammi didn't leave a message. She hung up and called again. This was so unlike her that I answered. She was crying hard; I couldn't understand what she was saying. Finally, I figured it out. Four men had come into Jalal's this morning and taken Hanif and Abba. They hadn't even let them make a call. Musa from the bakery next door had seen the whole thing happen and had phoned Ammi. He told her the men were dressed in suits and drove a black van; two of them were white and two were African American; the whole thing was over quickly. No, he didn't think to write down the license number. He was too scared. No, they hadn't hurt Abba or Hanif, not from what he could see, but they had been gripping them firmly by the arm.

I couldn't afford to panic—Ammi was upset enough—but my insides felt frozen. We'd heard about things like this. Government agents, some said the FBI, would pick up people from our community. Sometimes there was a reason; often there wasn't—at least not anything that was explained to the detainees. Some were released within a few days. For others, it took much longer. We knew men who had been deported, along with their families.

I told my friends what had happened, and Ali said right away that he would skip class and come with me. I was in no state to drive. Ali took me home. We picked up Ammi and went on to Jalal's. Musa was waiting for us, but he didn't have any new information to give. We went inside the office. Everything was in its place (my father was a tidy man); there was no sign of the upheaval that had turned our lives upside down.

We phoned friends, and friends of friends—anyone we could think of. They were shocked but not of much help. A few, I sensed, were afraid of getting too closely involved, as if our bad luck might be contagious. Finally, someone put us in touch with a lawyer who specialized in such cases. He had a hefty fee, though at this point we didn't care. Abba still hadn't phoned us. I gave the lawyer all of Abba's documents that I could find. One of Ammi's cousins came to stay with us because Ammi was getting hysterical, banging her head on the floor, calling on Allah to spare her husband, and I didn't know how to stop her.

Maybe the lawyer had friends in high places, or maybe the men who took him realized that Abba was innocent of whatever they had suspected him of doing, or maybe my mother's desperate prayers worked. After three days Abba was returned to Jalal's—with no more explanation than when he had been taken. Musa saw him sitting on the pavement beside the locked door of the office and called us. On Abba's face was the vacant expression of the men who sleep on the streets. By the time we got there, Musa had taken Abba into the bakery, had helped him wash his face, and had given him a glass of lime water. But Abba just sat holding the glass. I was afraid that Ammi would go to pieces, but although her face got very pale, she drew on reserves of strength that I didn't know she possessed.

Over the next days, she remained close to Abba. She ran her hands over each part of his body to make sure he hadn't been injured. She talked to him about old times—their courtship and marriage, the first house they had lived in, my antics when I was little. She sang children's lullabies. She assured him that we loved him and would take care of him. She told him he didn't have to talk about anything he didn't want to, and if he preferred to forget the last few days, that was all right with her. She would forget them with him. I don't know what a Western psychologist would have made of her methods, but my father responded to the constant flow of her soft voice. In a few days he was moving around the house, impatiently telling us he didn't need babysitters. One evening he even helped Ammi roll out chapatis like he used to. We thought the worst was over.

Then he had the stroke.

It happened when he was alone in the family room, watching TV. When Ammi found him, he had slipped to the floor, unconscious. By the time the ambulance arrived, parts of his brain had shorted out. When we brought him home, after a lengthy and expensive hospital stay, he couldn't move his left arm and leg.

AMMI AND I WENT BACK TO THE LAWYER; HE ADVISED US TO let things be. There were no signs of physical torture on my father. There weren't even official records of his having been arrested. Who would we go to, asking for reparation? It was a bad time for Muslims in America. It would be best if we didn't stir up trouble. Besides, we were better off than many. Take the case of Hanif, who hadn't been returned at all. No one knew where he was, or if he was alive.

To my mother, he said, "Sister, I tell you this not as a lawyer but as a fellow Muslim. What use is it to say, we are in the right and they are in the wrong? I could take your money and start a case, like I've done for several families. But all the cases are dragging on, with no end in sight. Better, if you have friends and family in India, to take Jalal-Miah—and your son, if he is wise—and retire there. The dollar still goes a long way back home, and you can get servants to help with Miah's problems. Best of all, among thousands who look like you, you'll draw no attention. Here, you are on their radar. For all you know"—he looked pointedly at my beard—"they're watching your son right now." He shook his head in a way that frightened Ammi.

When Ammi returned home, she requested her closest friends—a handful of people I had called Uncle and Aunty since childhood—to come over to the house; then she asked them what she should do. My father, who had always been fiercely independent, lay helpless in his bed upstairs. The thought that we were deciding his fate twisted my heart.

At this meeting, there were arguments and raised voices, cursing and tears, and contradictory counsel. But at the end our friends admitted that given my parents' situation, retiring in India wasn't a bad option. They didn't think my mother and I could keep Jalal's Janitorial going on our own. News of my father's "arrest" had already caused more customers to cancel their accounts. Abbajan's medical insurance covered many things, but there were still a lot of expenses that we had to handle. I didn't have a job—and even when I finished college, it was unlikely that I would get a good one right way. There wasn't going to be enough money for my parents to keep living here.

"Don't expect it to be easy," they warned her. "You enjoyed your visits to India as a rich NRI, with your pockets full of dollars. But living within modest means, with servants who don't show up in the morning and bribes that have to be paid to the right people in the right manner, is a different matter."

The uncles and aunties were not sure what I should do. They felt I wouldn't fit in in India after having been raised here. I had the

same doubts. Apart from lifestyle differences, there was another issue: This was my country. I was an American. The thought of being
driven from my home filled me with rage. Then again, if I stayed in
India, it would be a great support for my parents. Already Ammi
looked at me with longing. Farah would like that, too. Conflicting
loyalties warred in my head, keeping me awake at night.

UMA THOUGHT SHE HEARD A SOUND ABOVE, AS WHEN SOMEONE
turns over in an old, creaky bed. She stiffened and looked around,
but the others were engrossed in the story. *You're imagining things,*
she told herself sternly. She forced her attention away from the ceiling's mutterings and to the painful inevitability of Tariq's tale.

WITHIN THE WEEK, THOUGH I WARNED AMMI NOT TO RUSH
into decisions, she put our house up for sale and asked Farah's mother
to find her a small ground-floor flat not too far from their house.
After the phone call, Ammi spent a long time in the bathroom and
emerged with red eyes. Hard as it was for me to see the house I had
grown up in on the market for uncaring strangers to walk through
and comment on, it was harder for Ammi. The daily chore of taking care of my father—of assisting him into bed and out, placing
him in his wheelchair, helping him to the toilet—was taking its toll
on her body, too. My father didn't make it easier. Always a sweet-
natured man, he now developed a terrible temper. I was having
problems of my own: everywhere I went people seemed to stare at
me. Once or twice, I thought a black van followed me off the freeway into our neighborhood.

I e-mailed Farah, and she wrote back with concern, urging me
to move. She would make sure I settled into India. But her replies

didn't satisfy me. Living halfway across the world, Farah couldn't understand my frustration. The only person I could talk to was Ali. Ali listened patiently to my rants. When I broke down and wept, he wasn't embarrassed. In Eastern culture, he told me, it was okay for men to cry. He told me that to run away to India would be cowardly. I should help my mother with her move, then return to America. Bad things were happening here to our people, and we needed to fight them. He and several other young men rented a house, and they could fit me in, if I didn't mind sharing a room. He worked part-time at an electronics store. He could talk to his boss and maybe get me a temporary job there. He was more optimistic than the uncles and aunties about finding employment once we graduated. There were important people in the Muslim community, he said. People with pull. People who believed in helping their own.

I liked Ali's house, though it was in a bad neighborhood. It was an old Victorian with high ceilings and bay windows that looked out on an overgrown garden, very different from the cookie-cutter suburban development I'd lived in all my life. The living room was filled with pamphlets and handmade signs.

TARIQ'S VOICE WAS DROWNED BY A CRACK THAT MADE UMA jump.

"She's coming down," Cameron shouted. "To the doorway!"

There was a panicked milling. Uma realized that Cameron hadn't planned which doorway each of them would go to; that frightened her almost as much as the disintegrating ceiling. His asthma must have become worse; maybe it was impairing his thinking.

She ended up in the bathroom doorway with Malathi and Tariq. The water licked the tops of her calves and was, if possible, even colder than before. There was another crack. The walls shook. They were showered with plaster.

"Cover your heads," Cameron urged. "Don't breathe through—" His words disintegrated into a fit of coughing, which he tried to contain.

This was it, Uma guessed. She hoped it would be quick. Malathi was gripping Uma's good hand with both of hers. Uma gripped back. Tariq was praying, his eyes closed, his face unexpectedly serene. Uma wanted to pray, too, but all she could think was that if she had to die, she was glad she had someone's hand to hold while it happened.

It was not the end, however. After a few more cracks and a huge crash that made the floor shake, there was an eerie quiet. They stood in their respective doorways, breathing carefully through their teeth. Uma's tongue tasted of chalk. She was hallucinating. In her hallucination, a ray of light came down from the sky, like in biblical movies, and illuminated the desks where they had been sitting. Any moment, a booming Old Testament voice would bring them tidings of joy.

"Is that sunlight?" Lily whispered, her face full of wonder.

"I think so," Cameron said from the far doorway. His voice rasped painfully, but he held on to the flashlight. "Water, please—"

Malathi splashed over to the counter with the filled bowls. "They're full of dirt," she said. Dismay made her forget to lower her voice. The opening in the ceiling had created echoes. *Ert, Ert,* they called. Making her way to Malathi, Uma saw that chunks of plaster had crushed most of the bowls they had filled with such care. The few remaining bowls were full of debris. Only the water in the tea and coffee boiling pans, which had lids, might still be clean. Malathi rescued a bowl and took it to the bathroom sink to wash and refill. Her voice was panicky. "No water coming from the tap."

They crowded in the bathroom doorway. Mangalam shouldered his way in—it was his bathroom, after all—and jiggled the faucet. Nothing. He pushed against the faucet handle as hard as he could. The ancient top broke off in his hand, but no water came. When the ceiling collapsed, the pipe bringing water to the bathroom must have broken. Suddenly, their drinkable water had shrunk to what was in two saucepans, four mostly empty bottles, and the toilet tank.

Uma went back to the counter, cleaned out a bowl the best she could with one hand, dipped it into a pan, and took it to Cameron. She could feel everyone's eyes on her, trying to gauge how much water she was giving him and thinking, Shouldn't she have given less? She didn't care. She would give Cameron her share, if it came to that. When Cameron had drunk the whole bowlful, he stepped gingerly through the water—no telling what had come down with the ceiling and lay in wait under its dark surface—to check the damage on the other side of the room. He found a gaping hole in the ceiling—that's where the sunlight was coming from. He'd been hoping to find an opening to the world outside. Even if they couldn't reach it, seeing such an opening would have done them good. But arcing over the hole was a gridlock of broken metal with a gap large enough for only a single ray to make it through. He turned his attention to the ground.

Debris had fallen in a pile of Sheetrock and beams—and furniture: an office desk cracked in two across its middle; several chairs; a computer monitor, its glass unbelievably intact; a metal file cabinet bent into an L; and other objects too beat up to recognize. He felt around them gingerly. Then his fingers touched what he had been afraid of finding: a portion of a human body. It was an arm, sticking up through a gap between two rollaway chairs. He could tell from the rigor mortis that the person had been dead for hours. He stepped away, heart hammering, though this wasn't the first body he had touched, by any means. It was the asthma that was making him jumpy. He touched the inhaler in his pocket, longing to use it. But he had only one dose left. He had to save it for his story.

He decided he wouldn't tell anyone about the body.

THE COMPANY TOOK THEIR SEATS AGAIN. SUNLIGHT FELL ON some of their faces. Uma wasn't sure if she felt better because of that. The light seemed to be coming from very far away, and soon it would be gone.

Tariq wasn't in the mood to continue, but Lily wouldn't let him be.

"You can't stop here! Who were those people Ali was living with? Did you like them? Were they . . . terrorists?"

Tariq said, "They didn't tell me much about themselves—only that they were planning a march. They ordered pizza for dinner and wouldn't take any money from me. What I liked best is how close they were to one another. Like brothers. Watching one another's backs."

"Will you come back to America?" Lily persisted. "Will you live with them? What about Farah? What will happen to her if you come back?"

Tariq shook his head. He had no answers. "From having put up my story against the others, I can see this much: everyone suffers in different ways. Now I don't feel so alone."

Lily put an arm through his. "You could stay with us," she said, surprising Uma. "You remind me of my older brother. He's in my story."

"Very well!" Cameron said. "I can take a hint as well as the next person. Go ahead and tell your tale."

12

When I was too young to know better, I was a pleaser. That's what my parents tell me. Their story goes like this: "When you were little, you were so cute. You recited Chinese nursery rhymes whenever guests came over, whether anyone asked you or not. And now, look at you. We can't even get you to come out of your room to say hello."

Sometimes it's like this: "Whenever your mom made dumplings, you insisted on helping, even though you made a mess all over the kitchen floor. But now that you're old enough to be useful, you refuse to enter the kitchen, and you're always complaining that eating Chinese food makes you smell bad."

Or, "Remember that favorite dress you had when you were in kindergarten, pink with cherry blossom flowers all over it, and bows? You loved it so much. You insisted on wearing it to school every day. We had to hand wash it each night so it would be clean and dry by morning. Now—black, black, black, all the time. Do you even wash that T-shirt? And is that black *lipstick*?"

You get the idea.

My parents thought my metamorphosis from charming caterpillar to stinging wasp came from teenage angst combined with evil

American influences, but they were wrong. I gave up on being a pleaser because of my older brother.

My parents believed—and I secretly agreed—that Mark was the perfect child. In fact, he hardly seemed like a child at all. He was polite and obedient and serious about his studies. Most of his friends were from Chinese school. He wanted to become a scientist specializing in cancer research, and by ninth grade had already written a paper that went on to win a national science award. My parents would have preferred that Mark become a doctor or a businessman. (In addition to the supermarkets he inherited, my father owns a large Chinese import-export business that my mother helps him run. They're terribly proud of that business and were hoping to pass it on to Mark.) But they understood and admired Mark's humanitarian calling—and made sure all their friends did, too. I'd overhear them at Spring Festival parties: "Anyone can get a medical degree and make money, but to spend your life discovering a cure for those poor, suffering people—ah!" They would stop there, overcome by emotion, forcing the listener to complete the sentence: "Now that's true dedication."

"AND THIS IS THE YOUNG MAN I REMIND YOU OF?" TARIQ ASKED.

I KNEW IT WAS USELESS TRYING TO COMPETE FOR MY PARENTS' attention by being good. For a while, I tried to hate Mark, but my heart wasn't in it. When he had time (which wasn't often, what with his schoolwork and Kumon classes and music lessons and science fair projects), he let me come into his room and check out his old Dragon Ball Z cards or listen to his favorite bands (downloaded from illegal Internet sites, he confided to me). I would watch him play Knights of the Old Republic and give him advice, which he sometimes listened to. When I had trouble with homework, he tried to help, though most of his explanations went above my head. He spent weeks on science projects that awed me: elegant solar systems that rotated at different speeds around a sun, or intricate contraptions with beakers and burners that extracted water from ink. And he let me touch them. How could I *not* love him?

But I had to do something about my pathetic standing at home. I didn't plan on being seriously bad, like the girls the aunties gossiped about who ran away from home and got pregnant. I wanted to be just sufficiently disobedient to force my parents to notice me. I started with little rebellions—not making my bed, refusing to go to Chinese language class, coming down late for dinner so the family would have to wait for me, not turning in homework on time so the teachers would send home a note for my father to sign. I slept late and missed the school bus, forcing my mother to drive me to school. I acted up in class and got sent to detention, where I became friendly with kids who smoked in the bathrooms and got into fistfights and drank cough syrup to get high and cut themselves.

Soon I was getting plenty of attention at home. Gramma cried and talked about evil spirits; my parents yelled, grounding me, taking away my iPod, cutting off my allowance. It didn't satisfy me the way I'd thought it would; I only felt emptier. But I couldn't just turn around and become my old good-girl self. I was too stubborn. I started dressing in black and experimenting with cough syrup myself—thanks to Gramma, who catches chills easily, we always had some lying around. One day I skipped school and went to this tattoo parlor with Kiara and got my eyebrow pierced. Boy, did that get me a lot of parental notice!

Things were going downhill fast when Mark came to my room

one night. I told him to get out—I thought he was going to lecture me, like the others—but he didn't get angry. Instead he gave me a long, narrow box, and when I opened it, I saw it contained his old flute. I remembered that, although now he played the violin, for a while he had taken flute lessons. He gave me a stack of music books and offered to teach me. "Let's just keep it to ourselves," he said. I think it was the idea of having our own secret that appealed to me. I suspect he knew it would.

We decided to meet for lessons after school at a park in another neighborhood. Mark warned me that he would be able to teach me only the rudimentaries of flute playing, but the very first time I put my lip against the embouchure, I had the strangest feeling, as though I had done it before. And perhaps I had, in some other lifetime. How else did I learn so fast?

I loved our afternoons in the park and the walk back home together, when I gabbled on about school and my friends (ex-friends, really, since I no longer hung around after school let out). Mark raised his eyebrows at the cough syrup but told me that cutting was not cool because kids who started doing it often developed serious mental problems.

Soon there wasn't any more that Mark could teach me. He downloaded sonatas off the Internet onto his iPod for me. (Mine was still confiscated.) Bach and Handel and some Mozart. And he gave me a book about the lives of the great composers. I read and reread that book late into the night instead of doing homework. My favorite story was Beethoven's—not so much for his music (I prefer Bach) but for his tragic life. I thought often about his troubles: his beloved mother dying early, his alcoholic father, his dead brother's son, whose guardian he was, giving him all sorts of trouble. No one in his family appreciated him the way they should have. Mostly,

I admired his ability to keep going after he realized—early in his career—that he was going deaf. I would have thrown myself into the Danube, but he just went on composing.

I went to the park straight after school each day with Mark's iPod and my flute. I'd find a bench hidden behind some overgrown shrubs and listen and practice on my own until it turned dark. Sometimes kids stopped to watch me, but I knew what to say to make them move on fast. My grades didn't get much better. My parents yelled at me for coming home so late. And I still wore black. But inside, something had changed. I no longer wanted to waste my energy on being bad.

One afternoon, when I thought I was ready, I invited Mark to the park and played all the sonatas I'd learned for him, plus a few short melodies I'd composed. I expected applause when I finished, but he just sat there looking at me. Then he said, "Lily, you have a gift. You can't waste it. I need to tell Mom and Dad so they can get you lessons." At first, I refused, but Mark can be persuasive. Soon I was in our living room, playing the flute for my astonished parents and Gramma. I messed up a few times because I was so nervous. In spite of that I must have sounded pretty good, because afterward they all hugged me and my mother cried and said I should have told them. The next day they arranged for me to have lessons with Mrs. Huang, who everyone in Chinatown agreed was the best teacher around. My parents got me an expensive new flute, too (although they rented it from Brook Mays, just in case).

Just like that, I became the subject of much admiration at home and amazement at parties. ("Wah! Did you hear about that Lily? Learned to play Beethoven overnight, all by herself! Others practice until their fingers are bones, but that one, she's a born genius!" Gramma would rush in to avert the evil eye then: "No, no, she makes lots of mistakes still, not half as good as your Caroline.") I watched

Mark carefully to see if he minded my ascension, but he appeared relieved. He was busy with college preparations. He had been accepted to MIT and spent much of his time on the Internet, checking out professors' credentials and student ratings, deciding who he wanted to do work with. Dually blessed in their gifted progeny, my parents went around smiling all the time—humble smiles, of course.

Mrs. Huang was an ambitious teacher, and she pushed me. I didn't mind. I was hungry. I listened meekly when she scolded me about having learned things the wrong way. I even stopped composing my own music—though I missed it—because she said that I must first get a full classical education. When she entered me in a local contest, I was nervous about playing in front of strangers. But I won. She entered me in a more important contest. I won again, and this second time I was less nervous. I began to realize that I was better than the other players. I enjoyed the attention of the audience and my parents' excited hugs afterward. I asked Mrs. Huang for more competitions and practiced feverishly for them. I put away my dark clothes and Goth makeup and became positively suburban, additionally delighting my parents. Mark was away at college. It was his first semester, but neither my parents nor I paid much attention to how he was managing so far from home. We were too busy winning (a bigger high than entire bottles of cough syrup). And Mark was Mark, after all. We knew he would perform superbly.

When I e-mailed him details of my success, he wrote back congratulating me. At the end of the note, he added, *Don't do too much too soon.* I thought it was a strange thing to write. I felt exactly the opposite. Music had come to me so late. I had to struggle to catch up with all those boys and girls who had been practicing since prekindergarten. How could it ever be too much?

But one Saturday morning, just a day before a major state-level competition, I woke up with a heaviness in my fingers. Actually, I felt heavy all over. I didn't want to go into the room my parents had set aside for my practice (Mark's old room). I didn't want to play Bach's Sonata No. 5 in E Minor, which was supposed to have been my opening piece, though it was one of my favorites. I wanted to call a girlfriend and go to the mall and giggle over girlish things—but I didn't have a friend to call. My obsession had pushed my friends away.

When I realized that, I wanted to cry. Instead, I called my brother.

Mark's voice on his cell phone sounded sleepy, although on the East Coast it was long past noon. I was surprised because he'd always been an early riser. I asked him what he'd been up to—we hadn't spoken in a while—and why was he still sleeping. He said he'd been out late the previous night.

"Were you partying?" I asked. It was a joke; Mark never partied. His idea of a good time was meeting his geeky friends at the local Borders for a latte and discussing lesser-known scientific theories.

"I guess you could call it that," he said.

Intrigued and amused, I asked if he partied often.

"Hey, listen," he said abruptly. "Can I call you back? I have a terrible headache." Before I could respond, he hung up. I waited around a couple hours, but he didn't call.

My conversation—actually, nonconversation—with Mark made me feel heavier. By this time, it was afternoon and I definitely should have been practicing for the contest. Instead, I sneaked out of the house, took the 38 down to the ocean, and went for a walk, hoping the salty, stinging air would clear my head and help me figure out what was going on. Music had been my life for the past year. I heard it in my head while I went through the boring necessities of daily existence. The pieces I was dying to compose as soon as my teacher gave me permission flitted around in my sleep like colorful birds. Then why was I feeling that I couldn't care less if I never saw my flute again? And Mark—was something wrong with him, as I felt in my gut, or was I just projecting my own gloom? Should I tell my parents about our chopped-off conversation, or would that be betraying him? I decided to wait until Mark came home for Thanksgiving and I had a chance to see him face-to-face.

I WAS HOPING THAT NEXT MORNING I WOULD BE BACK TO NOR-mal, but by then a numbness had spread across my lips, and my fingers felt like they belonged to the Tin Man. I told my mother I didn't feel well, but she said it was an attack of nerves and piled me into the car with all my musical paraphernalia. I'll cut the painful details short: halfway through my first piece, I froze and had to be called off the stage. My parents took me home and put me to bed, sure I was coming down with the flu. Gramma felt my forehead, which was cool, declared that my spirit was sick, and burned some special incense in my room. She was closer to the truth. I'm not sure if the incense did its job, but the next morning I told my parents I didn't want to enter any more contests and that Mark was in some kind of trouble. As I expected, both statements made them go ballistic.

At that time I was pretty ballistic myself, but now I don't blame them too much. They'd tried hard to be good parents. They'd dedicated evenings and weekends to schlepping Mark around to his activities. They'd supported my sudden and expensive love affair with the flute. Most important, during all those years when we thought I wasn't good at anything, they hadn't nagged me about it. (For Asian parents, that's as close to sainthood as you can get.) Now, it was as though they'd been handed a gold medal only to have it snatched away.

You can imagine the shouting matches. They took away my new flute and canceled my lessons. I retaliated by going back to black and putting on my eyebrow ring. Then they forgot about me because they got a call from Mark's advisor. They didn't discuss it with me, but by eavesdropping on their agitated conversation with Gramma, I gathered that Mark was failing his classes. I caught snippets of phrases: fallen into bad company, drinking habit, cutting class. Mark's advisor had told them that this sometimes happens to kids from strict, traditional homes—they can't handle the sudden freedom. I couldn't fit my brother into a cliché like that. I was sure there was more behind his disaster. That weekend my stunned parents put a CLOSED UNTIL FURTHER NOTICE sign in their office window (the only other times they'd done that was when my mother went into labor) and left for Boston.

Monday morning I knew that if I had to sit through a day of meaningless chatter in class, it would drive me nuts, and I would do something everyone involved would regret. So I took my backpack and hurried like I was late for the school bus, but once I was out of Gramma's sight, I went to the park. I'd packed Mark's old flute, and I sat on my favorite bench behind the overgrown bottlebrushes and played the Moonlight Sonata and some nocturnes that seemed to suit my melancholy mood. When I got hungry, I ate the sandwiches I'd packed. Then I took a nap. When I woke up, I played my own melodies, closing my eyes and making things up as I went along.

I don't know how long I played—my lips were hurting, but in a good way—when I felt hands on my face. I must have jumped a mile high and yelled loud enough to be heard across the park. When I opened my eyes, there was no one. I remembered Gramma's stories about the spirits of the dead, and my hands started shaking. What if Mark had killed himself and his spirit had come to say good-bye? Then I saw the boy, hiding behind a bush. He must have run back there when I started screeching like a pterodactyl. I beckoned to him to come out, and when he did, I realized that he had Down syndrome. I'd seen Downies at the park a couple times, holding hands and walking, with an adult on either end. Maybe they came from a special school nearby. The boy—he was about ten years old— must have gotten separated from the group. He came up to me a bit nervously, but when I said I was sorry for scaring him, but he'd scared me, too, he told me he liked my music. I asked if he wanted to hear some more. He nodded and settled himself on the grass near my feet.

I started playing something sad that I'd heard in my head as I walked along the beach after my conversation with Mark. But as I made my way through it, I found out that it wasn't sad all the way through. It had leaps and trills and a ribbon of joy that kept looping back. After a while, the other boys heard the music and wandered over and sat down, too. My boy (that's how I thought of him) might have felt proprietary, because he scooted up and put his hand on my knee. He smelled like strawberry jam. I played the melody for a long time, discovering something new with each pass-through, and then it was time for us to go home.

UMA THOUGHT HER BRAIN WAS SLOWING FROM A LACK OF FRESH air. After Lily finished, she found herself thinking of her father— but shouldn't she have remembered him right after Tariq talked about his Abbajan? Shouldn't she now be considering how she had always wanted a sibling, and how for years she had held a grudge against her parents for having deprived her of a ready entertainment that all her friends possessed?

During his college days in India, her father had played guitar. He fancied Elvis and was considered by his classmates to be quite a singer. He had told Uma this when she was about twelve, and she had collapsed in giggles, unable to imagine him as a slick-haired performer. Incensed, he had enlisted her mother's aid. She had corroborated his story, telling Uma that was one of the reasons why, when the matchmaker had come with a proposal from his family, she had agreed to see him.

"Your mother, now, she was very fashionable as a college student," Uma's dad had said, sneaking a hand around her mother's ample waist as he spoke. "She wore go-go glasses and stiletto heels and sleeveless sari blouses, and sometimes she skipped class and went with her friends to Metro Cinema to see American movies. The day I came to see her, she had painted her nails deep pink to match her sari. If I hadn't had that guitar, you'd still be a speck in God's eye."

Uma had been intrigued by the images. They seemed equally fantastic: herself floating around in God's eye and her pink-nailed mother floating around Calcutta in go-go goggles, discarding suitors at will. She had watched her parents, him balding, her plump and matronly, dressed in department-store clothing, leaning into each other with satisfied expressions, and felt a sorrow for the glamorous young selves they had discarded.

Her parents, however, still had a few surprises up their polyester sleeves, one of which her father would reveal during her first semester of college.

THE NINE SURVIVORS ATE THE LAST OF THEIR FOOD AS SLOWLY as they could, hunched against the dropping temperature. The hole in the ceiling was making the room even colder. They held their chewy bars and apple slivers close to their mouths as though they were afraid the morsels might disappear along the way. Cameron didn't distribute the food this time. From where he sat, his spine wilting against Uma's good arm, he raised an eyebrow in query at Malathi and Mangalam, and they cut things into the right number of pieces and gave them out. Uma noted that there were more snacks now than she had originally counted. People must have taken things out of their secret stashes and put them in the pile when no one was watching. There were a small bag of carrot sticks, one whole-wheat roll, and three small white-chocolate truffles, quite delicious, that Mangalam dissected with extra care. But all was gone in a few mouthfuls.

Cameron was whispering instructions in Uma's ear. She announced that they could use the facilities one last time. The water would have risen almost to the lip of the toilet bowl by now. (What would they use for a bathroom after this? she wondered.) Since the bathroom door could no longer be pushed shut, people would have to wait outside Mangalam's office to allow the user privacy.

A few people struggled into their wet shoes and climbed off the table gingerly. Mr. Pritchett, Uma noticed, stood at the end of the line. Hadn't he just gone? But he was so proper that maybe the possibility of having to pee into a pitcher—or whatever it was that they would be reduced to doing next—made him nervous.

Alongside her, Cameron had stiffened. He, too, was watching Mr. Pritchett. When he whispered to Uma, she held up her broken arm and called out, "Mr. Pritchett, please, could you come here for a moment?" How could she have forgotten those cigarette breaks?

Mr. Pritchett looked irritated, but he could hardly refuse a cripple, could he? When he came near them, Cameron stretched out his hand and said, "Your cigarettes and lighter."

"You don't trust me?" Mr. Pritchett said, his shoulders belligerent. "You think I'd be stupid enough to light up and endanger all of us?" Uma was about to call Tariq, who was dozing on the adjacent desk, but Mr. Pritchett said, "You're wrong, you suspicious bastard!" and threw a gold lighter and a crushed pack of Dunhills down onto the desk. He marched (as much as one can march in freezing, calf-high water) back to the bathroom line.

AS SHE WAITED IN LINE FOR THE BATHROOM, MRS. PRITCHETT was trying to remember something. Lily's passion had touched her and drawn a memory almost to the surface. Something about her mother's kitchen. But the cold water clutched at her legs with icy fingers, making her joints ache. The last few times, it had been hard to climb on and off the desk—her arthritis was acting up—but she hadn't wanted to ask for help, hadn't wanted anyone to know her body was betraying her. Dusty air coated her tongue, and a nagging smell she couldn't quite place distracted her.

Mr. Pritchett distracted her, too. She could feel him at the rear of the line, emitting negative energy. She'd followed, out of the corner of her eye, the exchange between him and Cameron, the flinging down of the cigarettes and lighter. A great sympathy had risen up in her. She knew addiction, the way every brain cell focused on the forbidden substance, the way the nerves started to vibrate, guitar strings resonating to unheard music. She was planning to take a pill—maybe two—as soon as she was in the bathroom, so that when her turn to tell the story arrived, she would be at her best. She wished she could have shared the pills with Mr. Pritchett, but of course she couldn't. She couldn't even tell him how she felt about the kitten. There were people standing in line between them, and it would have embarrassed him.

The memory she'd been groping for came to her: she was sitting at that sunshine-yellow linoleum kitchen counter with her best friend, Debbie, each with a piece of celebratory peach pie in front of them. Mrs. Pritchett—Vivienne—had baked the pie. She had loved baking. The feel of warm risen dough against her palm. The joy of apples sliced for a pie, so thin that you could see through them. She had been good at it, too. Good enough for Debbie and her to plot all of senior year about running Debbie's dad's bakery once they graduated.

"Viv," Debbie said, "I've got great news!"

"Don't tell me—you're getting married," Vivienne said. It had been their standard response since ninth grade.

Debbie rolled her eyes. "Stupid! Dad said yes! He'll let us run the bakery, on a trial basis, for six months."

Why was Vivienne's smile less dazzling than it should have been?

An excited Debbie didn't notice. "We'll be in charge," she said. "Managing the employees, deciding the menu, buying the supplies, fixing prices—everything! Dad will teach me how to do the books. Mr. Parma will stay on and bake the bread, but you can make all the specialty items. If we do well, after some time Dad will let us buy the business from him. We won't have to put any money down. We'll pay him each month from the profits. What do you think?"

It's perfect, Mrs. Pritchett wanted to say, trying to forestall her younger self. *Let's go for it!* But in the memory, Vivienne raised her face, flushed with happiness and guilt, and Mrs. Pritchett knew with a sinking of the heart that she was going to turn her best friend down.

A LITTLE WHILE AGO, MRS. PRITCHETT HAD BEEN DISTRAUGHT because time was running out. What if she died before she got to tell her story? Now, having taken her pills, those small, round blessings, those miracles of science, in the privacy of the bathroom, she was equanimous and expansive. At the hospital, before leaving, the night nurse had said to her, *If not in this life, then the next.* Mrs. Pritchett repeated the statement to herself like a mantra. Even Mr. Pritchett's announcement that he had constipation and would require more time in the bathroom, so could they please go back to their seats and give him some space, had failed to embarrass her.

But as she waded back to her desk, several realizations struck her. First, Mr. Pritchett never had constipation. Second, the door to the bathroom was being pushed shut, gradually and with great effort. Third, the odor that had been tugging at her subconscious was gas. Fourth, when Cameron had demanded Mr. Pritchett's smoking supplies, Mr. Pritchett hadn't been surprised. He had acted angry, but it hadn't been the real thing.

She grabbed the arm of the person closest to her, who happened to be Mr. Mangalam. "I think Mr. Pritchett's planning to smoke in there," she whispered (she couldn't bear to betray her husband to the whole company). "You've got to stop him—I smell gas."

Mr. Mangalam sloshed through the water, as swiftly and gracefully as anyone could, and threw himself at the half-shut door. Mrs. Pritchett's stomach knotted with dread as the door resisted. But finally it swung in with reluctance, bumping Mr. Pritchett, catching him in the act of lighting a cigarette. He staggered sideways, cigarette and matchbox flying from his hand and into the water. Mr. Mangalam landed on top of Mr. Pritchett. Both were soaked through immediately. Mrs. Pritchett saw Mr. Pritchett swing a fist at Mr. Mangalam's head, but his heart must not have been in it; Mr. Mangalam avoided it easily. Mrs. Pritchett was afraid Mr. Mangalam might hit back, but he pulled himself up heavily, using the sink as support, and then helped Mr. Pritchett to his feet.

The men made their dripping, shivering way back to the desks.

Mr. Mangalam mumbled something about having tripped in the dark. Mrs. Pritchett saw disbelieving looks, but no one wanted to pursue the matter. His voice an amphibian croak, Cameron instructed the two men to get out of their wet clothes. People gave them the blue rags to wipe themselves down, then handed over all the disposable tablecloths and any clothing they could spare. Cameron and Tariq took off their undershirts. Mrs. Pritchett insisted on giving Mr. Pritchett her sweater, and Tariq fetched the prayer shawl he had in his briefcase: he had put it up on the counter a long time back, Alhamdulillah, without thinking about it. He put the shawl into Mangalam's hands. Everyone looked away as the men changed into their motley wear and spread their wet clothes over the file cabinets—a futile act. Nothing would dry in this damp mausoleum.

The thin ray of light from the hole in the ceiling was fading. Uma asked Cameron if he wanted to tell the next story. She was afraid he might not have the strength to do it later. But Cameron pointed to Mangalam. Mangalam's teeth were still chattering. He would need a few minutes. Mrs. Pritchett searched in her purse and came up with a travel-size bottle of lotion, which she rubbed as vigorously as she could into both men's hands. At first Mr. Pritchett made as though to pull away, but then he allowed his wife to chafe some heat into his palms. A faint smell of lavender spread through the room, reminding Uma that it had been her mother's favorite scent. Before her mother's birthday, Uma and her father would go to a specialty store downtown and get her a big bottle of lavender water from France. She remembered the heft of the bottle, its elongated, dark blue neck. Somehow, when she was in high school, the tradition had foundered. Uma couldn't remember why.

"You wouldn't happen to have your flute, would you?" Tariq asked Lily.

"I do," she said. She felt around in her backpack, which she had placed behind her, and took out the slender silver instrument.

"Are you sure?" she asked. "It'll use up oxygen."

Tariq urged her on with a small jerk of his chin, and no one objected. She played a melody, short and serene, and the light fell through the ruins above them and shone on her for a few seconds before it died away.

13

I was born into a poor family in a small South Indian town, the first son after three daughters. Upon examining my birth stars, the astrologer told my parents that I would rise high in the world, and that my face would be my fortune. Interpreting this to mean that they would rise with me, my delighted parents made sure I received the best of everything as I was growing up—from extra helpings of food to new clothes on Pongal to fees for the best school in the area—even if it meant that my sisters had to do without. As you might imagine, I grew up spoiled, believing that I deserved everything my parents scraped together for me. In my defense, however, I should inform you that I was the sharpest child in my school and possibly the most handsome. And though I could have done well in class without expending much effort, I pushed myself to excel because I took seriously my role as savior of my family.

My hard work paid off: I received a generous scholarship to one of the leading universities located in faraway Delhi. I began my college career by studying assiduously and ranking high in exams, but I quickly realized that academic achievements were not enough to open the door to true success. The offices of the city were filled with brilliant men rotting in mediocre positions. I was determined not to become one of them. I could not afford to. Although the family never brought up the matter, I knew they were waiting for the long investment they had made in me to pay off. Two of my sisters were still unmarried, and with every passing year their chances of finding a husband shrank—unless we could dangle a substantial dowry as bait. My grandmother suffered from a kidney problem that would soon require expensive treatment. The old family home was falling apart. My father patched the roof each monsoon season and waited stoically for the day of my graduation. The only person who didn't seem to want something from me was my mother. Maybe because of that, I wanted to give her something. I settled on a pair of gold bangles. (She had sold hers to buy me clothes for college.) On my way back from classes, I often paused outside the local jeweler's window, evaluating patterns, imagining the look on her face when I presented her with the velvet box.

BUT FIRST I HAD TO FIND THE RIGHT KIND OF JOB. TO DO THAT, I needed to know—and know intimately—people in high places. I researched where such people were to be found. Several of the venues, such as the Tennis Club or the Polo Club, required expensive skills that I lacked. Finally, I discovered the Film Club.

At the Film Club the children of the rich—some of whom had aspirations toward stardom and others who fancied themselves future directors and critics—congregated twice a month to watch and discuss foreign movies that the father of one of the members procured through his connections. I made it a point to read up on the movies ahead of time so that I could make intelligent and occasionally provocative comments about them. (In the course of this activity, I discovered, to my surprise, that I enjoyed reading.) In a short while, I was considered an expert in many fields, and Film Club members sought my opinion on various issues. People liked my looks, too—my fresh countenance and my athletic physique, which I maintained through a careful exercise regimen.

After the film, it was customary for members to go out for dinner to the posh Imperial Hotel, where they took turns paying for the group's dinner. Soon I began to join them. The hotel's restaurant was sinfully expensive. But I saved money for a month, eating only rice and sambar, which I cooked on a kerosene stove in the secrecy of my room, and at the planned moment I casually plucked the bill out of the waiter's hands and said, "Folks—my treat today."

It was at one of these dinners that I met Naina, the only daughter of a high-level government official. I wooed her cleverly, presenting her with love poems—signed with my name—that I copied from anthologies I knew she would never read, and exerting just the right amount of pressure on her hand during our evening walks in the Lodhi Gardens. I hope you will not think too badly of me. My heart beat hard when I did these things, and I thought that was a sign of love. But perhaps it was desperation—I was six months away from graduating and my grandmother had been hospitalized. Finally, on an excursion to the Taj Mahal—timed so that we would be there under the hypnotic glow of a full moon—I confessed my feelings for her, insisting immediately afterward that she forget me. My origins were too humble. She would never be able to persuade her father to accept me.

This veiled challenge had the desired effect. Naina went to her father and insisted that she would marry no one but me. Her father did not like this. But love for his child was the single chink in his armor. He hired private detectives to research my background. They found nothing objectionable in it other than poverty. Impressed by the ambition that had brought me this far in life, he invited me to his office where, after an hour of grilling, he agreed to the marriage. He even offered to find me a suitably high position—he thought I would do well in the government's Protocol Department—and advised me to take the appropriate examinations so that this could be managed. The one thing he expected of me, he said as we shook hands in farewell, was that I keep his daughter happy. Failure to do this, he said, smiling jovially, could be dangerous to my health. I was not sure if this was a threat or a joke. In either case, I did not worry about it. How hard could it be to keep a woman happy? I thought. I did not know that Naina would undergo a Jekyllean transformation soon after our wedding.

THE FIRST SIGNS WERE SMALL: NAINA ASKING ME TO FETCH HER a drink at a friend's party, her tone more an order than a request; Naina deciding on deep red as the color theme for the luxurious new flat her father had given us as a wedding gift, even though I preferred something more restrained; Naina flipping through the numerous invitations we received, deciding which ones to accept and which to snub; Naina spending hours shopping for new shoes at a scandalously expensive store and settling on a pair that cost as much as my salary for a week. (When I remarked on this fact, she reminded me that she was paying for it with her own money. This was true. In addition to a trust, she had a hefty allowance out of which she paid all our household expenses so that I was free to use my salary however I desired. She was generous that way.)

I put up with these rumbles. All her life, Naina had been given everything she wanted as soon as she wanted it. I expected that it would take her time to settle into domesticity. Meanwhile, I focused on my job, which was to oversee hospitality for visiting governmental dignitaries. I liked conversing with powerful people from around the world. I liked my office staff, who treated me with a deference I had never before experienced. Every month, I sent most of my paycheck to my parents, who had by now repaired the roof, paid the most urgent medical bills, and made plans for my middle sister's wedding. It was a happy time.

A happy time, even though Naina refused to go to my backwater hometown to attend my sister's wedding. She pointed out that she had already booked tickets for us to attend the Cannes Film Festival. I controlled my temper and requested that she consider coming with me instead, because this was important. She asked if I was crazy. We had our first fight—but those were the early days, and we made it up. Afterward she told me (as part apology) that she would be miserable at the wedding and that would make everyone else miserable, too. So she went to Cannes with her best friend, Rita, and I went home to face my family's questions.

THE EVENT THAT CAUSED AN IRREPARABLE RIFT IN OUR MARriage occurred the next year, when my parents wanted to visit. I tried to discourage them, offering to travel home again, but they were longing to see my fancy new flat—and my fancy new wife. When I told Naina, she shrugged and said that they could come if I really wanted it, but she wasn't going to have them staying with us. I could put them up at a hotel. Not to worry, she would pay for it.

Those of you familiar with Indian traditions will realize what an insult that was to my parents—and to me. But I couldn't say anything. Naina's last sentence made me aware of how beholden I was to her. It was her flat I was living in, her food I was eating. Even the job I held was due to her father's string-pulling. I was ashamed that once I had considered these indications of good fortune.

The next day, I stayed back in my office after work; when the other employees left, I phoned my parents to inform them of what

Naina had decreed. They did not express the hurt they must have felt. They told me not to worry; they would come another year when it was more convenient. But I knew the truth. They were proud people; they would never ask to visit again. My mother added that she had made a box of Maisoorpak, my favorite sweet, and that she would mail it to me. She hoped Naina would like it. After I hung up, I sat with my head in my hands. When I could no longer escape the fact that I had made the biggest mistake of my life by marrying Naina—yes, I confess it—I started to cry.

That was when someone knocked on the door. A hesitant female voice asked if I was okay. It was Latika, our department's accountant, who had been working late. Passing by my office, she had heard my sobs. Her concern made me break down further. She fetched me water, rummaged through her handbag and found me a handkerchief to wipe my face, and told me things would surely look better in the morning. I told her I didn't think so. Before I knew it, I began pouring out my marital troubles. She pulled up a chair and listened, not trying to offer any solutions.

I couldn't help noting how different Latika was from Naina. She was no beauty, but in her simple sari and minimal makeup she exuded a glow. If Naina was a flashing disco light, Latika was the moon in a misty sky. Behind her glasses, her eyes were understanding, and I felt that she knew the meaning of struggle. The handkerchief she gave me was frayed at the edges, and I was impressed that she hadn't minded sharing it with me even though I would see this. The act made her seem at once brave and vulnerable—and real in a way that most of the people I had been mingling with recently were not.

I must have talked to her for half an hour, moving from my anger toward Naina to the subject of my parents and how much they had sacrificed for me. In return Latika told me that her parents had died in a train accident a couple of years earlier. She still missed them every day. Her only remaining family was her younger brother, whom she was putting through college.

When I apologized for having delayed her and offered her a ride (I drove a BMW that my father-in-law had given me and that—until that day—I had been rather vain about), she refused. The buses were still running, and the bus stop was right across from the ladies' hostel where she roomed. But I insisted, pointing out that it was raining. We sprinted through the rain across the empty street to the parking garage. We were soaked and laughing by the time we reached the car. An hour back, I wouldn't have believed that anything could have made me laugh on this day. As I drove Latika to her hostel, I felt that, perhaps to balance out my misfortune, the universe had offered me a friend.

I'm not sure when our friendship metamorphosed into love. Neither of us had intended it. Latika considered the husband of another woman out of bounds. When she figured out what was happening, she tried to push me away in distress. But what had blossomed between us was too strong to resist. Still, our relationship never became physical—Latika insisted on that. We understood the necessity of secrecy. At work we pretended we were no more than colleagues. But each day after work, for one precious hour, we went to movie theaters, that old refuge of sweethearts in crowded Indian cities. We chose buildings with small screens and poor air-conditioning because they would not be as crowded. We went to a different one each day and sat in the back of a darkened hall, holding hands and whispering. As the months passed, we dared to dream of a future together in a city far from this one, a future that would include my parents and her brother.

I went to my boss and, in confidence, requested a transfer to a smaller branch in the south of the country—for family reasons, I told him. He advised against it, warning me that it was a huge step back from which my career would never recover. I didn't care. My ambition, once a conflagration, had become a mild hearth fire. The day my transfer was approved, I asked Naina for a divorce. I pointed out that we were incompatible. She loved parties and shopping, holidays in expensive locales, and running the high-end boutique she had opened recently. The things I cared for—my job, my friends, my books, my family—she found dreary. Why not admit we had both made a youthful mistake and go our own ways?

Naina stared at me, eyes wide with shock. For a moment I thought she looked stricken. Then she stalked into her bedroom and slammed the door. In a few seconds I could hear her voice, low and furious, on her phone—probably bad-mouthing me to one of her girlfriends. I didn't care. I felt a great lightness at having taken this step toward my freedom. I went to my own room—we had started using separate bedrooms some months back, and though we still had physical relations, those times were rare. Using my personal line, I called Latika and told her what had transpired. She was a bit scared but mostly excited—she already knew about my transfer. We decided we would talk more after work.

The next morning I was in my office, fine-tuning details for the visit of a Ghanaian minister, when I heard a commotion. Stepping out, I saw four policemen hurrying Latika down the corridor. Her hair was disheveled and there were streaks of dried tears on her cheeks. She shot me a wounded, accusing look as she passed me. My heart began pounding. I grasped the arm of a policeman and asked him what the problem was; he shook me off, saying he was not at liberty to discuss details. The corridor was filled with employees who stared and whispered, enjoying this bit of drama. I wanted to run after her, but the presence of those staring eyes stopped me. I went back into my office, where I summoned my office boy. From him I discovered that early that morning the police had arrived with a warrant for Latika. Apparently, a large sum of money was missing from accounts that Latika managed, and she was suspected of having embezzled it. She was being taken to the central police station for questioning.

I grabbed my briefcase and started for the stairs. I intended to rush to the police station and do what I could to help Latika. I was certain she was innocent; this mistake could be cleared up soon. But on the way, my boss's secretary, an older woman who had been with the company for many years and was privy to high-level secrets, stopped me. My boss wanted to see me. Immediately.

I told her I needed to leave right away on a personal emergency, and that I would see him as soon as I got back.

She shook her head. "If you don't see him now, you may not have a job when you get back."

Her tone stopped me. I followed her into my boss's office. He didn't waste time with niceties. "I got a letter from high-up this morning," he told me, "stating that your transfer has been revoked." He did not explain. Instead, he suggested that I return to my room and focus my energies on the Ghanaian minister.

When I stepped out, I had to hold on to the secretary's desk. My head was whirling. In less than an hour, my world had fallen to pieces. What was going on?

The secretary looked at me with wry sympathy. "Looks like you've made someone powerful very angry. If I were you, I'd make amends fast. And I'd stay away from Latika."

Understanding flashed through me. Naina hadn't called a friend last night. She had called her father, and he had struck with the immediate intelligence of a hawk that knows how best to mortally wound its prey.

I left my briefcase on the floor of the secretary's office and drove like a maniac to Latika's hostel. I bribed the gardener and learned that an hour before, the superintendent had received a phone call. When she hung up, she was very agitated and had Miss Latika's belongings packed and brought to the gate. She instructed the gate-keeper to give them to Miss Latika but not let her into the hostel. Soon afterward, Miss Latika had shown up in a police van. She had picked up her things and told him she was leaving the city. One of the policemen had stopped her from saying more. She had given the gardener a ten-rupee note as baksheesh when she left. Folded into the note was a letter for a gentleman named Mangalam.

More money changed hands. I got the letter. It consisted of only one sentence: *For both our sakes, don't look for me.* When I crushed it into a ball, it seemed as though I were crushing my dreams. And not only dreams but also the part of me that was tender and moral. Latika had called it up. Without her, it could not survive.

Standing outside the dilapidated building, I was forced to admit that I had brought upon Latika trouble so deep that she might never recover from it. And this: though Naina didn't want me for herself, the thought of my being happy with another woman stung her like poison ivy. She would fight to keep me tied to her for life, and in that battle her father would be her ally.

That evening Naina and I dined together as though nothing amiss had occurred. As I watched her compliment the cook on the Chicken Makhani, rage flowed through my veins like exhilaration. Liberated from the scruples that Latika had lovingly woven around me, I felt a plan taking shape. I would begin by flirting with Naina's closest friends, women too well connected for her to ignore or harm. I would use my charms to embroil these women in affairs, and flaunt these affairs so all of Delhi's rich and famous gossiped about them. If in the process I broke a few hearts, it didn't matter, as long as Naina became the laughingstock of high society. I would shame her and her father until in desperation they would do one of two things, and at this point I didn't care which. They would either hire a thug to kill me, or they would make sure I went somewhere far away. In this way, I would gain my freedom.

CAMERON HEARD THE END OF MANGALAM'S STORY, BUT IT WAS also a kind of not-hearing. In his head he had drifted into another place, in another dimension. Tall yellow flowers grow wild around the crumbly brick of the walls, all the way up to the locked iron gates. Cameron has no trouble recognizing the gates. Hasn't he been looking at their photo for years? The road leading to the gates—no more than a gravel path—is mud-red. Cameron's feet slip-slide on it as he walks. He wishes there were something to hold on to, a rail, a bush, another person's arm. The wish surprises him. It is so un-Cameron-like. For years now he's prided himself on doing without support, on being the one others come to for help. But his backpack is so heavy. He wants to drop it, but he can't. The backpack is filled with gifts. Without the backpack, Seva might not like him. He hoists it higher onto his shoulders, though that makes it harder to draw breath. Around his heart, there's a sharp, hot squeezing, like scorpion pincers. He's encountered scorpions before, on desert missions. He hopes there aren't any here in the foothills, because beyond the gates the children in their patched blue uniforms are playing barefoot.

The boys chase a soccer ball around the yard. From the articles he's been reading to prepare for this journey, Cameron knows they call soccer something different here. But holes have opened up in his memory, and he can't remember what. The girls play crocodile, jumping onto the porch of the old building with shrieks of delight and terror so that the girl who is crocodile can't get them. Their legs are thin and scabbed, but when they run they're transformed into forest flashes of golden brown. Seva runs the fastest; the crocodile will never catch her. When she reaches the gate, she swings up on it. *Seva,* Cameron calls. *Seva!* She looks out through the bars, an inquiring frown on her face, as though she can hear but can't see him. Behind her the mountain range is wrinkled and friendly, like the head of an elephant. The air smells of cow-dung fires. A goat bleats to be milked.

He drops the backpack and runs to the gate. He wants to touch her determined fingers, the nails black with dirt. But the orphanage bell is ringing. It summons the children to study hour. They make a ragged, reluctant line at the pump so they can wash their hands and feet. A teacher in a faded sari appears on the porch and yells at Seva to get off the gate, but she hangs there for an additional moment, listening, a perplexed expression in her eyes.

Seva, he shouts, *it's Cameron.* He's only a foot away from her now. He can see the gap between her top teeth, which are a little crooked. One of her braids has come undone. Flecks of rust from the gate coat her forearms. She has a muddy smudge on her cheekbone. He reaches through the bars to wipe it off.

Seva! the teacher thunders.

Coming, Mam, she says. She jumps down from the gate, agile as a monkey, leaving Cameron's finger to caress the air.

"THAT SUCKS, MR. M," LILY SAID. "TO FINALLY FIND SOMEONE you love so much and then lose her like that. No wonder you were pissed off. I'm glad you got away."

Now that he had finished his story, Mangalam's teeth began to chatter again. He hugged himself. "I got away geographically," he said. "But not legally. Or psychologically. Naina's still my wife, and

I can't forget that. Maybe today, in a while, I really will become free."
He glanced up where the collapsed ceiling had been, and Uma, following his eyes, caught a movement there. A shattered light fixture,
still attached by its chain to something, had begun a small, swinging movement. Why would it do that?

"It wasn't all Naina's fault," Mangalam continued. "I started the
cycle of wrongdoing. I used her to get what I wanted. It's only fair
that she became the cause for losing what I wanted even more. Karma's wheel is intricate."

"What do you mean, karma's wheel?" said Mrs. Pritchett. She
leaned across her husband toward Mr. Mangalam.

"Remember how I flirted and enticed purposely, intending to
snare Naina's friends? Well, after I achieved my purpose and was
sent away to America, I found I couldn't stop behaving like that
toward women—even those I respected and felt a genuine liking
for." Here he glanced at Malathi. "It was like those stories we tell
children to frighten them into goodness: if they grimace long enough,
their muscles will freeze, and when they want to smile, they will
not be able to."

Mangalam turned toward Malathi and spoke as though they
were alone. "I think we might die here—perhaps in the next few
hours, if more of the building comes down or the air deteriorates
further. . . . I don't want to die without telling you that I'm sorry for
my behavior."

Malathi said, "I accept. And thank you for translating my story,
which I chose partly to jab at you, the kind of man I thought you
were."

Cameron had been coughing intermittently, but now he had a
prolonged fit that left him gasping. Uma tried to hold him upright
and Lily hurried over to help. He had to push their arms away to get
at his pocket and extract the inhaler, which he used. When he held

his breath, Uma found that she, too, was holding hers. He handed the inhaler to her—so frighteningly light—and she put it back in his pocket. Another puff and he might as well throw it away. "Tell your story," she said to Cameron.

"I can't," he whispered, rubbing his chest. "It isn't ready."

She knew what he meant. Hers wasn't ready either.

Then Mrs. Pritchett cleared her throat.

14

I apologize in advance for my story. I know it will cause my husband pain. The way I see these events is not how he views them; it cannot be. I only hope that he—and all of you—will see by the end why I had to tell this story.

You've been speaking of events that shatter lives in a day's time: wars, betrayal, seduction, death. In my case, my life was turned around by a man I didn't know helping his wife take off her coat.

THAT FATEFUL DAY BEGINS WITH MRS. PRITCHETT ENJOYING A cup of lemon tea in her morning kitchen, closing her eyes and breathing in the tangy steam. She believes in life's small pleasures. Around her, the kitchen gleams: immaculate granite counters, a purring Sub-Zero refrigerator, a blue ceramic bowl she made in pottery class. The bowl is filled with apples and pears, her husband's favorite fruits.

Mrs. Pritchett has sent her husband off to his office on a wholesome breakfast of oatmeal with almonds and brown sugar and a glass of freshly squeezed orange juice. Until he returns in the evening, the day lies ahead of her, luxurious as a stretching cat waiting for her to stroke it. She makes a mental list: go into her dewy garden and pick an armful of irises; tidy the house in preparation for dinner guests, Mr. Pritchett's old clients, grown into friends over the years; visit the local market to pick up strawberries for an English trifle she's planning to create. After shopping, she may stop for lunch at the little deli nearby. Their sandwiches are excellent, made with bread they bake each morning in the back. At teatime she'll meet her monthly book club, intelligent, pleasant women, several of them in their late sixties like her; she is ready for the meeting, with a page of notes on *The House of the Spirits*. When she gets home, she'll put on a Satie CD and lie down on the couch. (This need for rest would have irked her when she was younger; she accepts it with equanimity now.) Then it'll be time to prepare dinner—an easy task. The lamb has already been marinated, the greens washed and patted dry.

It does not strike Mrs. Pritchett that her life is small and contained, filled with bourgeois pleasures. If it did, she would not consider that a bad thing.

SHE IS RUNNING LATE, AND THE LITTLE CAFÉ IS EMPTY WHEN she gets to it, the lunchtime crowd gone. This disappoints her for a moment; she loves to people watch. But no matter. She orders ham and melted cheese on rye and bites into the crusty bread with vigorous pleasure. Then she sees the couple walking in. They're old; the husband has age spots on his face and trembly hands with which he guides his wife. She has aged worse than he. She wears thick, Coke-bottle glasses and shuffles with painful slowness, leaning on a cane, one of those ugly aluminum quadruped things. Mrs. Pritchett watches them with a mix of pity and fear. One day soon, she and her husband will come to this.

The couple has reached a table. The old man lets go of his wife's arm and pulls a chair out for her. He helps her off with her coat, an action that takes some maneuvering as she shifts her cane from one hand to the other. But he is patient, and when it's off, he hangs it carefully on the back of her chair. He flicks a speck off the sleeve before he turns back to his wife and helps her sit down. The couple discusses the menu, the woman pointing with sudden animation to items while the man inclines his head toward her to hear better. Then he nods gravely and summons the waitress. Mrs. Pritchett dawdles over her sandwich; she is curious about their order, which turns out to be a sugar-dusted lemon square and a decadent, oversize éclair. The man cuts each in half so they can share them. It's the flicking of the speck off the sleeve that gets Mrs. Pritchett—the caring behind the gesture, even though his wife with her poor vision would never have noticed whatever was on the coat sleeve.

THROUGHOUT BOOK CLUB, MRS. PRITCHETT CAN'T STOP THINKing about the couple in the café. In her distracted state, she forgets to bring up her best points during discussion. At home, the Satie makes her want to weep. She stares blankly at the oven while the lamb roasts, trying to figure out why she is so obsessed with the old man and his wife, and when she finally understands, she cannot move. By the time Mr. Pritchett returns from the office, she has made a decision. After dinner, when the men swoon over her trifle and the women clamor for the recipe, which she writes down for them on monogrammed notecards, she tells Mr. Pritchett that she has a terrible headache. Would it be okay if she slept in the guest room? He agrees easily, as she knew he would.

In the room that has rarely harbored guests, she thinks about the children Mr. Pritchett and she could never have. This not-having has been a dull ache at the back of her mind all her life, but today she's happy about it in a bitter way. If there had been children, she could not have done this. She takes from the pocket of her robe a bottle of sleeping pills—they belong to Mr. Pritchett, who occasionally suffers from insomnia—and takes the entire bottle, along with two glasses of wine.

At first all goes well. On the bed she lies on her back, her fingers linked over her chest like an image on a sarcophagus. The pressed sheets smell of lavender. She feels herself suspended like a jellyfish in the darkening waters of her mind. A little more, a little more. But then her body, wiser perhaps than she is, rebels, forcing her to double over with cramps. She starts to vomit and can't stop. Mr. Pritchett, who has been catching up on some work—there's always work to catch up on, even though he's seventy and could have retired years ago—hears her and comes running, and she ends up in the hospital, getting her stomach pumped.

WHAT TERRIBLE DISCOVERY DID I MAKE THAT PUSHED ME INTO this desperate action? It was this: my husband did not love me the way I needed him to.

Don't misunderstand me. Mr. Pritchett was a good husband. He provided me with everything I needed and many things I did not need. At dinner he listened (though often with only half his attention) when I told him about my day. How can I complain? When he spoke of his achievements—new companies he'd acquired as clients, or old clients whose financial disasters he'd adroitly avoided—I struggled to hide my own boredom.

There were many things we enjoyed together. Mr. Pritchett was proud of the beautiful and expensive house we lived in, and now that I've heard his story, I understand his pride better. He loved to show it off to people he knew, and I loved to show off my cooking skills. And in return we got invited to beautiful, expensive homes with pleasant people in them. (But when I was about to kill myself, I couldn't think of one person among them whom I would miss, or who would miss me.) We went to the theater and had dinner afterward in a little Italian restaurant on Columbus where the food was superb and the maître d' knew us by name. We went to the movies, mostly action films and sci-fi, which he liked and I didn't mind if there wasn't too much gore. Early in our marriage we used to travel. Europe, Canada, even New Zealand. One year we went on an Alaskan cruise. But it was hard for Mr. Pritchett to be away from the office. He would carry his computer with him everywhere. And when I saw how he struggled upon returning to catch up with his clients, I didn't feel like suggesting further trips. My favorite activity was lying in bed after dinner, reading, he with his business journals, me with a novel, snuggled under a quilt that I had made.

But after I saw the couple in the café, a great dissatisfaction washed over me. I remembered the old man tilting his head attentively, listening to his wife making her menu choice. Her eyes had shone through her thick glasses as she watched him cut up their desserts for sharing. There was nothing like that tenderness in my life. And without it, what use were the things I'd built my days around? My garden, my home, my activities and friendships, even the time Mr. Pritchett and I spent together—they were all so many zeroes. With the "one" of love in front of them, they could have been worth millions, but as of now, I was bankrupt, and it was too late to start over.

THE FIRST DAY IN THE HOSPITAL, I MOVED IN AND OUT OF A haze that was alternately pain and numbness. On the second day, I began to feel a great shame. I refused to talk to the people waiting to see me: my doctor, the hospital psychiatrist, a social worker, and my husband. I spent the day with my face buried in my pillow, my arms aching with IV needles, plotting how I could do this more efficiently once I was released.

I wasn't sure when the night nurse came into my room. I awoke and found her standing at the foot of my bed. The lights were off and she left them that way. In the glow of machines I could only see a silhouette, short and thin. Her hair was tied back neatly in a bun. The darkness had turned her uniform gray. When she greeted me, from her accent I guessed—because Mr. Pritchett had many clients from that country—that she was Indian. I pretended to be asleep. Being a nurse, she could probably tell I was awake, but my pretense didn't annoy her. She hummed softly to herself, a foreign-sounding tune, as she stood there. I waited for her to do nurselike things—check the machines, feel my pulse, give me a shot—but she just stood there. Then, in a whispery voice, she told me that this was her last night at the hospital, and I was her last patient.

I hadn't expected that. Surprise made me blurt out, "Are you retiring?"

"You could say that," she said.

"What will you do now?"

"Some people think I should go back to my birthplace," she said. "But I've decided to go where no one knows me. I want a new life."

Moving to live where no one knew you, shucking off your worn-out life like old snakeskin! The idea ran through me like a shiver. And though I'd been determined not to give anything of myself away in this place filled with concrete and chemicals and cheerlessness, I found myself saying, "That's what I want also. A new life. This one's too painful."

"Why?"

Maybe it was her casual tone. Or the fact that we would never see each other again. I said, "It's like *The Matrix*." (I wasn't sure she would be familiar with the movie. I'd gone to see it only because Mr. Pritchett insisted—though then I had been captivated by it. She nodded, however.) "All this time I thought everything around me was beautiful. But in reality I had been squeezed into a cramped, loveless cell. I chose death. I couldn't see any other way of breaking out."

"Death is a breaking out of sorts," she said. "But you won't necessarily end up in a better place. Especially if you kill yourself. Terrible karma, that. You'll just have to go through everything you tried to escape, in a different form. In any case, this husband whom you consider to be the bane of your existence, he came to you because of your own desire. Don't you see it?"

Her words shot through me like voltage, charging the dead battery of my brain, bringing to life a lost memory. I was astounded because what she said was true.

———

IT IS THE DAY AFTER HIGH SCHOOL GRADUATION. VIVIENNE SITS in her mother's Formica kitchen (lemon yellow, baby-chick yellow, color-of-hope yellow), eating the world's best peach pie with Debbie. Debbie has just told Vivienne she has persuaded her father to let them run his bakery for six months.

"We'll be in charge of everything!" Debbie ends, smiling all over her good-natured, freckled face. But instead of the squeal of joy Debbie is waiting for, Vivienne can only say, in a hollow tone, "That's wonderful, Debbie. But I have some news, too."

"Don't tell me—" Debbie starts. "You're getting—" Then something in Vivienne's expression silences her. Vivienne holds out her left hand, which she has been hiding in her lap until now. On her finger is a ring.

"Lance proposed, and I said yes. He's got a job offer in Tulsa.

He wants us to get married next month, before he moves." She talks fast to keep Debbie from saying the things she doesn't want to hear. Debbie doesn't think Lance is right for her—too intense, too serious, his black eyes boring into whomever he looks at. "He wants too much," she told Vivienne once.

Debbie also thinks Vivienne hasn't known Lance long enough. (He started working for Pete Albright, who owns a secondhand car dealership, two months ago. A week after he moved to town, he came into the bakery where Vivienne and Debbie work after school to buy pumpernickel bread. He ended up asking Vivienne out.) But that's exactly what Vivienne finds exciting about Lance: he doesn't talk about the usual boring things—his family or where he grew up. That's all behind him and of no importance, he tells her. Only the future matters, and about that he has a lot to say. The high-powered jobs he's determined to get, for instance, or the mansion he plans to buy for his wife.

And that's just fine with Vivienne, thank you, because she has lived in the same house since she was born: three bedrooms, two baths, aluminum siding, dripping kitchen faucet, dark, practical carpets that stubbornly hoard odors. She has gone to school with the same kids since kindergarten. Her parents' friends, whom they meet for church picnics or bridge, have known her since she was a tantrum-throwing toddler. She's ready to take a little risk, to follow the yellow brick road into romance and a house on a hill with all-white carpeting. (Tulsa, they've both decided, is only a stepping-stone.) She's ready to want too much, along with Lance.

So now she speaks to Debbie about decorating their beautiful new home, baking her best desserts for Lance, holidaying in exotic destinations, eating at restaurants where the menu is in French and the wineglasses are crystal. And having babies, lots of babies. Already she's imagining the birthday cakes she'll create, confections extravagant as Disneyland that will be the talk of the neighborhood.

"You'll do fine without me," she ends, trying not to look at Debbie's fallen face.

(Debbie will, indeed, do fine. She'll get one of her other friends to join her, and Debbie's Delights will become a hit in their hometown. But Vivienne? How will Vivienne do? In forty years, when she looks into the ledger of her life, at the profit and loss columns, what will she see?)

"I want you to be the maid of honor," Vivienne says. "Will you? Please please?"

And because ultimately a girl can't resist the tinsel lure of weddings, the happily-ever-after she's been conditioned into dreaming of since her first memory, Debbie examines with some envy the minuscule diamond in Vivienne's ring, and agrees.

THE MEMORY SEEMED TO SPOOL FOREVER, BUT IT MUST HAVE taken only a moment. When I came out of it, the nurse was holding my hand.

"What are you doing?" I asked.

"Feeling your palm," she said. "That gives me a sense of what's waiting for you."

The machine light tinged her hair green, but her features were in shadow. I felt heat radiating from her fingertips.

"Is it like palmistry?"

"Not exactly. It's possible for you to break out, if you really want to. But changing your karma will not be easy. You'll have to be alert and intelligent at every step."

Much as I wanted to break out, I wasn't sure I possessed these prerequisites. Karma-changing sounded complicated, and every part of me—body and nerves and heart—felt overwhelmingly stupid.

Still, because I liked the sound of her voice, I asked, "What do I need to do?"

"Stop blaming your husband," she said. "And yourself. Accept. Forgive. A path will open."

I didn't like the sound of this advice. Maybe Mr. Pritchett had sent her to talk to me. Maybe she wasn't even a real nurse.

"Your husband didn't send me," she said, startling me. "I came because you need help, and I need to help you. Let me tell you something that happened to me. Some years back, I had a supervisor I really disliked. She was a harsh woman, always finding fault. I was positive that she hated me. I should have ignored her. Or quit. But I obsessed over it until I did some bad things—to her and then to me." She shook her head. "I shouldn't have spent so much energy hating her. I should have focused on the little things I loved."

I scowled in the dark. Hadn't I been focusing on little things all this time? And hadn't the biggest thing then slipped away?

"What I want is to go somewhere I've never been," I said, "like you, to start a new life."

"You don't want to be like me," she said.

I was only half listening. "I'm not sure where to go," I said. "Can you tell which would be the best place for me?"

"I don't think going anywhere will help."

"Why not?" I asked angrily.

"You'll still be carrying yourself. Even into another lifetime, you'll carry your old, tortured self." Was it my imagination, or did her fingertips turn chilly as she spoke? "Remain where you are and work on your heart. Once you're dead, it's much more difficult."

Was this a joke? She seemed serious. "What I'm telling you is, don't try to kill yourself again. I have to go now. Remember, if you change inside, outer change will follow." At the door she waved good-bye. I tried to see her face, but the light from the passage shone in my eyes.

A few minutes later, another nurse came in. This one was square and bulky and carried a clipboard. She turned on the night-light, checked my vitals, and forced me to take a pill. When I grumbled about her disturbing my sleep by coming so soon after the first nurse, she pursed her lips and wrote something on her clipboard. I asked for a damp towel to wipe my face, and while she went to fetch it, I glanced at the board. In the comments section at the bottom, she had written *delusional*.

WHEN I RETURNED HOME, I TRIED TO RISE ABOVE LETHARGY and follow the first nurse's advice. (Had she actually been a nurse? Was she even a real person?) But her words had grown indistinct, a landscape seen through smoke. The smoke seeped inside me. Was it the result of the numbing medications the psychiatrist insisted I take, or was it a deeper malaise? She had said something about enjoying my days, and I tried. The fact that I was alive was a miracle. But the seeping smoke had filled my cavities. It was hard to feel thankful with Mr. Pritchett hovering, bags of worry under his eyes. And harder still to admit that it was I (a foolish I, a too-young-to-know-better I, but I nevertheless) who had brought calamity upon myself by choosing to marry, against the advice of friends and family, a man I had not understood. One thing had changed: I no longer wanted to commit suicide. But secretly, I increased the dosage of my medication. The numbness brought some relief. Still, I was carrying my old unhappy self inside, I didn't know how to get away from it, and I felt guiltier. So when Mr. Pritchett showed me the picture of the Indian palace, those curtains delicate as spiderwebs blowing in a foreign breeze, and asked if I wanted to go there, I was struck dumb with joy. It was as though the universe had opened a door.

Now that I'm probably not going anyplace, I, like Mr. Mangalam, have a confession to make. This is why I was so excited about going to India: Once I got there, I planned to leave Mr. Pritchett. I planned to dive into that roiling ocean of one billion people, all our karmas fitting together like jigsaw puzzle pieces, and begin anew.

MRS. PRITCHETT'S ADMISSION FILLED UMA WITH A PRIMAL SORrow. They were about to die. It was now clear that the entire group believed this. The sorrow infiltrated her lungs. Ramon! she called in her mind. In answer, a memory came, a summer walk she and Ramon had taken in the hills. They had climbed up a trail of slippery orange gravel, impeded by picnic supplies. When they reached the top, the puckered golden skin of the bay stretched below them. They had spread a sheet on the narrow, bumpy ledge and eaten chutney sandwiches and oranges and densely sweet chocolate pan de huevos. Then they had held hands and watched the sky until the clouds turned purple.

Uma looked down on their intertwined fingers and was surprised to see that Ramon's were as brown as hers. But this was not right. Ramon was lighter skinned. In this not-quite-a-memory, Uma's eyes moved up his brown arm, his shoulders, and his neck, until they alighted on his face. She gasped because the man was not Ramon at all. He was Indian. His features shifted as she watched— now a mustache, now a pair of high cheekbones, now square-framed glasses over wide-set eyes—but his Indianness was never in question. Watching him, she realized what she must have guessed deep down when her mother had interrupted herself during their phone conversation. "Enough time for—" her mother had said. Now Uma was able to complete the sentence: "for us to introduce you to some nice Indian men." Was this subterranean knowledge the reason she hadn't told Ramon where she was coming today? Did she *want* to meet the nice Indian men her parents were even at this moment lining up for her?

Had she been only playing at love, all this time? Was that the kind of person she was?

LILY WAS TRYING TO WHISPER, BUT THEY ALL HEARD HER. "Gramma, do you think that woman was a ghost?"

The word hung in the air, papery. Uma thought she felt presences around them—not malevolent or sorrowful, but startled by their sudden weightless existence.

"I think yes," Jiang said. "When I was young, I heard stories. Spirits that died in the place where you are, coming back to warn you."

Lily said, "So many people must have died in this quake. Perhaps they can save us?"

MR. PRITCHETT SAT WITH HIS HEAD BOWED. HE WOULD NOT look at anyone. If it had been possible for him to go somewhere and never see any of the group again, he would have done so. But their world had shrunk to three desks. *Hell is other people,* Uma thought on his behalf.

It was completely dark now. Cameron had to switch on the flashlight again. For a moment it didn't work. Had water leaked into it?

Give up Seva, said the voice inside his head, *and I'll fix the flash-*

light. Cameron ignored the voice. He shook the flashlight hard until it came on. He shone the beam around to check for problems. He trained the circle of light for an instant on the cubicle wall, beyond which the dead man lay in the water. Cameron's chest hurt. But no more procrastination was possible.

15

When Cameron first met the holy man, he didn't recognize him as such. Partly, he didn't fit Cameron's concept of holy men: no beads, no robes, no beatific expression on a bearded face. And partly, Cameron was distracted; it was the thirtieth anniversary—or as close to it as he could figure—of his son's death, and with each passing year, the event weighed more heavily on him.

They were traveling on a crowded Muni. Cameron was on his way to the hospice where he volunteered one afternoon each week. So was the holy man, though Cameron did not know this. The man, whose name was Jeff, stood holding on to one of the bus handlebars, swaying as the vehicle made a wide turn. He was white, with pleasant, nondescript features; he wore jeans and a freshly laundered shirt. His head was shaved, but it was currently fashionable for men to shave their heads, so Cameron barely noticed it.

Cameron stared out a window, trying to occupy his mind with observation. The passing scenery was painfully familiar, so like the landscape of his childhood, the ugly streets he had labored to escape: storefronts with grills over the doors and windows, piles of garbage, men passed out in doorways. Dealers hung out on street corners, keeping an eye out for customers, or for cops. Even without opening the window, Cameron knew what it would smell like: rotting food, sour armpits, piss, marijuana, and the desperate hilarity of young men who waited for night. But when the doors hissed open, it was to let Cameron—and Jeff—out into sunshine and a happy burst of music and the not-unpleasant odor of Sesame Fried Chicken from Tang's Carry Out. From across the years he could hear Imani's voice, so clear that he had to sit down on the bus-stop bench and put his head in his hands: *You already decided you going to leave, so you can't see nothing good even if it up and smack you in the face.*

Jeff paused to give him a concerned look. "You okay? Need some water?"

Cameron considered telling the stranger to mind his own business, but he held up a hand to indicate he was fine. When Jeff moved on, Cameron went back to thinking about Imani even though he didn't want to. She was like a scab that he couldn't help picking at.

They had both been in their senior year of high school when he met her at a party. He usually avoided the kind of parties his friends threw, with liquor and loud music and making out in the stairwell and fistfights or worse in the alley behind the apartments. They weren't even his friends—just guys he happened to know because they went to school together or lived in the neighborhood. But on this day he had just sent off the last of his college applications and was feeling celebratory. And perhaps a bit nostalgic. Soon all this would be behind him. He was certain of getting into a good college. His grades were excellent; his recommendations enthusiastic; he was on the track team, and for the last couple of years, he had taken care to stay out of trouble. Following the advice of his biology teacher, who had become a mentor, he volunteered regularly at the local hospital. His counselor had declared that all these credentials, added to Cameron's unfortunate background—impoverished, orphaned, first-generation college applicant—would probably snag him a scholarship. At first Cameron had resented the counselor's patronizing manner. Like some second-rate prestidigitator, the counselor tried to turn the painful truths of Cameron's existence into advantages. Cameron had wanted to say something cutting, to walk out of the man's office, slamming the door behind him. But he had held on to his temper. If doing so helped him get where he needed to go, Cameron could put up with a little patronizing.

Cameron wanted to be a doctor. He guarded this fragile dream jealously, not confiding it to anyone except his biology teacher. His friends would ridicule it, and even his well-meaning, churchgoing aunt, with whom he had lived since his parents had died, would shake her head in warning and say, "Boy, you aimin' above your station." Blindsided by infatuation in the months following the party at which they had met, he had ventured to share his goal with Imani, but that turned out to be an error.

At the party, he'd had a couple of beers. When he first saw Imani being pushed into the middle of the room by a couple of other girls, he didn't recognize her because she went to a different school. She resisted her friends, but when someone turned off the music, she squared her shoulders, stood tall, and began to sing. She was good, definitely, but not so exceptional in this community; almost every family had a member in a church choir. So what was it about this girl that captured his attention and his breath? Her hair was too nappy, her skin too dark. She looked good in the red sweater she wore over a black skirt—but several girls there looked better. Was it the passion with which she sang, eyes closed, leaning into the song? Or the song itself, the haunting, dragged out notes of "My Man He Don't Love Me"? Cameron had never heard that song before; it would go deep into him, lodging like a guinea worm, emerging whenever it wanted to. It pulled him across the room to introduce himself to

Imani, to offer to get her a drink, to listen with fascination to her chatter, though later he couldn't remember what she had said. By the end of the party, he had—most uncharacteristically—exchanged phone numbers and set up a movie date for the next evening. Maybe that's why the relationship was doomed from the first: the person Imani fell for wasn't the real Cameron.

Their romance sped through winter into the beginnings of spring. He rushed to get his homework done before he went to his job at the grocery, where he was a stocker, so he could pick her up after her shift at Burger King. Sometimes on Friday nights they went to the movies or to a club. Mostly they spent hours in his beat-up Chevy, parked on a quiet street where they wouldn't be disturbed by gangs or cops, talking or listening to music or singing along with the radio—or groping. Evenings when she knew her mother wouldn't be home, they went to her apartment. He fixed her grilled cheese sandwiches and listened to her sing; she initiated him into the mysteries of the female body. Tangled together in bed afterward, he felt an easefulness that was foreign to him. Usually, he had to be constantly doing something, pushing himself. But at these times he felt he could lie there forever.

Then, as the oleanders began to bloom and the orioles started flying back north and universities began sending acceptance letters, Cameron and Imani's relationship grew strained. After graduation, Imani was going to increase her hours at Burger King (her mother said it was time she helped with the rent) while she took classes part-time at the local community college. She couldn't understand why Cameron couldn't do something similar. The manager at the grocery liked him. Her friend Latisha, who worked one of the cash registers there, had informed her that he'd offered Cameron a position as assistant manager—with benefits. "In a couple years," Imani told Cameron, "we be saving up some. Get our own place. Get married." She offered him a shy smile. When Cameron said that he would find that kind of life stifling, she flinched as though he'd slapped her in the face. On the increasingly rare occasions when she sang, the blues tunes he had loved earlier seemed loaded with reproach: "Crazy He Calls Me," "Lonely Grief."

They argued almost every time they met. Imani would cry and invoke sayings from her grandmother, a Jamaican obeah woman; Cameron would feel guilty and attempt to console her. If they were at her apartment, they would end up in bed. On the day he learned that a prestigious private college had offered him admission and a sports scholarship, she came into the grocery to say hello. Exhilarated into garrulity, he told her his news. She called him an Oreo, speaking loud enough for his coworkers to hear and snigger. It was the last straw for him—that she would want to ruin the moment of his greatest achievement. When he took her out to the parking lot to tell her this was the end, she informed him that she was pregnant. He could see she was scared, but beneath the fear was a kind of triumph: now he would have to stay with her and take responsibility for the baby.

Cameron was furious—and terrified. The ghetto seemed to be closing in on him. He told her that he refused to be manipulated. He was going to college. If she thought she could stand in his way, she was mistaken. He recommended an abortion. He would scrape together the money to pay for it. He couldn't do any more than that.

At the mention of abortion, she stopped crying and grew very quiet. "You want to kill our baby?" she asked. "It so important for you to get away from your people?"

He started saying that the mess he saw every day around him was not his people, and he wasn't alone in wanting to get away. All around him young men were enlisting in the army, being shipped to the jungles of Vietnam. But she was wringing her hands. No, she was making some kind of a complicated design in the air with her fingers. Was Imani putting some kind of voodoo on him? He shook off the ridiculous idea.

"It do you no good," she said. "No matter where you run, you be ending with ashes in your mouth." She walked across the parking lot. He considered hurrying after her, grabbing her by the hand, saying he was sorry. But that would reopen the coffin of their relationship, and he didn't have the energy to go through the ups and downs of the last months again. She would probably come running to him soon enough—for the money, if nothing else.

Over the next weeks he waited—at first with trepidation, then with concern, then with a strange disappointment—for her to make contact. She didn't. One day Latisha cornered him in the canned foods aisle and told him Imani had had an abortion the week before. He couldn't bring himself to ask Latisha—whom he didn't like—if Imani was okay. Instead he inquired if Imani needed money—could Latisha ask her? Latisha gave him a hard look and walked off. Cameron felt terrible, but the rush of getting ready for college didn't allow him time to dwell on the whole complicated mess.

REMINISCING ON THE BUS STOP BENCH HAD MADE CAMERON late, and this annoyed him. He jogged the last few blocks (though jogging through this kind of exhaust-laden air sometimes brought on his asthma) and arrived at the hospice sweaty. The sweat wouldn't matter too much since he worked in the garden.

When he had started volunteering, they had tried him with the inmates (that's how he thought of the patients, prisoners with a life sentence). He sat with them, read to them, adjusted pillows. But watching the seemingly interminable process of dying made him nervous and snappy, and after a couple of incidents the management had asked if he could do something with the barren strip of land behind the building. Now the Pacifica Hospice Care boasted a garden, lush with lavender and daylilies, where patients could be wheeled in to watch the hummingbirds flit around brightly colored hanging feeders.

As he hurried down the passage to the back, where gardening supplies were kept, Cameron was surprised to see Jeff emerging from a patient's room. Jeff tried to engage Cameron in conversation, but Cameron sidestepped him with a curt hello. When, a half hour later, he saw Jeff wander into his garden (that's how Cameron thought of it), Cameron felt a frisson of annoyance. Was the man following him? Cameron turned his back on the intruder and went on planting sweet alyssum. But Jeff sat on a bench peaceably, ate a sandwich, and watched the clouds. When he finished eating, he sat very still with his eyes closed. After an hour, he left quietly. Cameron, intrigued by the stillness, made some inquiries and learned that Jeff was a lay Buddhist priest. The management had asked him to come in and minister to their Buddhist patients.

In the following weeks, Cameron saw Jeff every time he came into the hospice. Jeff ate his lunch in the garden and meditated there. He always gave Cameron a friendly nod but made no further attempts to talk. (Cameron was surprised to feel a twinge of disappointment at this.) One day, Jeff didn't eat but sat rubbing his eyes tiredly until Cameron couldn't stand the suspense and asked what was wrong.

"Louie died," Jeff said.

Cameron suggested that maybe that was a good thing. Louie, a skeletal young man with AIDS, had been suffering for months.

"He was so afraid of death," Jeff said. He punched the bench in frustration. "Nothing I said could comfort him."

Cameron abandoned his weeding and sat beside Jeff on the bench. That was how their friendship began.

TO HIS BITTER ASTONISHMENT, CAMERON DID NOT DO WELL IN college. First, he developed severe allergies that deepened into asthma. It could have been from moving to a different part of the country, but he couldn't help thinking of it as punishment. The Bricanyl cleared up his breathing at first, but soon he had to increase his dosage for it to work. It felt like he was moving underwater. He couldn't perform as well as before. Imani's words echoed in his bones: *no matter where you run.* The coach kept him on for the year, but his scholarship wasn't renewed. His brain, too, felt submerged. He sat for hours with textbooks that seemed to have been written in a foreign language. In class, where he was often the only black student, he fell dull and unprepared. The privileged kids with their smart answers intimidated him into silence, which his teachers took as indifference. Outside of class his touchiness pushed away the few students who tried to befriend him. By the time he understood that he should have gone to a large state college where there would have been more of "his people," his grades had plummeted and he had no money. Ashamed to write to his biology teacher, who might have given him better advice, he quit school. Keeping his health issues secret, he joined the army—and was plummeted into the last desperate days of the Vietnam War.

CAMERON BEGAN TO SPEND A GREAT DEAL OF HIS FREE TIME with Jeff. Jeff had a small apartment in the Mission District and taught Comparative Religion at a local college. He also volunteered at a small Tibetan monastery, helping with everything from paperwork to fixing leaks to chauffeuring the monks, who had fled from Tibet to a small Himalayan village before arriving here. Some days, Jeff cooked, odd dishes with flat noodles and tofu and seaweed, or mushrooms that plumped up when you soaked them in water, dishes that Cameron was distrustful of at first but grew to like. Jeff was no saint; he tended to impatience and took it hard when things didn't go the way he wanted them to. But Cameron admired the quickness with which he was able to return to cheerfulness.

Jeff had a way of listening without interruption or advice that Cameron appreciated. As they sat on the balcony of Jeff's apartment with steaming mugs of coffee, he found himself telling Jeff things he hadn't shared with anyone. He went backward, beginning with his current job. He was the head security guard for a large bank building downtown, but each day the gun he carried at his hip seemed heavier. He lived in a tiny one-room place in a too-expensive neighborhood so that from his window he would be able to see the ocean. Every morning he tucked his inhaler into a pocket and went for a run. With the wind whistling in his ears, he could forget the decisions he regretted. He had to take pills at night to sleep. He hated insomnia but feared sleep because of the nightmares. None of his activities since he left the army—helping at the hospice, serving food in soup kitchens, donating money to organizations that rescued abused children—had stopped the nightmares. The worst was that of a tiny child afloat in an oval room. The boy would open his black eyes and look at Cameron without reproach, and that was the hardest thing.

Cameron told Jeff about his deployment to hot, mosquito-infested countries supposedly threatened by Communism, where he had been feared and detested because of his uniform. He described the men he had killed—sometimes apathetically, because their lives hadn't seemed as real as his own. Jeff grew white around the mouth, but he put a hand on Cameron's shoulder and left it there.

When Cameron had told Jeff everything he could remember, all the way back to his parents' death in a car crash when he was twelve, he asked about Imani's curse. Jeff didn't believe in curses, but he did believe in consequences. He felt that Cameron had done what he could to expiate his wartime acts, but the abortion was unfinished business.

Cameron knew he couldn't go looking for Imani to ask forgiveness. She was probably married; his reappearance would cause more harm than good. He was too old and set in his ways to adopt a child and become a full-time parent. Then Jeff recalled that the monks had spoken of orphanages in the hills of India. What if Cameron contacted one and sponsored a boy? When the time was right, he could visit him. Perhaps when Cameron saw this child in person, when he caught hold of his hand and felt the metta that upholds the universe flowing between them, he would be healed.

Buoyed by new hope, Cameron contacted the orphanage. They were slow to respond; he had to stop himself from sending reminders, from taking a plane to the nearest city and hiking up to the gates. To succeed, his offer must appear to be a casual act of philanthropy, not a desperate yearning. (The authorities were cautious; Jeff had told him stories about foreigners and child trafficking that explained why.) Finally the orphanage sent a photograph, along with details. Not a boy, as Cameron had requested, but a scrawny girl left outside their gates a few years back. It did not matter. As soon as he saw the blurry black-and-white picture in which she wore a too-large frock and squinted into sunlight, he knew she was the one.

He sent in the necessary money to become her sponsor and requested permission for a visit. But the orphanage informed him that they did not want to rush things. People sometimes tired of their charity, and if the children had had contact with them, they felt additionally rejected. Cameron could write letters to Seva—that was the girl's name. They would be translated and read to her. In a year or two, when she learned to write, she would send him notes in Hindi. Meanwhile, could he fill out the enclosed forms for a background check and have recommendation letters sent directly to the orphanage?

Impatience—and that old anger—had boiled up in Cameron, but he followed the instructions. Each month he wrote to Seva. Each year, the orphanage sent him two photos of her, taken at activities such as lunch or games, which he pored over hungrily. Since last year, he had begun to receive, at random intervals, lined sheets filled with a child's scrawlings that the owner of his neighborhood Indian grocery deciphered for him. Cameron could tell that Seva had a mind of her own. In addition to the requisite sentences thanking him and wishing him good health, she informed him of various occurrences in her life: the orphanage cat's newborn babies had been eaten in the night, by a coyote, the cook said; her friend Bijli had ventured into the bushes at the edge of the playing field in spite of being warned and now had a terrible itch; she had done well in most of her exams except math, which was very difficult for her to understand; Anil had pushed her into the mud when they were marching during P.T. class, so she had pushed him down, too, and the P.T. teacher, Mr. Ahuja, had made them stand out in the yard all afternoon as punishment; Mr. Ahuja had a big mole with hairs sticking out of it on his left cheek.

Cameron was concerned when he heard of the punishment, but Jeff consulted the monks and assured Cameron that this discipline was fairly mild compared to what was customary at many such schools. Still, Cameron thought it was time he went and saw Seva. Perhaps he would have a little discussion with Mr. Ahuja while he was there. He wrote a stern letter to the orphanage, hinting that he might switch his support to a more forthcoming organization. The orphanage sent a speedy reply: Mr. Grant was of course welcome to visit. When Cameron informed Seva, he was coming, he received an ecstatic note listing all the things she would take him to see once he arrived. He carried it around in his wallet. He applied for an indefinite leave from work and for a one-year visa from the Indian government. He suspected that, as a single male, and an African American at that, he would never be given custody of Seva. But as he scoured Toys "R" Us, filling his suitcase with gifts he thought an eight-year-old would like, he wondered if he might just stay on in the hills. Perhaps he could persuade the orphanage to fire Mr. Ahuja and take him on as the P.T. teacher?

Then the earthquake struck and—

16

It was as though the giant in the earth had heard Cameron speak his name. Before he could complete his sentence, before his listeners could compare his story to theirs, before they could feel admiration or sorrow or thankfulness, the building shuddered and groaned. Something crashed upstairs, and above their heads a ripple went through the ceiling as though it were made of paper.

"Aftershock!" a voice yelled. Someone started to scream. Someone else was crying. One man began a cryptic prayer, "God, let it end, let it just end fast!" As she plunged through water, making for a doorway, Uma wondered, What did the praying man want finished—the earthquake, this imprisonment, or their lives? *Wait a minute,* she wanted to protest. *I haven't told my story yet.*

In her doorway, there was only one other person: Mr. Pritchett, who had abandoned the shawl Tariq had loaned him and was shivering in his underwear. Stripped, he was a lot smaller than Uma had taken him to be. He held on to both doorjambs with outstretched arms, his limbs thin and ropy like those of aged Christian martyrs in medieval paintings. Uma had to duck under his armpit to find shelter. The water came halfway up their thighs, and as soon as that the building stopped shaking, Uma became aware that her legs were growing numb from the cold water, though her arm still throbbed. She considered submerging it in the water. Then it struck her that there should have been another person in her doorway. Peering through the gloom, she knew who it was and called his name. *Cameron! Cameron!*

Cameron lay curled on the table, fetal position. Uma thought he looked like the unborn child he had dreamed of. When he heard her calling his name, he opened his eyes and gave her the same, reproachless, infant look. He had been holding on to the flashlight, which contained their last batteries, and he raised his fist slightly, as if to say he would keep it safe until he could hand it to her. Though chunks of plaster covered the table and dotted his face and arms, he appeared unhurt.

Uma waded back to the table through the black water, their own Mnemosyne, pool of memory, drawing their dearest secrets out of them. The ceiling looked as if it was holding, but even if it wasn't, she couldn't bear to leave Cameron by himself. They were all going to die anyway, unless a miracle happened soon. When she put an arm around him, Cameron's body felt colder than normal—but what was normal anymore? His heart fluttered like a snared bird. She could hear wheezing with each breath he drew. He gave her a small, blanched smile. Against his silence, the comments about hope and forgiveness that she had planned to offer seemed platitudinous. Who was she to speak, anyway? Hadn't she wronged the people closest to her: Ramon because she had not cherished him as he cherished her; her mother because she wouldn't listen to the cautionary lessons she tried to teach Uma; her father because when he needed someone to talk to, she had turned away. *Forgive me,* she said to them in her head. But it did not provide her with the same satisfaction as hugging a plump maternal body, or rubbing her palm along a jaw sexily stubbled with a night's growth of beard, or leaning against a no-longer-muscular chest and breathing in the distinctive smell, familiar from childhood, of Old Spice cologne.

THE AFTERSHOCK SEEMED OVER. OTHERS VENTURED OUT OF their doorways and checked for damage, looking up worriedly at the ceiling. Jiang, whose face was flushed and feverish, told Uma they should make Cameron sit upright; it might improve his breathing. Lily helped them prop him up. The smell of gas was distinctly stronger, but no one commented on that. They climbed back onto their tables, drawing their knees up and trying to dry their legs with the rags that had once been a sari colored by hope. Mangalam examined the water level and said that at this rate, the water would reach the level of the tables in an hour; they would then have to collect chairs from the other side of the room, place them on top of the tables, and sit on those. These tables could accommodate only two chairs each. Three people would have to take their chairs into Mangalam's office, where the table was larger. But there was time for the last story before the group split up.

"I DID NOT MISS MY PARENTS AT ALL," UMA BEGAN. "WHEN I went away to college, I guess you could say I was heartless and self-centered, like many young people. My mother took it hard, but my father—"

Before she could continue the chronicle of her filial perfidies, there were noises above. Everyone cringed, but these were not the rumbles of an earthquake. There was a tapping and banging, a crash like furniture toppling over. They thought they heard engines revving, a door slammed shut.

"It's people!" Tariq said. "Rescuers!" Everyone looked up, elation battling disbelief on their faces. They gripped one another's arms. Mrs. Pritchett and Lily cupped their hands and yelled for help, and the others joined in. But there was no answer from above. The clang-ings grew quieter, as though receding. When a large chunk of plas-ter fell into the water, it scared them and they stopped shouting.

Tariq stood on the table, craning his neck. He wanted to see through the hole in the ceiling. But the angle wasn't right. "I'm going to go to the other side of the partition," he said, "climb on a chair or something, and figure out what's going on." He jumped down, splash-ing water in every direction.

"I'll come with you," Mangalam said, taking the flashlight. "We can tie a strip of cloth on a post and wave it through the hole."

Mr. Pritchett, who had struggled into his pants, hurried after them. Uma, too, longed to follow, but Cameron was propped up against her good arm, and she didn't want to move him.

"Warn them," Cameron whispered. "There's a dead body in the water—fell from upstairs when the ceiling collapsed." She peered at him in shock. Until this moment, in accepting that she might per-ish, she had thought she understood what death meant, but it had only been an abstraction. This body, within fifty inescapable feet of where she was now, bloated and rubbery and beginning to decay, made death a touchable horror.

Cameron nudged her. "Don't shout—people might panic. Go after them. I'll be okay."

"Go, I'll watch him," Malathi said from Cameron's other side. Uma felt Malathi's firm, bangled arm come around Cameron's torso. She was humbled by Malathi's calmness in the face of what they had just heard.

The thought of stepping into the water where the dead man lay filled Uma with revulsion, but Cameron was waiting. She climbed down gingerly but couldn't stop herself from shuddering. She walked around the partition and stopped at the edge of the room. Mr. Pritchett was bent over, clearing debris from an area that lay directly under the gash of the collapsed ceiling. That, she guessed, would be where the dead man fell. She imagined the heavy drop. She hoped he had died before falling, that he didn't have to drown in liquid blackness. Tariq and Mangalam were dragging a sofa through the water. They meant to stand it on its side. One of them would climb on it while the others steadied him.

"After I make some space here, we'll need to find a rod to tie a cloth to," Mr. Pritchett said. "Can you give me a hand?" He reached into the water.

"Stop!" Uma snapped. "Move away!" But it was too late. In the beam of the flashlight Mangalam aimed at her, she saw the shock on Mr. Pritchett's face. The dark water splashed up as he let something heavy fall and backed away. She heard him retch and stumble in the dark. There was another splash. She gritted her teeth and hurried past the corpse toward him.

"I touched it," Mr. Pritchett said to Uma, between heaves, as she tried to pull him up.

"Hush. It's all right," Uma said. She rubbed his back.

"What's wrong?" Tariq called from the other end of the room. When she told him, he dropped his end of the sofa and cursed.

Among them, Mangalam seemed the least affected. He seemed calmer, if anything. Cameron's decline had forced him to take up the responsibility that should have been his in the first place. "We can avoid that area," he said. "Let's set up the sofa here. It won't give us as good a visibility, but it'll do. We have to hurry. If someone's up there, they'll move away unless we let them know we're trapped here. Mr. Pritchett, we need you to hold one side of the sofa. Uma, fetch that rod from near the wall."

Thus rallied, they did what Mangalam said. Uma found that

she was able to function if she kept her mind on the task at hand and didn't think of the water flowing from the corpse toward her, contaminating her with deadness. In a few minutes, they upended the sofa. Tariq climbed on, lifted the rod as high as he could through the hole, and waved the makeshift flag vigorously. Uma trained the flashlight on the blue rag. When they shouted for help, the group in the other room joined them, like a Stygian chorus. Plaster fell again, but they continued. What did they have left to lose? There was a loud noise upstairs like an explosion. Then silence. When their throats grew raw and they were sure there were no further noises above, they gave up, one at a time. Some of them sobbed for a bit. Some sat wordlessly, devastated. To have been extended those minutes of hope only to have them snatched away was the cruelest cosmic joke, the final insult.

The batteries were dying. In the dimming glow of the flashlight, Uma saw her companions crumpled into themselves, avoiding one another's eyes, hands balled by their sides or covering their faces. Mangalam brought forth a bottle with bourbon still in it and passed it around. A couple of people took desultory sips, but even such a conjuration didn't perk them up much. It was getting harder to breathe. Uma remembered an old science lesson from middle school. Gas killed people by displacing oxygen, which was lighter. When enough gas settled in the basement, they would suffocate.

Too many problems, all beyond her solving. There was nothing to do but go on with her story.

WHEN IT WAS TIME FOR ME TO GO TO COLLEGE, I CHOSE A PLACE far from home, although I knew my parents would have preferred it otherwise. It wasn't that I had a bad relationship with them, or that they were tyrannical, in the way Indian immigrant parents sometimes are. I was just eager to strike out on my own, without their protective presence. It never struck me that my presence might have been protective for them, too. The college I picked was in Texas: expensive and private, with a reputation that a parent could brag about. Still, the key lure for me was its distance from home.

My mother took my absence hard. Though she was a successful manager, fairly high up in her company, she defined herself mostly as a mother and homemaker and took more pride in a made-from-scratch Indian dinner than in acquiring a new customer. My first month of college, whenever my mother and I spoke on the phone, she would dissolve into tears while insisting I describe every detail of my day. My father admonished her to pull herself together. He kept his questions brief and basic—how was my health, was I able to keep up with the workload, did I need money—and he was satisfied with monosyllabic answers. He always ended his conversation with a joke about prospective boyfriends—mostly the same joke—while my mother remonstrated on the other line. I was thankful that my father was handling my departure so well. I admired his suavity. Up until this time I had been closer to my mother, but now I felt a subtle shift in allegiance.

The student population at the college was different from my high school but not drastically so. I loved the lush campus with its tropical foliage and old Southern elegance; the single dorm room that I could decorate as I wanted; the small literature symposiums where famous professors treated me as an adult, which, deep down, I wasn't certain I was; the coffeehouses that remained open until two a.m. and where students held heated intellectual discussions; and the partying, which was available in hot, medium, or mild. My mother's cautions must have rubbed off on me; the pleasures I chose were innocuous ones.

One evening, a couple of months into the semester, my father phoned me. This was unusual on several counts, though I didn't think about that until afterward. Our family calls usually occurred over the weekend, when cell phone minutes were free. Generally my mother initiated them. And it was barely five p.m. in California, which meant that my father, who worked late, was calling from his office.

My father had never wasted time with small talk. "Now that you've settled down in college and done so well in your first midterms," he said, "I can tell you this. I'm planning to get a divorce. You mother and I no longer have anything in common except you— and we've launched you successfully into the world." He paused for a moment, and I wondered (as though he were a stranger) what he was feeling. If he was nervous.

"All my life I've done what other people expected from me," he continued. "Whatever time I have left, I'd like to live it the way I want. Do you have any questions?"

It struck me that he did not see how ridiculous his last sentence was. I wanted to laugh, but I was afraid that once I started I might not be able to stop. Apparently he took this to mean that I had no queries, because he went on.

"I haven't told your mother anything yet. I suggest you don't call her until I've had the chance to break the news to her. I'll do it over the coming week." He became aware of my silence and added, "I'm sure you're upset, but try to see it from my point of view. Is it fair to ask me to remain in a relationship that's killing me?" While I pondered his choice of gerund, he said his good-byes, promising to phone me back with an update.

After he hung up, I lay down and tried to understand what had just happened. For some moments, I wondered if I had dreamed my father's phone call. All these years I had been sure, in the unthinking manner in which we skim over the absolutes of our lives, that my parents had a good marriage. They had approached their joint activities—child-rearing, entertaining, traveling, movie-watching, gardening—enthusiastically. Within the boundaries prescribed by the culture of their birth, they had expressed affection, kissing in the morning when they left for work, putting their arms around each other in photographs, admiring a new outfit, sitting close on the couch as they listened to Rabindra Sangeet CDs. They often read together on that couch, my father laying his head in her lap as he turned the pages of *Time,* my mother absentmindedly stroking his hair as she read a Bengali novel.

Had that not been love? If it had—and I would have bet my life on it—how had it crumbled overnight? Could all the things of the world crumble so suddenly? What was the point, then, of putting our hearts into any achievement?

Amid these metaphysical questions, a couple of practical ones popped up from time to time: Was there another woman involved? And, what would happen to my mother when my father told her? But that last question was rhetorical. I already knew she would not survive the blow.

I SPENT THE NEXT DAY, AND THE NEXT, IN BED, FIGURING things out. I had a single room; there was no roommate to wonder what was wrong. I did not brush my teeth or bathe or eat, though I did drink three cans of Coke that were in my mini-fridge. I did not attend my classes. This was a first, and deep down, the old me worried about consequences. But the new me merely shrugged and turned on the TV. My cell phone rang. I checked the number, and when I saw it was my father, calling from his office again, I turned it off.

On the third day, I resisted the urge to go and see my professors and, pretending I had been ill, pick up my missed assignments. Instead, I went on a rambling drive around the city and lunched at a fancy Italian restaurant I'd been eyeing for weeks. The food was as excellent as I'd hoped. I ordered too much, along with wine, but instead of asking them to pack the remains, I ate everything. Back in my room, I slept away the afternoon, feeling decadent and full of ennui, like a Roman patrician. I awoke with a headache and recalled that my weekly kickboxing class was that night. I considered skipping that, too, but fortified myself with ice water and a double dose of Tylenol and went to it.

The kickboxing class was held in a part of town my parents would have termed seedy, with tattoo parlors and adult video shops. (But enough of my parents. I would exorcise them from my mind.) I had learned about the class from a flyer I'd been handed at a café I had stopped by one day, out of curiosity. I'm not sure what made me try the class, or what made me keep going back. Perhaps it was that the other students were so different from me.

In class, I usually ended up next to Jeri, a waif-thin woman with hair of a redness I had not encountered before. Her ribs showed through her tight black leotard top, the same one every week. She worked at a used-clothing store named Very Vintage. She wore a lot of eye makeup and yelled viciously every time she punched, but she had a gamine charm. From some angles, she looked about thirty years old; then suddenly she would smile and be transformed into a teenager. I couldn't resist smiling back or listening after class as she regaled me with the latest treacheries of her boyfriend, whom she was always on the verge of leaving.

This evening, Jeri's smile held a frenetic cheerfulness, and halfway through class, during water break, she leaned over and whispered, "Guess what, I dumped the SOB!" Later, as we changed out of our drenched clothing in the women's locker room, she said, "I'm ready to leave this god-awful hellhole. I have a girlfriend in New York—said she'd set me up with a job and let me stay with her until I find a place of my own. If I had a car, I'd be gone like this." She snapped her fingers loudly.

"I have a car," I heard myself saying. "And I'm ready to leave, too."

"No shit!" she said. "Aren't you going to college or something?"

"Not anymore," I said.

It took us only a few minutes to decide on the details. She would go to Very Vintage tomorrow afternoon and pick up last week's pay. I would bring the car at four p.m. to the address she provided. By then, she would be packed and ready. We'd hit the road. She would pay for half the gas.

I tossed and turned most of the night from an illicit excitement akin to fever. Or was it satisfaction at a well-executed revenge? Toward morning I dozed off and didn't hear the alarm. I had barely enough time to stuff some clothes in a carry-on suitcase and put a shoe box full of CDs in the car. I felt a pang as I looked around the room; I had decorated it only two months ago, with posters of Impressionist paintings, a batik wall hanging, and three potted plants. But I told myself I had been a different girl then. On the way to Jeri's, I stopped at the bank and took everything out of my checking account—over a thousand dollars—in small bills. I divided the money into stacks and hid them in various places—inside the glove compartment, under the floor mat on the driver's side, in my cosmetics case. Right now I didn't feel like trusting anyone.

I need not have rushed. When I reached the ramshackle house where Jeri rented a room, no one was there. I parked in the shade of a large mimosa, dozing again, dreaming in snatches. Images of past birthdays came to me, always with a pink cake that my mother had decorated with strawberries (though my birthday was in winter) proudly displayed on our kitchen table. The tables changed as we moved into different houses. The number of candles on the cake increased. But always there were the strawberries that my mother scoured the markets to find because I loved them. And always there was the ritual of a family photo afterward. My father would set up the stand, put the camera on timer, and run over just in time to be in the picture. Later we crowded over the photos, laughing at the imperfections that made them more fun: someone's mouth hanging open, a dab of icing on someone's cheek, the top of someone's head sliced off by the edge of the photograph. But in my memory-dream, the expression on my father's face had changed. He waited in stoic impatience for me to go to college, do well in my first midterms, and set him free.

I was startled awake by Jeri rapping on the car window. She was full of righteous indignation. The manager at Very Vintage had refused to pay her—had, in fact, berated her for quitting without giving notice, even though she told him it was an emergency. She had berated him right back. Finally, he gave her half of what he owed her, the miser, and threatened to call the police if she didn't leave. She had packed just one bag—that's all she cared to take—and some provisions for our journey, both solid and liquid. But it looked like she might not be able to spring for her part of the gas. She scrunched her nose in apology.

I told her it was okay. We would manage. Her eyes glinted as she considered the financial implications of my statement. (Was I a rich girl?) She disappeared into the house to fetch her things. By the time she returned, the sun was setting. She threw a suitcase into the trunk and, with great care, placed a brown paper bag on the floor of the passenger seat, between her legs. I saw the necks of two bottles—whiskey, I guessed, or rum. Jeri directed me to the neighborhood grocery where, true to her promise, she ran in to pick up supplies:

potato chips with onion dip, sugar cookies, Coke and 7Up, ice in one of those disposable Styrofoam chests, and a stack of cups.

Ten minutes later, we were stopped at a red light on the access road to the freeway when Jeri said, "Oh, look!" A young man with a duffel bag stood by the side of the road, his punk hair streaked with blue. His cardboard sign said, NEED RIDE NORTH, WILL SHARE GAS. Before I could stop her, she had rolled down her window.

"Where you going?" she called.

"Where *you* going?"

"New York."

"Sounds good to me," he said.

"Wait a minute," I said, but not too forcefully. I was fascinated by his hair and his ragged black shirt, declaring to all the world that he was angry, young, and poor. He sported a lip ring and was as emaciated as Jeri. I had never shared a vehicle with a person like him. I imagined the expression that would cross my father's face if he knew what was going on. Jeri twisted in her seat and threw open the back door. I thought I saw them exchange a brief look of complicity and wondered if she had planned this. Uneasiness flashed through me, along with images of my body dumped under an overpass with a slit throat, but the light had changed. People behind us were honking. My cell phone rang. I looked at the caller ID. It was my father. The young man jumped in, and we were on our way.

THEY STARTED DRINKING BEFORE WE LEFT THE CITY LIMITS, seven and sevens with more whiskey than 7Up, though they drank them slowly, elegantly, the ice cubes clicking within the Styrofoam cups. Jeri passed a cup to me and I propped it up between my legs and took a sip once in a while. I got a buzz almost immediately. I hadn't eaten all day.

We followed the freeway east. The strip mall lights grew intermittent, then were gone. We were passing long fields of something tallish, young corn maybe? There was no moon, and around us the land felt ancient and unaltered and secretive. We saw no other cars. Jeri said, "Toto, I don't think we're in Kansas anymore," and climbed into the back seat to keep Ripley company. That was the name the young man claimed. ("I'm Ripley—believe it or not.") They crunched chips as they discussed people and places they hated in the city we had left behind. Jeri passed a bag of Cheetos to me, along with another filled Styrofoam cup, but the Cheetos were oily and made me want to throw up. Or maybe that was the Seagram's to which I wasn't accustomed. Later, there were carnal sounds. My eyes strayed to the rearview mirror, but it was too dark to see much except shapes lumped together and moving jerkily. The car wobbled over the median. Once, twice. I wondered how it would be if I let it go all the way to the other side, maybe even into the dark gash of ditch that ran alongside the road, if the shock of the tragedy would weld my parents back together. I stored the idea in my mind under *distinct possibility*, but for the moment I pulled to the right and declared I needed a break.

We climbed out shakily to use the facilities. I insisted on gender separation: boys in the right-side field, girls to the left. Jeri and Ripley humored me. The crop wasn't corn—another mistake on my part. It came up to our armpits and had seeds, like wheat or wild grass. Ripley passed his hands over the stalks and announced it to be barley, but he was an unreliable narrator.

Later we sat on the hood of the car and Ripley rolled us joints. I had tried marijuana at parties before, but only a puff or two, and never in combination with alcohol. I took long drags, which made me cough. Jeri showed me how to hold the smoke inside my lungs for maximum effect. After a while, we lay back against the windshield and looked up at the sky. The stars were exceedingly bright. In a few minutes, they began pulsating. I put my hand over my breast. It was pulsating in the same rhythm. Someone else's hand was on my breast, too. I didn't push it away. I closed my eyes. Inside my eyelids colors were swirling, my very own living kaleidoscope.

Suddenly Jeri shouted, "Holy shit! Would you look at that!"

My eyes startled open, and the sky was full of the same swirling colors I'd seen within my eyelids. Swatches of red mostly, but also greens and yellows. I forgot to breathe. Curtains of misty light swept across the horizon, punctuated by bursts of brightness. It was like something out of *The Lord of the Rings*.

Ripley was trying to say something, but his tongue didn't seem to be cooperating. Finally, his vocabulary muted by reverence, he burst out with, "It's an effing aurora borealis." It seemed sublimely plausible. There are more things in heaven and earth than are writ of in our geographies. We watched the aurora. Maybe for minutes, maybe for hours. Eventually, the spectacle turned my companions amorous and they made for the backseat. They invited me to join them. When I declined, Jeri narrowed her eyes at me, trying to gauge whether I was insulting them and whether they should do something about it. But Ripley said, "Whatever," and slammed the car door shut.

The aurora gave a little shiver, then continued displaying its splendors. I walked into the field. The stalks of bearded barley were hard against my back. The hairy ends tickled my cheek. I rolled around, flattening stalks as I went until I had cleared enough space to see the aurora clearly. All around me was a musty, muddy odor, moles or raccoons or something more secretive. I had never before lain down on the bare ground at night. I pressed my palms against it. How foolish humans were to travel the world in search of history. Under my shoulder blades and over my head were the oldest histories of all: earth and sky. Strands of light—not the reds and greens I had thought earlier, but hues I had no name for—enacted their mystery. Soon, I fell into the deepest sleep.

WHEN I AWOKE, THE AURORA WAS GONE, LEAVING A TRACE OF redness in the sky, like embers in a fireplace after a party. My clothes were wet with dew. My head was clear. I returned to the car and, scooping up chilled water from the ice chest, washed my face. Jeri and Ripley were asleep in the backseat, limbs askew, mouths open. I'd been afraid of them earlier because they knew so many things about living that I didn't—but I wasn't scared anymore. Something had happened as I lay in the field, watching the sky, an understanding that I couldn't control the lives of others—but neither could they control mine.

I swung the car in a wide U-turn and started driving back to the city. My CDs were in the back, so I turned on the radio, low, to keep myself awake. After a while, the news came on. There had been a major explosion in one of the chemical factories to the east of the city. Twenty fire engines had been dispatched to tackle the blaze. The situation was now under control, although residents close to the factory had been advised to keep doors and windows closed and to drink bottled water until informed otherwise.

This explanation of my aurora was disappointing, but no matter what its source, the dance of lights over the night field had given me something facts couldn't take away.

I was almost at the city limits by the time Jeri and Ripley woke up. There was much loud-voiced remonstrance and banging of fists and questioning of my sanity and spewing forth of profane threats. I bore these with equanimity. I was in the driver's seat, after all. I took the exit where we had picked up Ripley, stopped at a gas station, and asked them to get out. Something must have changed in my demeanor, because they did so without further ado. In all the turmoil, no one brought up the aurora.

I drove back to the dorm, took a shower, ate some dry cereal, and got to my classes on time. I hadn't missed much; it wouldn't be difficult to make up the work. Friends looked at the circles under my eyes and surmised I'd had the flu; I didn't deny it. I gathered up the money—I hadn't spent even a dollar—and returned it to the bank.

Later I listened to the messages that had piled up on my cell phone. There were twenty-two—eighteen of them from my father, increasingly frantic as he tried to figure out if something had happened to me. I thought of how he had almost ruined my life. Then I thought, no. I was the one who had headed for the brink; I was the one who had pulled back from it.

When he called that night, I picked up the phone. When he asked where the hell I'd been, I responded with a cool silence that lobbed the question back at him. He must have sensed that same difference in me that had made Jeri and Ripley leave quietly.

"What I told you about, a few days ago," he said. "All I can say is, I don't know what came over me."

He wanted me to express thankfulness, but I would not oblige him.

"Maybe I'd caught a bug or something," he said.

I didn't reply.

"What I mean is"—he spoke too fast, the words tripping over one another—"I'm no longer planning to ask your mom for a divorce. In fact, I want you to forget all about that conversation we had." He must have realized the absurdity of this request, because he amended it. "I'd appreciate it if you don't bring this up with your mother." There was a pleading tone in his voice.

I agreed. Reassured, he asked his regular questions about my health, coursework, and financial stability, and I offered my usual monosyllabic answers. The status quo thus restored, he hung up with relief.

But things were not the same. The relationship between my parents and me had shifted. I was driving, seeing them in my rear-view mirror: smaller, shrunken; my mother trustingly oblivious of the fragility of the relationship on which she had based her life; my father without the courage to follow through on what he had—selfishly, illicitly, but truly—desired. Later I would forgive, but for now, I pulled away from them. Perhaps this distancing would have happened anyway, in time. But I felt rushed into it, as though I had yanked off a scab before the wound was healed, leaving behind a throbbing pink spot, the slow blood oozing again. And when I entered relationships of my own, I was careful to withhold the deep core of my being, the place in my mother that would have shattered if she had learned of my father's betrayal.

I didn't realize—until this earthquake, until today—that my withholding was a worse kind of betrayal, a betrayal of the self. It was time for me to change.

THERE WERE SOUNDS AGAIN UPSTAIRS, A CLANKING, ADVANCING noise, as though a different giant—this one in iron shoes—had decided to take a walk. It could be rescuers; it could be parts of the building getting ready to collapse. No one jumped up. It hurt too much to hope indiscriminately. But their eyes were alert. They were aware of the possibilities and ready to accept them. While Uma had been busy telling her story, people had moved around some. Tariq sat between Jiang and Lily, and both of them had laid their heads on his shoulders. Mangalam had come over to Uma's table and placed his arm around Malathi. Mrs. Pritchett had wrapped Mr. Pritchett in the black shawl, and he hadn't objected. Cameron, who had been pressed closer against Uma by these rearrangements, patted her knee as if to say, *Good job*.

But what they didn't know was that the story wasn't over yet.

A RAIN OF PLASTER BEGAN TO FALL, COVERING THE LITTLE BAND in grayish white until they looked like statues carved from the same material. Uma knew she had only a few minutes to find the right words to describe how, long after she had graduated and moved back to California for further study, the past had resurrected itself in the form of a phone call. It was Jeri on the line, her voice like old sandpaper. Uma hadn't recognized her until she identified herself.

Jeri said she was dying. She didn't give details. Nor did she ask for money, as Uma at first supposed she might.

"Hey," she said, "remember that aurora we saw that night we almost went to New York? That was something, wasn't it?"

Uma agreed.

"Remember," Jeri said, "I was the one who pointed it out? You guys wouldn't even have noticed it without me, you were that stoned."

"Yes, that's right," Uma said.

"People never believe me when I tell them about it. They say I must have been smashed and imagined it. Or it must have been something else, something ordinary. But it was an aurora for real, wasn't it? Because if it wasn't, I want to know."

There was no time to hesitate. Uma said, "It was an aurora."

"You telling the truth? People lie to me all the time. I'm sick of it. I want the truth about this one thing before I die."

"I'm telling you," Uma said. "It was an aurora."

Jeri laughed, then coughed a horrible, hacking cough that went on and on. When she could speak, she said. "I knew it! All those SOBs, trying to mess with my head. Feels good to hear you talk about it. I screwed up my life big-time, a lot of ways. Did a lot of stupid stuff. But at least I saw one amazing thing."

Then she hung up. Uma never heard from her again. But her thoughts kept returning to their surreal night together, an experience she would never have had but for her father's fateful phone call. She wondered if she had done the right thing in lying to a woman who had seemed to want only one thing from her: the truth before she died. Or had it not been a lie? Weren't the lights an aurora, their magic transforming Uma, giving her the courage to turn her life around, because she had believed them to be so? Uma suddenly felt it was crucial that she ask the company what they thought of this.

The clankings grew louder. The giant was on his way down. As they waited to see what would happen next, Uma began the end of her story.